THE END OF TERROR

THE END OF TERROR

Bruce Howitt

IGUANA

Copyright @ 2019 Bruce Howitt
Published by Iguana Books
720 Bathurst Street, Suite 303
Toronto, ON M5S 2R4

Editor: Beth Werner Kallman
Front cover design: Ruth Dwight

ISBN 978-1-77180-378-6 (paperback)
ISBN 978-1-77180-379-3 (epub)
ISBN 978-1-77180-380-9 (Kindle)

This is an original print edition of *The End of Terror*.

This book is dedicated to all those who have suffered at the hands of terror.

"The whole history of the world is summed up in the fact that, when nations are strong, they are not always just, and when they wish to be just, they are no longer strong."

— Winston Churchill

"The whole secret lies in confusing the enemy, so that he cannot fathom our real intent."

— Sun Tzu, *The Art of War*

CHAPTER 1

Vienna, July 2015

Anyone observing the many guests transiting in and out of the lobby of the Hotel Palais Hansen Kempinski would hardly have taken note of the very trim and neat-looking visitor. He was just over six feet tall, probably 180 pounds, with a muscular frame. With his short, dark, curly hair, piercing ice-blue eyes, and bronzed skin, he appeared to be just another upwardly mobile businessman used to international travel. In fact, he was one of the most senior field operatives of a highly secretive Israeli intelligence agency. Ari Lazarus was a special retribution operator, which is a euphemism for *assassin*.

In the course of his career with this agency, he had travelled to Vienna on "business" several times. For Ari, stepping out of the lobby of the Palais Hansen Kempinski onto Schottenring was a litmus test of his attitude and feelings for the old and venerable city of music.

His previous visits to Vienna had all been about his work. With all its beautiful architecture and music, Vienna was a veritable sewer for men in Ari's profession. This day, he was here on vacation with his wife, Leah, and daughter, Esther. They had been begging him to take them, and this was his first real family vacation. He was actually considering retirement.

When Ari, Leah, and Esther boarded Austrian Airlines Flight 858 at Ben Gurion Airport for the four-hour trip to Vienna, he was mentally trying to deal with the fact that he was going back to Vienna. The whole flight he was deep in thought, recollecting why he so intensely disliked it there.

Once they landed in Vienna, they took a taxi to the hotel, and Ari made a great effort to engage with his wife and daughter, both of whom had noticed how distant and removed he had been since they left their apartment in Tel Aviv. Even while they waited to board their flight, he had been in another world—sitting and staring out of the terminal building windows, uncommunicative. Of course, for both Leah and Esther, this being their first trip together as a family was a most exciting time.

Leah had grown up in Jerusalem and Tel Aviv and never been to the grand cities of Europe. Ari was not excited about her choice of Vienna, but he had acceded to her request and decided to make the best of it. He agreed partly because he wanted to exorcise the demons of his past experiences in Vienna, and because Esther, who had just entered her teens, was so excited that they were finally able to vacation together.

After they checked into the Palais Hansen, Ari finally began to relax. He had chosen the Palais because it was one of the best hotels in Europe, with an outstanding reputation for elegance and comfort. Designed by the famous Austrian architect Theophil Hansen in the nineteenth century, the hotel was a magnificent example of opulent living from that era. Now it had been modernized, and the two luxury connecting rooms Ari had booked were beyond Leah and Esther's wildest dreams. He had decided that their first real vacation together would be first class all the way. The rooms were opulently but tastefully furnished, and the hotel services were impeccable. Esther and Leah squealed with delight when they inspected all the toiletries in the finely constructed baskets on the shelves above the commodes in their respective rooms. There was every imaginable lotion, shampoo, conditioner, two brands of body cream, and several other assorted goodies.

Ari woke at his usual 0630hrs., showered and dressed, then went for a walk around the hotel neighbourhood, leaving Leah and Esther to get themselves ready for the day. As he left their room, he told Leah—who was still half asleep—that he would meet her and Esther in the lobby at 0830hrs.

Ari, even though he was on vacation and considering a career change, could not rid himself of his training and instincts. He walked along the main Schottenring and crossed the street twice, checking for any surveillance. He was still not one hundred percent sure that he hadn't been spotted as a person of interest by the Austrian security at the airport, or whether the Russian SVR or Iranian VEVAK had made him when he checked into the hotel. After an hour of conducting a detailed surveillance check he returned to the Palais Hansen pretty much convinced that he was in the clear.

As a senior operative of one of the world's most secretive organizations, Ari had been on the front lines of many secret and deadly retribution operations inside Europe, North America, and the Middle East. He was well aware that several intelligence agencies, although they did not have an accurate identity on him, might consider him a person of interest. Those that concerned him most were active in Europe in general and in Austria and Germany in particular. Both the Russian SVR and the Iranian VEVAK had several hundred agents located in Europe, with many of them in Vienna and Berlin. Whenever Ari travelled to European capitals, he was acutely aware that these other intelligence agencies were on the lookout for Israeli operatives. So far, he and his colleagues had avoided any exposure to the opposition. He intended to keep it that way.

His plan that day was to find a café and spend an hour or so with Leah and Esther watching the world go by, enjoying the wonderful Viennese coffee and pastries for breakfast. While he walked back to the hotel, he glanced up and down Schottenring and identified an old-style Viennese café with heavy damask tablecloths and immaculately attired waiters, all too eager to serve the many tourists thronging the famous street. This would be their breakfast destination.

Before Ari strolled back into the lobby, he performed one more check of his surroundings and was still satisfied that he was clear and clean. He found a comfortable wingback chair and sat observing the ebb and flow of guests and visitors moving through the elegant structure. He was quite surprised at the international flavour of the clientele. Many were from Europe and easy to identify by their language, dress, or behaviour; there were Germans, French, Italians, Swiss, and a great many North Americans, which he easily distinguished between Americans and Canadians. The Americans mostly were brash and confident, and in many cases, overweight; whereas the Canadians were more conservative and reserved and looked a great deal healthier. He was intrigued by the number of Asians, both Japanese and Chinese, who, unusual for them, were not in large tour groups, but travelling as individuals or couples. Added to the mix were many obscenely wealthy British tourists and businessmen, immaculately dressed and comporting themselves with the assured arrogance of their long-dissolved empire.

In sharp contrast to the British were the Russians—all fabulously wealthy and not shy about flashing it around, along with their rudeness and crudity. For Ari, assessing these fascinating surroundings and the polyglot of people was all part of his job, one which he could never seem to drop.

Soon, Leah and Esther exited the elevator bank and, beaming with anticipation, converged on him with great anticipation for their first day of sightseeing. Leah affectionately planted a good morning kiss on his cheek. "Ari, my dearest, I'm starving. Let's go to the restaurant for breakfast. I had a quick cup of coffee from the machine in the room, but I am so hungry!"

"Sweetheart, I've checked out the hotel coffee shop and it is nothing special. I was out walking earlier and saw this authentic Viennese restaurant just down the street from here. They appear to have a wonderful pastry offering, plus all kinds of other great-looking items, so we can walk there. It's about five minutes."

Esther gave her father a warm embrace. "Good morning, Abba. That sounds fantastic. I could not sleep last night thinking about all the places to visit while we are here. Ima and I talked about them this morning. St. Stephen's Cathedral is one of our musts, and the Vienna State Opera. We have to visit the Belvedere Palace and Museum, as well as the Hofburg Imperial Palace. I read that it was the home of the Austro-Hungarian Emperors and also once the home of the Imperial Arch-Duke Ferdinand and Sophie, Duchess of Hapsburg.

"Did you know their assassination in June 1914 began the horror of the Great War? Before the end of the Great War in 1918, it was considered one of the most magnificent lived-in palaces in the world and is still described as one of the largest palaces ever constructed. It is also home to the famous Spanish Riding School and numerous museums. The floor concierge gave us maps and directions; they are all within easy walking distance or a short cab ride from here."

As they walked to the Café Schottenring, Esther was breathless with excitement. "Abba, do you think we could arrange a tour of the Lipizzaner horses at the Spanish Riding School? They have a tour tomorrow at 11:00 a.m. I know you and Ima will love it. Please, Abba!"

Ari grinned as they made their way into the café. He selected a table on the outside terrace and said to Leah, "You know, I have to thank you for pushing me on this vacation. Listening to Esther and her excitement is such an experience. Wow! You are a genius for suggesting Vienna!"

Leah squeezed his hands across the table and gave him one of her electrifying smiles, the one that had made him fall in love with her when they first met.

Ari was glad to have this time with his little family. Even though he despised the Viennese people because of their history during World War II and their participation in the Holocaust, he made peace with himself to enjoy all the sights and sounds with his wife and daughter and let the past be forgotten, at least temporarily.

One of the two waiters in the café immediately brought over a pot of coffee and a jug of hot milk. As he waited, they studied the breakfast menu and ordered a tray of assorted pastries. The other waiter doubled as a barman; Leah and Esther were fascinated that people were coming in and ordering alcoholic beverages so early in the day.

The waiter returned with a small cart and they each selected two different pastries from the large assortment offered.

Leah and Esther were beaming adoringly at their husband and father. Ari returned his warmest smile and all three realized a degree of contentment they had not experienced as a family unit in a long time.

CHAPTER 2

Vienna, March 12-13 to November 8-9, 1938

As the Third Reich prepared for the Anschluss into Austria, Drs. Ephraim and Miriam Lazarus listened to the insanity of Adolph Hitler on the radio.

"The man is deranged. These rantings are not those of a normal person," Ephraim muttered more to himself than Miriam.

"We Austrians cannot be serious about turning over our country to this madman!" Miriam said. "How could we accede to this Anschluss nonsense?"

Ephraim despondently replied, "It would be that or a one-sided military confrontation, which we would lose in half a day."

"But what does he want?"

"Lebensraum—more space for the Germanic people. He's absolutely nuts."

"I'm scared, Ephraim. No good will come out of this."

"Perhaps we should liquidate all of our assets and move to England or North America—Canada or the US."

"Sure, Ephraim my dear. And how much do you think we would get? Hundreds of Austrians will be trying to leave Vienna; they will all be selling. We'd get twenty pfennigs on the schilling. No, we will stay and surely Hitler's own people and government will realize he is a dangerous madman and remove him. After the horror of the Great War, no one in their right mind wishes for a repeat of that slaughter. I'm sure he will be removed. He has to be!"

And so, after they had considered leaving Vienna and moving to England, the United States or Canada—where they had distant relatives on Miriam's side of the family—they decided that their station in life and professional qualifications would keep them immune from the street rabble being whipped up by Hitler and his Nazi thugs.

Before the Nazis and Hitler came to Austria, they had enjoyed a good and cultured life in Vienna. Ephraim, a third-generation Austrian, was considered one of the foremost leaders in his discipline in Europe. His father had been an officer in the Austro-Hungarian Army and had fought courageously on the Western front before being wounded on the Somme in 1916.

Ephraim was an internist and general surgeon on faculty staff at the hospital attached to the University of Vienna. The second-oldest medical school in Europe was world renowned for its alumni's achievements in science, medicine, and the arts.

Miriam and Ephraim had met when they were both completing their studies. For Miriam it was love at first sight when they were introduced at a mutual acquaintance's dinner party. Ephraim was tall and extremely good looking—sophisticated in a subdued way. Miriam was gregarious, with a warm and endearing personality; she was also a stunningly beautiful woman. After she received her doctorate, she secured a position as a pediatrician in a vibrant practice in the city.

Thus, they were completely stunned when on March 13, 1938, the Nazis invaded Austria in the Anschluss and all of their hopes and dreams were shattered. The Medical University of Vienna, one of the finest medical schools in the world, saw 65% of its faculty and students dismissed because they happened to be Jewish.

Not only were the Lazaruses dismissed from their professional positions, but they ultimately lost their beautiful apartment, on which Miriam had laboured so hard to make into a fine home. Along with thousands of other Viennese Jewish families, they were subjected to daily ridicule and hardship as the Nazis slowly tightened their suffocating regulations around the "Jewish Question."

Neither would never forget that terrible evening of November 9, 1938, forever to be known as Kristallnacht, when the Viennese police and German storm troopers crashed into their apartment, shouting and screaming at them to gather some belongings. "No gold, no jewellery, no furs, leave the silver and artwork. Just take your stinking Jew clothes and get out!" Nothing could have prepared them for this.

Miriam stood and looked on in abject horror and terror, whispering finally to her husband, "Why, why? What have we done to deserve this?"

"Shh! If we antagonize them, it will be worse."

A German sergeant screamed, "Quiet, you Jew bitch! Just your clothes!" He leaned right into her face and screamed at her again. His foul alcohol- and smoke-infused breath almost caused her to retch.

"Filthy piece of Jew shit! Move! Move! Now!"

Ephraim and Miriam were given less than ten minutes to pack some meagre belongings into a suitcase each before they were brutally hastened out of their home. The Germans ransacked the apartment as the Lazaruses were being shoved down the stairs to the lobby. Ephraim, in attempting to assist Miriam, was brutally beaten across the back and head with a rifle butt wielded by a vicious young SS trooper barely out of his teens. In the lobby, they saw their Jewish neighbours standing in a complete state of shock, some like Ephraim, bleeding from a face or head wound. Two of their neighbours, Simon and Yehudit Weissman, who were in their late seventies or early eighties, had been brutally beaten. Simon was bleeding badly and Yehudit, a tiny, frail woman, was struggling to aid him. They were stricken by fear and incomprehension.

"What have we ever done to these people?"

A Nazi officer in a black SS uniform screamed at her, his face red and contorted with hate and rage. "Silence, you Jewish whoring piece of shit, or you will get the same as your filthy Jew husband! Move! Move! Raus!"

As he turned on his heels, he struck Simon across the face with his riding crop, leaving a vicious welt across Simon's cheek and causing him to fall. Simon Weissman was a retired neurosurgeon. He and his wife had never been exposed to violence or discord.

Outside the apartment building, trucks were lined up in the street. The Lazaruses and their neighbours were violently shoved into the trucks. Other neighbours were leaning out of their windows or standing silently on the sidewalks, watching. Some snickered and called out, "Serves the dirty Jews right! They were never any good! *Greedy bastards!*"

Eventually the trucks transported them to the main rail station. Here, they were packed into stinking cattle cars with hundreds of other Jewish families from across Austria.

The complete transformation in environment was shocking and traumatic for all of the victims. One day most of them were living a cultured and sophisticated life. The next they were packed along with over a hundred others into filthy trains with just one overflowing bucket for a latrine, no food or water, and no place to lie down.

Ephraim held Miriam tight to him. "Miriam, you must stay with me. Don't fall down or try to lie down."

"I am so afraid, Ephraim. What is going to happen? Where are we going?"

Ephraim used his strength and size to bully his way to the outer wall of the cattle car, where there were some gaps in the board slats. Here he and Miriam were able to at least get a minimum of fresh air. Using his muscular frame to protect Miriam from being crushed by the other prisoners, Ephraim held her close so her face was exposed to the openings and she was able to breathe fresh air.

"Take deep, slow breaths," he urged.

They were held in the cars without any food or water or any opportunity to empty the latrine bucket. Many of the prisoners—for that is what they had become—relieved themselves where they stood. The stench of urine and feces was overpowering, and the crowded conditions meant that people were standing in their own foulness. They endured these conditions for three full days before they finally arrived at the Dachau concentration camp, and during that horrific time over thirty of their fellow victims died in that cattle car.

CHAPTER 3

After Hitler invaded Poland in 1939, those inmates who had survived Dachau were sent to Mauthausen in 1941 and then on to Auschwitz in 1942. Once again, they were exposed to the brutality of the Nazis. They spent several more days of hell in the filthy cattle cars as they were transported to the extermination camps, where most perished in the gas chambers or died from malnutrition and vicious beatings.

When Ephraim and Miriam stepped off the cattle car at Auschwitz–Birkenau, they were given a cursory examination by a snarling SS officer whose face they would never forget. He was screaming at all the victims, and as the soldiers under his command herded captives into two lines, Ephraim and Miriam were at least thankful they were not separated. They noted with trepidation that mothers and children were being sent to one line while husbands and fathers were kept in the same line as Ephraim and Miriam. The SS were enlisting the aid of huge, vicious German shepherd dogs to help separate and direct the prisoners into the respective lines. Some unfortunates among them were savagely bitten by the awful beasts for not moving fast enough or trying to stay with their spouses and children.

Risking a blow from a rifle butt, Ephraim whispered to Miriam, "The bastards are culling the young and weak. Miriam, you must stand tall and look strong."

Once the transport had been emptied, the two lines were marched off. Ephraim and Miriam were led to the barracks that would be their hellish home for the next thirty months. The line of women and children with the old and weak went straight to the gas chambers. Ephraim didn't say anything to Miriam, but he had watched as the

Weissmans—who had managed to survive Dachau and Mauthausen—were brutally herded into the line that was sent to the gas chambers.

They were interviewed by an SS doctor, had their heads shaved, and then a number was tattooed on their left arms. Ephraim was given a lice-infested, striped pyjama-style uniform and a cap to wear, and Miriam was provided a shapeless grey dress. In their separate barracks, they were forced to sleep four persons to a bunk, which were stacked three high down each side of the room. There were separate communal latrines for men and women where they would have to sit. Beneath the bench was a trench which gathered the human waste and flowed it out to a noxious pit at both ends of the hut. There was no such item as toilet paper or water to cleanse oneself.

For Miriam, the indignity of having to perform her private business in open public was soul-destroying. During the day, the inmates were subjected to meaningless work, and on occasion, marched out of the camp to work in a factory or field. Daily beatings served to cull the weaker prisoners from the population.

The Lazaruses knew they had to be strong and that the other line of prisoners had gone straight to the gas chambers before the continuously belching ovens. The weaker inmates were eventually sent there. The food allowance was never more than a crust of stale and maggot-filled bread with an occasional bowl of greasy water masquerading as soup. Occasionally, a piece of turnip or potato would be included.

The psychological stress on both of them was almost insurmountable. Miriam and Ephraim tried to administer rudimentary medical care to the inmates around them. They did this at great risk and with no drugs or instruments.

On more than one occasion, Miriam was randomly selected to accompany two SS guards to their living quarters. When this occurred, Ephraim was petrified she would not return. Fortunately, she survived each time. Once having arrived at the centre, she was taken to the sleeping quarters of some of the officers. During one of these visits she was gang raped six times and one of the SS officers was particularly vicious and used his riding crop to assault her both vaginally and anally.

Two female guards dragged her back to her barracks, where Ephraim waited nervously for her to return. She bled for several days, progressively growing weaker each day. Ephraim's assistance to other prisoners earned him and Miriam some sympathy, and several gave some of their meagre rations to Miriam to help her gain back some strength.

At the end of their second year, Ephraim and Miriam had survived. They had seen and heard the US Air Force fly over on their way to bomb the German forces on the Eastern Front, and everyone, including the guards, understood there was a big change coming in the direction of the war.

Many of the original guards had been sent to the Eastern Front to stem the Soviet forces advancing on Poland and Germany. Their replacements were mostly young boys in their teens or older men.

At the end of 1944, there was an influx of Hungarian prisoners, and from them Ephraim and Miriam heard that the Allies were relentlessly closing in on victory. The rumours of the Normandy landings were confirmed; the American and British forces were right on the western German border, poised to cross into the Fatherland. In the East, the massive Soviet Red Army had crushed the Germans at Stalingrad and were rolling the Nazis back across Russia and eastern Poland.

Rumours were confirmed that a huge tank engagement at Kursk had destroyed most of the German tank forces in the East. Then, in January of 1945, the SS removed many of the healthier prisoners and marched them back toward Germany to work in forced labour camps. Ephraim and Miriam were among this group and miraculously survived the 50-kilometre march in deep snow and freezing temperatures to Gliwice. Hundreds died from cold and malnutrition. Any prisoner that failed to stay on their feet was summarily shot by the guards. Some dared to try and run away into the forests that lined the road. The dogs either killed the prisoners or they were immediately shot on capture and left to die where they fell. Many of these prisoners were the Hungarians, as they were the most recent arrivals and therefore had more strength and stamina.

CHAPTER 4

Haifa, Israel, May 1949

Ephraim and Miriam Lazarus looked out at the Port of Haifa. Along with hundreds of other Shoah survivors from the displaced persons camps of Europe, they were entering Palestine—now Israel—on a decrepit, rusting merchant ship that slowly made its way to the dockside. Several dozen expectant Israeli citizens lined the dock, anxious to reconnect with loved ones previously believed lost.

The Lazaruses were not happy about their lot in life. The conditions on the ancient freighter had been less than ideal. The latrines on board had been designed to accommodate perhaps twenty to thirty crewmen, yet there had been over four hundred passengers on board. There were limited water and rations available, and the Mediterranean Sea had not been kind. The seas were rough, and the sun had been beating down on the passengers during the four-day voyage from Bari, Italy. They had been sent by train down to Bari from the temporary DP camp where they had been staying near Padua in the North. The stench of vomit, urine, and feces inside the ship was horrendous from overflowing toilets and there were no maintenance crews to clean up the stinking mess. Ephraim and Miriam found a small covered area near the fantail of the ship and spent most of the journey there, trying to escape the noxious odours that emanated from every part of the ship.

"We should have considered America or Canada, perhaps even England, if this is any indication of where we are going," Ephraim complained to his wife.

"You know that wasn't possible. The Canadian government was still keeping unofficial quotas on Jewish refugees and so were the English. We would probably have had to wait in that depressing DP camp another year or two."

"But we could have tried. Your relatives in Kansas could have helped us gain admittance into the US."

"Sure, Ephraim. They hardly know of us and getting admitted to the US is not easy. We don't have any jobs or money, and they for sure wouldn't want the financial burden. Israel is our best hope. It allows us the opportunity to get out of this cesspool of anti-Semitic Europe. Even now, after everyone knows what the Nazis did to the Jews during the Holocaust, the Europeans don't like us or want us. Did you see the way the people in Bari sneered and insulted us as we went from the train station to the ship?"

Ephraim and Miriam had somehow survived the hell of Auschwitz–Birkenau. Both were strong and in good health before they were rounded up. Ephraim had continued his love of fencing and horseback riding after he had graduated and physically was very fit. Miriam practised and taught yoga, and as a result was also healthy, fit, and strong. Both had a deep faith and made a commitment to each other to do whatever it took to survive. This was no more apparent than when they were marched in freezing, snowy conditions from Auschwitz to Gliwice some 50 kilometres back toward Germany in January 1945, where they were then put on trains back to the concentration camps in Austria and Germany. They were destined for Buchenwald when their train was shunted onto a siding to let the trains carrying Nazi troops fleeing the Russian Army get back to Germany. Eventually they were sent back to Mauthausen and worked as slave labourers in the factories set up around the camp.

The Americans arrived in May and the prisoners were liberated. Ephraim and Miriam knew their lot would lie in the West, so they somehow made their way west out of Austria before the borders closed and the Russians took over. They finally arrived in the Allied section of Germany. Here they spent almost three years recovering in a displaced persons camp. They had no desire to go back to

Austria and Vienna. Both were shocked at the virulent anti-Semitism that had risen its ugly head in Vienna as soon as the Anschluss occurred. Neither could forget the look of sheer hatred on the face of a young Viennese policeman. He had once been a helpful, smiling, city beat cop, but when he aided the Germans in breaking down the door to their apartment, he was a violent, hateful, screaming anti-Semite.

Now in their late thirties, they wondered about their future in this new land. They stood at the deck railing of the rusted old freighter that had slowly limped across the Mediterranean Sea to bring them to Haifa. Ephraim and Miriam were in awe as they looked out at the green hills of Haifa and its surrounds. The stark contrasts of the land and many aromas of the Middle East—falafel, spices—the noise and energy of a new country, and the polyglot of different ethnic groups all held them entranced.

Hundreds of eager, searching faces lined the docks, seeking out loved ones thought lost in the horror of the Shoah (Holocaust). This caused Ephraim and Miriam a great deal of pain and sadness.

They had arrived in Haifa all alone, with no idea of where they were going or what they would do.

"You know full well we would have to wait another two or three years in that dreadfully depressing DP camp. Canada still has a strict quota on admitting Jewish refugees. The English are not our best of friends, particularly since they were basically chased out of Palestine by our fellow Jews."

"Miriam, you know how irritated I become when you repeat yourself. I know all that, but at least we could have approached your relatives in Kansas to maybe sponsor us into the US."

"No, Ephraim! They hardly know who we are, and we don't have any financial means at all. Remember, we are lucky to be alive with the clothes on our backs. Just the way we had to leave Vienna on those stinking cattle cars. There is no way we could expect them to sponsor us and assume financial responsibility for us, two virtual strangers they have hardly ever heard from! No, my dear. We are here in Eretz Yisroel. We will enter this young country as thankful survivors and make the rest of our lives here. There will be no more discussion on what if we went here or there. We're staying in Israel!"

Ephraim placed his arm around Miriam's shoulder and hugged her to him, sighing, "My darling, Miriam. As always, you are right. You are so practical."

They both committed to never forget the atrocities and dehumanization they had witnessed in the camps, but they also believed deeply that they had to move on with their lives.

CHAPTER 5

They were immediately shown to a temporary canteen, which served them an assortment of fresh fruit and vegetables with a selection of hot and cold drinks. This was a cornucopia they had not experienced since they left Vienna all those years ago.

Once fortified with some wonderful food, they began the admission process to Israel. It was a slow and gruelling process. They were first shuffled to a tent where officials from the Jewish Agency registered them. They were asked the details of where they were originally from, which camps they had been in, and how they had survived and arrived in Israel. This was traumatic for Ephraim and Miriam. After this interview they then went to another area where they lined up to await their turn at a table. There the interviewers wanted details of their families, and if possible where they may have been during the Shoah.

Ephraim provided as much information as he could, even though it was terribly painful to go into.

After all the documentation and forms were completed, the Lazaruses were directed to a large Nissen hut, where people from the Joint Commission served them another magnificent meal. There were salads, hot and cold dishes, and something they had not experienced since Vienna—real kosher food. It was the first time since they were dragged from their Vienna apartment all those years ago that they had the opportunity to select from an endless menu of delicious food. After their rescue from the camps and subsequent time in the DP camps, the food they experienced had been mostly bland and institutionalized. The offering on the dockside at Haifa was incredible.

After their meal, they were processed to another tent and tables, where Ephraim and Miriam were told that they were now citizens of Israel. Since they had no family or relatives living in the country and both were still recovering, they had no thoughts about where to go or what to do next.

Miriam turned to Ephraim, "Thank goodness we are off that stinking ship. It will be weeks before I get the odours of urine, vomit, and human waste out of my nostrils."

The Joint Commission people who interviewed and registered them were kind and understanding. One of the Joint officers, Ariel Glucksman, was an astute and caring woman. Ariel had been born and raised in New York City and had made Aliya (emigration to Israel) immediately after nationhood was declared in 1948. She was a typical brash, extroverted New Yorker from Brooklyn. Something in Ephraim's eyes and bearing drew Ariel to this tall, strong man. The fierce attachment that Miriam and Ephraim showed for each other suggested that they were a very special couple.

"It's Miriam, right?"

"Yes. Yes, Miriam Lazarus, and this is my husband, Ephraim."

"Hi, I'm Ariel. Ariel Glucksman. I made Aliya right after Independence, and I live and work on Kibbutz Yagur, not far from here."

After she completed their registration, Ariel suggested they accompany her to Yagur. Since they had no relatives or friends in Israel, they could at least get grounded there and begin their lives again instead of being shuffled from one settlement camp to another while getting fully processed.

CHAPTER 6

With Ariel's help, Ephraim and Miriam began their first days in Israel at Kibbutz Yagur, some five miles east of Haifa.

Yagur was one of the oldest and most well-established kibbutzim in Israel. Soon, they both realized that after all the terrible experiences they had endured, the simple life on Yagur was for them.

Ariel was one of the most popular persons at Yagur and she adopted Ephraim and Miriam as if they were her own family. The Lazaruses were both special people and Ariel was quickly drawn into a deep friendship with Miriam. Miriam's genteel toughness and Ariel's brash New York style were such opposites that, somehow, they attracted each other in a unique way. They quickly became inseparable. Ariel gave guidance and encouragement to her new friends as they settled into their new home.

When Ariel agreed to marry a true Sabra, Yitzhak Blum, most of the whole kibbutz was invited to the wedding, and Ephraim and Miriam were treated like family.

On account of the mentoring and genuine love that Ariel and now Yitzhak showed to Ephraim and Miriam, the two couples became solidly integrated members of the kibbutz. The genuine feeling of inclusiveness and acceptance buoyed the Lazaruses in no small way.

Every Friday night, the Lazaruses and the Blums shared a table and celebrated the Sabbath. For Miriam, it was always a special moment. Nothing moved her more than helping Ariel light the Sabbath candles and say the blessing over the candles. It recalled similar celebrations long ago at her parents' and grandparents' homes in Vienna.

At Ariel's suggestion, Ephraim began working in the orchards. This was hard physical labour, but Ephraim thrived on it. At one Shabbat dinner, he said, "When Ariel told me she thought a complete change would be good for me, I had no idea how soul-lifting and stimulating working in the outdoors would be. Frankly, picking fruit and pruning trees has healed my soul." This was from a former urban-dweller who had never set foot in an orchard in his previous life. The healthy outdoor environment and abundance of healthy food agreed with Ephraim, allowing him to regain his mental and physical health.

Kibbutz Yagur was recognized as one of the major growers of fruit in Israel. Ever since its founding in 1922, Yagur had been a central part of the history of Palestine and then Israel. In 1946, the British Army raided the kibbutz and uncovered a large arms cache that was used by the Haganah in their fight against the Mandate occupation. It was this discovery—and their inability to counter the other efforts of the Irgun and the Haganah—that convinced the British government in Westminster that their struggle to hold on to the Mandate was doomed, and the sooner they removed themselves from Palestine, the better.

Many original kibbutz members had more than one skill, and their diverse backgrounds soon made them recognize that exporting fruit would only provide limited income. So, they put their combined skills to work and founded what would eventually become one of the largest fruit canning enterprises in Israel, exporting their products all over the world.

Ephraim eventually showed a mechanical aptitude he never knew he possessed and became one of the lead hand/managers of the kibbutz canning facility. He relished the idea of going to work each day, studying the intricacies of the machinery employed in the canning process. He treated them as if they had been patients in his medical practice in Vienna. He nurtured them and repaired them with a skill that only a former physician could apply.

The knowledge that he was aiding the development of the economy of Yagur gave Ephraim immense satisfaction. It surprised him and Miriam when he revealed a latent entrepreneurial talent he had never realized he possessed. He was always developing new improvements to the canning lines and their specialized equipment. The kibbutz had some of the machines he designed patented, and eventually they were sold all over the world. Ephraim's skills and efforts made a great deal of money for the kibbutz. The success he had achieved in a relatively short time brought him immense pride and comfort.

On Sundays, he would teach in the kibbutz school. Even though he was a doctor by training and an engineer at heart, Ephraim was above all an incredible teacher. He taught the senior students for a three-hour period each week. At first Ephraim's remit was to teach his class the basics of science and math with the intent of preparing the students for the many opportunities that were opening up in the medical and electronics industries, but he quickly recognized that these were much too dry and boring for the group. He switched up the course to one about life and getting along in the world, efficiently and creatively weaving not only science and math, but also music and literature into the program. Needless to say, Ephraim's Sunday program was the one most anticipated and sought after.

In the meantime, Miriam became wholly immersed in aiding young children in reading and writing Hebrew. She had developed a special bond with Ariel from their first meeting and by now the two were inseparable. Ariel was able to encourage Miriam to use her first love of pediatrics to help her teach language and writing to the kindergarten and early grades.

Neither Miriam nor Ephraim had believed they would ever have children after the physical atrocities forced on her in the camps. It was a miracle she had survived, and the healthy invigorating kibbutz life and special relationship with Ariel rejuvenated her. Many times, Ariel would say quietly to Miriam when they were alone together, "Don't ever give up. At least enjoy the lovemaking each and every time. Men like nothing more than a good schtup after a hard day's work. Don't chase Ephraim away. He adores you and even if you are not able to get pregnant, give him a good schtup!"

Then, in 1952, Miriam gave birth to a healthy boy, whom they named Eli, after Ephraim's late father. It was only while they were in the DP camps that Ephraim had learned, through the services of the Jewish Agency, that his father and mother had both perished in a death camp at Sobibor.

The birth of Eli and the utter joy and happiness he brought into their lives was heartwarming to see for all their friends and fellow kibbutzniks, most of all Ariel. Once in a while, she would give Miriam a knowing smile and they would keep their little secret about 'a good schtup.'

As he grew from baby to young boy, then young adult, Eli's parents wanted much more for him than kibbutz life. By the time he was twenty, Eli had finished his education at the Technion in Haifa and joined the IDF (Israeli Defense Forces) for his compulsory three years of service. After finishing as a lieutenant in the Tank Corps, Eli served on the Golan during the Yom Kippur War in 1973 and distinguished himself so much that he attracted attention from the senior brass in the army, who prevailed on him to become a career officer. Eli accepted and eventually rose through the ranks. He was a fearless warrior, yet gentle and empathetic, not to mention extremely handsome. He was considered to be one of the most eligible bachelors in Israel at the time.

CHAPTER 7

Golan Heights, October 6–9, 1973

The combined Arab armies attacked Israel on October 6, 1973 in what became known as the Yom Kippur War. Eli was commanding a squadron of tanks on the Northern flank of the Golan. The Syrian Army attacked the Israeli forces with an overwhelming force of 50,000 soldiers, plus 1,200 tanks and artillery.

Eli was attached to the 7th Brigade, commanded by the legendary Lieutenant Colonel Avigdor Kahalani. Over three days of intense fighting, some of it hand-to-hand combat, he and his troops drove off the Syrians, destroying large numbers of their tanks and artillery pieces. It was during this desperate battle that Eli's courage and leadership came to the attention of his superior officers. At one critical point, his squadron of eight remaining tanks was about to be surrounded by a far greater force. With ammunition running low and little fuel, Eli ordered his tanks to charge the Syrians, destroying twenty Syrian tanks as they advanced on Israeli positions. Eli had been ordered to withdraw from the Valley, but he ignored the command and later claimed poor radio reception. Instead he spoke to each of his tank commanders, code names David 1 through David 7: "Leader to Davids, line abreast on me and full speed at these bastards!"

The eight tanks quickly fell into line and raced at the Syrian tanks, firing cannons and machine guns, causing heavy enemy casualties. At one point, David 2, commanded by Sergeant Yossi Ehrlichman, radioed, "David 2 to Leader, we're out of fuel. I'm going to laager here and target whatever I can get a clear shot at. We have about fifteen rounds of 105 mm left. Over and out."

Eli felt despondent when he realized that Ehrlichman's crew was his youngest and least experienced. Speaking to his driver, he said, "Those kids are beyond heroes. They have just signed their own death warrants and we cannot aid them. God help them."

He continued to urge his remaining force forward, destroying armoured personnel carriers (APCs) and tanks, chasing the Syrian and Moroccan enemy back to their own lines.

One of his tankers, David 3, called out, "David 3 to Leader, Yossi in 2 just took a direct hit! *Oh God! Oh God!* The whole fucking tank just exploded in a fireball!"

Eli managed a quick look over at the burning mass of molten metal and was hard-pressed not to throw up. He knew the youngsters, and worse yet, their parents. As a tight little command, they were a close-knit family; or had been. "May their memories be for a blessing," he said in a broken voice.

David 3 replied, "Baruch dayan ha'emet (Blessed is the true judge)."

The Syrian force directly opposed to Eli's consisted of over 120 tanks when the battle commenced. Within two hours, the Syrians withdrew, leaving behind on the battlefield, soon to be known as the Valley of Tears, over fifty blazing tanks, dozens of burned-out APC troop carriers, and more than four hundred dead soldiers.

After a tense 72 hours, when the survival of Israel lay in the balance, Eli and his fellow tankers fought off and defeated a far superior (in numbers) Syrian Army. At the height of the battle for the Golan, Israel possessed a total of 120 operational tanks. The Syrians and the Moroccans had over 1,200.

In recognition of his success on the Golan, Eli was quickly promoted from lieutenant to captain in the IDF tank forces, eventually rising to the rank of Tat Aluf, in command of all the IDF tank forces.

CHAPTER 8

In 1976, Eli travelled to Canada and the United States as part of an IDF delegation, speaking at synagogues and other institutions about Israel's role in the Yom Kippur War.

As he began his address on a Thursday night to the congregation of the famous Temple Emmanuel in Westmount, Montreal, he took a moment to connect with the audience. Sitting a few rows in front of the stage, he noticed an incredibly beautiful young woman. She had lustrous auburn hair and brilliant green eyes and was one of the most stunning women Eli had ever seen. Sophie Grantzman was fascinated by the handsome Israeli soldier.

Then, Eli began to give his talk. He described to the assembled people of Westmount how the survival of Israel hung in the balance for a nerve-wracking 72 hours. He spoke of the acute shortage of 105 mm shells for the tanks and artillery. Eli told the audience how Golda Meir had flown to Washington, DC to beg President Nixon and Secretary of State Kissinger to get the ammunition to Israel or Israel would likely be defeated. Eli explained that the Israeli military was down to less than a 48-hour supply of this critical ammunition. His praise was effusive for the American Air Force, who on Nixon's and Kissinger's orders rushed the supplies to Ben Gurion Airport. Eli also told how ordinary civilians came to the airport to assist in unloading the US Air Force planes, driving the critical cargo straight to the battlefields because the situation was so desperate.

He modestly described his own role in the battle on the Golan Heights and how young, way too young, Israeli tankers selflessly drove into battle to confront the Syrians. Some of these youngsters were not even in their twenties. Eli became emotional when he told how one of the tanks under his command had run out of fuel and how the young commander, Sergeant Yossi Ehrlichman, had manoeuvred their tank into a position where they could fire effectively at the enemy. Yossi and his tank eventually became a sitting target for the Syrian tanks, and sadly the young crew's tank received a direct hit that turned it into a fireball, but not before they had destroyed two enemy tanks and three APCs. Eli often relived the scene in nightmares, hearing the gut-wrenching screams amid the explosions as it became a mass of shattered steel and detonating ammunition.

He captured the audience with his soft but authoritative speaking style, and many gasped when they heard just how desperate the fighting on the Golan had been and the terrible sacrifices so many young Israelis had made. Most had no idea how close Israel had come to being overrun and defeated. Eli gave many in that audience, finally, a close connection to the real dangers of the neighbourhood Israel lives in.

After he finished, the audience was invited to a reception, where Eli was the congregation's guest of honour. As he circulated among the members, he was constantly looking for the gorgeous young woman he had seen in the audience. Eventually, he and Sophie were introduced by the synagogue president. For the rest of the evening, the two of them only had eyes for each other. As the gala concluded, Sophie and Eli exchanged contact information. He informed her he was a house guest of the synagogue president, Chaim Miller. Sophie gave him her details, and both knew they would see each other again. Then, on a whim, she invited him home for Shabbat dinner the next evening, Friday, much to the chagrin of the Millers.

Sophie was a gregarious knockout, and she was swept off her feet by the handsome IDF officer. Never in her life had she been so physically smitten by a man. From the very minute she set eyes on Eli, all of her physical senses were energized. At first, she was so totally shocked that she felt ashamed. Quickly shedding that thought, she set her focus on getting to know the magnetic Israeli.

Sophie had grown up in Montreal, in a typical middle-class family in the town of Mount Royal. Her grandparents had arrived in

Montreal from Romania and Russia in 1910. Both were essentially penniless when they met at a synagogue social a few months later. Sophie's grandfather, Abraham, was very industrious, and her Grandma Rebecca was a brilliant seamstress. Within a short time, they had created and grown a booming teen-clothing manufacturing business, which became a well-known brand name across Canada and the United States. Sophie's father, Arnold, had taken over when Grandpa Abe and Grandma Beckie retired and moved to Florida, and Arnold had greatly expanded the business.

For the whole Shabbat evening, it was all Sophie could do to keep from touching Eli's arm or cheek. She was also acutely aware of her mother, Rhoda, keenly observing the change in her daughter. Sophie had spent years with many boys chasing her, but never had any one of them caused such a change in Sophie. When dinner was over, and Sophie announced she would drive Eli back to the Miller home, Rhoda and Arnold were quite overwhelmed by their daughter's being so smitten. She came home later that night and told her parents she was going to marry the dashing young man, which came as no surprise to Rhoda.

Eli was only in Montreal for another week, during which Sophie and he tried to see each other as much as they could. Because of their respective time commitments, they only spent a few hours together, but both knew their lives would forever be entwined. Sophie showed Eli the historic quarter of Old Montreal and the original Jewish Quarter just north of the mountain. Eli was fascinated by the eclectic vibrancy of the city.

He returned to Israel and his duties, but he and Sophie wrote regularly and spoke often on the phone.

CHAPTER 9

A year later, in 1977, Sophie made Aliya to Israel and joined the IDF herself. This came as no surprise to her parents. The transition was relatively easy, since her grandparents had encouraged her from an early age to study and speak both Yiddish and Hebrew. She was also fluent in French, so languages were a nonissue for her.

By this time, Eli had been promoted to command a new tank school in the Judean desert, commuting on weekends to Tel Aviv. He and Sophie remained in constant contact with each other and when their leaves and time permitted, they met up, usually spending weekends in Tel Aviv, mostly in bed.

Their first time together was an experience like no other for Sophie. Eli literally swept her off her feet as they entered their hotel room, and she was so overcome with passion, it was only a matter of minutes before the floor was littered with their clothes. Sophie had never experienced such physical pleasure before Eli. Lying snuggled up to his bare chest, she was practically purring like a cat. Sweat glistened on their torsos and the pungent aroma of sex surrounded them. Gazing into Sophie's eyes, Eli murmured, "My little swallow from Canada, you are the most beautiful person I have ever known."

"I'm not a bird, you big goof." Sophie giggled.

"Listen, little girl, I know we have to go back to our units in a few hours, but let me tell you, I will never let you go. I will love you all the days we are apart and twice as much on the days we are together. You are my soulmate, my destiny. Without you I cannot be and do what I have been called to do for our beloved Israel. I will need you by my side forever."

"Oh my, Eli, you must know that I fell in love with you from the first minute I set eyes on you, when you gave that talk at the synagogue in Montreal. After the time you came for Shabbat dinner, my mother knew even before I told her that I was going to marry you. She had already told my dad that I would have eyes for no one else and that I would eventually marry you. So, Soldier-Boy Lazarus, when are we getting married?!"

After their passionate sex-filled weekends, they would both return to their units and anxiously count the days to their next encounter. Whenever Sophie returned from one of her weekends with Eli, her fellow soldiers would tease her. She looked radiant and they all guessed as to how she had spent the weekend.

It wasn't long after she finished her first year in the IDF that Sophie got her wish. She married Eli in 1978.

CHAPTER 10

Eli and Sophie settled into married life and soon had a son, Ari, in 1979. Very soon after Ari began to grow into a young child and then a young adult, they both realized he had a unique talent and ability—a photographic memory. Show him a face, a book page, a mathematical problem, and Ari had the memory or answer forever imprinted in his mind. As a soldier and then a member of 9, he could recognize a terrorist from a picture that he had seen only once while perusing files years earlier. After finishing high school, Ari served his mandatory three years in the IDF infantry, his final year with the counter-terrorist forces, Mista'arvim, where he participated in some highly secretive and classified missions. The Mista'arvim was a unit of special forces within the IDF whose remit was to clandestinely enter hostile territories—usually the Gaza Strip, Judea and Samaria, and the bordering states of Lebanon, Jordan, and Syria—to root out and eliminate known terrorists who had attacked Israel or Israeli citizens.

Ari's father, Eli, was aware of some of the unit's missions and many times had to wrestle with the fact that he and Sophie's only son was in harm's way; yet he could never divulge even to Sophie his angst and concern for Ari's safe return.

One such mission was led by Ari in 1999. Arab jihadi terrorists had slaughtered a young family on a beach north of Haifa. The four PLO terrorists had come down from Lebanon looking for opportunities to attack and kill Israeli civilians. Their plan had been to land on the beach and move inland to a small town near Rosh Hanikrah, then detonate explosives and shoot up the residents as they left a community centre and synagogue. As they landed their boat and prepared to move off, they were surprised by a family who were spending a day there. The father, Nahum Rivkin, immediately recognized who and what they were and desperately tried to alert the authorities as well as protect his family. His cell phone call reached the local police station, who alerted the IDF and Border Police, but it was too late for the family. The terrorists strangled the two children — Sarah, aged five, and Joseph, three. Then they disemboweled their mother, Shifra, in front of Nahum as they held him down and forced him to watch. Finally, they almost beheaded him by slitting his throat from ear to ear, leaving him to bleed out on the beach next to his slaughtered wife and children. The terrorists quickly departed before security forces could apprehend them; they returned to Lebanon believing they had struck a blow for the greater good of the Arab world and for the freedom cause of the PLO.

This heinous crime shocked not only Israel but most of the Western world. Ari's mission, given to him by the commander of the Mista'arvim himself, was to seek out these despicable men and terminate them wherever they were found.

Ari knew that the terrorists had come down the coast by high-speed Zodiac boat from Lebanon, because Israeli naval radar had identified the passage of the Zodiac in both directions. Naval intelligence had been able to track the group of four jihadis fleeing up the coast and determined that the boat had originally commenced from and then returned to the small coastal village of As-Sarafand.

Six Mista'arvim under Ari's leadership, Rasalim (sergeants) Micha Flosberg, Nahum Sharon; Rabatim (corporals) Alon Gold, Baruch Feldner, and Turalim (private) Avram Almein followed the same route up the coast into Lebanon. There they disembarked at a small cove a few miles south of As-Sarafand and carefully concealed the Zodiac under some rocks and foliage.

As-Sarafand was about 22 miles north of the border. The Israelis waited until daylight, then slowly and carefully made their way to the town. To any casual observers, the pairs of Arab men dressed in thobes and keffiyehs walking along the road toward As-Sarafand were merely workers journeying into town looking for employment. Once there, they walked about and began to gather clandestine intelligence on the four terrorists. This was not difficult to do. The terrorists had been hailed as heroes of the resistance and the townspeople were openly praising them. It didn't take Ari's team long to locate the terrorists with big mouths. When Ari and his men ambled through the town square in pairs—so as not to attract too much attention—they soon had their targets in plain sight.

The young men of the area gathered to show off, discussing the terrible state of the poor Palestinians, passing out candy, and waving flags about their impending conquest of Israel. Ari and his group could hardly believe their luck; sitting at an outdoor café were the four perpetrators, front and centre and easily identifiable, smiling and boasting of their heroic feat. They were surrounded by several young men who ultimately, one day, wished to emulate them.

Listening to their bombast and jubilation of their "heroic" mission sickened Ari and his team.

Around noon, Sergeant Sharon and Ari meandered across the square to another café and sat at an outdoor table so they could observe the four individuals.

Ari and Sharon ordered tea and pastries, keeping the four Arabs in sight. Ari spoke quietly on an open channel to Sharon, so all their men could hear. "Just look at these pieces of shit. They seem to think killing babies is heroic. Sergeant, we are about to change their minds for good. Listen up, everyone! Almein, you casually join them and get them comfortable with you. We will be watching to see if any others join them."

Private Almein, whose parents were Iraqi Jews, Mizrahim, looked more Arab than most Ashkenazic Israelis did. He was fluent in several dialects of Arabic. He wandered over to the four young men and congratulated them on their achievement. He was immediately embraced into their gathering and, for the next hour, they all regaled each other with tales of bravery and conquest. Avram Almein was at times the most boastful and soon was acknowledged as a leader among them.

Ari and Sharon stood and left the café and slowly walked around the square looking for any threats.

Sergeant Flosberg and the two corporals stayed in the background, awaiting a command signal from Ari via their earpieces, which were hidden by the traditional keffiyeh headdress they all wore. As the afternoon progressed, the men began to disperse, and the four terrorists and Private Almein were suddenly the only patrons remaining in the café they had been sitting in.

Ari and Nahum Sharon soon recognized that a Toyota 4x4 parked adjacent to the café belonged to the terrorists. This would be most useful in their extraction from Lebanon.

With whispered communications, Ari detailed the plan. "Gold, Flosberg, move on the café. Get close enough, wait for me and Almein to jump these bastards, and then do your part. Feldner, Sharon, you get that 4x4, it's theirs. We'll use it to make our way out of here."

Like in a well-rehearsed ballet, the Israeli commandos, led by Ari, moved in on the terrorists. Private Almein, Sergeant Flosberg, Corporal Gold, and Ari would each kill one of the terrorists with garrotes and the uniquely deadly two-edged Israeli commando combat knives.

Ari positioned himself behind the largest, oldest, and undisputed leader, whom he recognized as Ali-Mohammad Abu from some earlier Mossad file he had seen. Quickly, Ari pulled Abu's head back, exposing his throat. One firm slash with his knife and Ari ended Abu's life. A gush of arterial blood spurted from Abu's neck all over the table and the three remaining terrorists. Gold used his serrated garrote on one of the other men, who didn't even have a chance to stand up from the table as his buddy Abu's blood covered everything. The other two jumped to their feet as soon as Ari slashed Abu, each attempting to grab a Makarov pistol from their waistbands. They were dead before they had their hands on the butts of their weapons.

Private Almein and Sergeant Flosberg each expertly stabbed the two terrorists in the eye with their commando battle knives, instantly penetrating their brains and killing them. As soon as the four killers were dispatched to the seventy-two virgins, all six of the Mista'arvim piled into the Toyota with Corporal Feldner at the wheel. They headed back to the cove where they had landed two miles from the centre of town and uncovered the Zodiac they had hidden on the deserted beach. Ari ordered his men to carry the Zodiac down and into the water. As soon as they had launched the vessel, Gold and Sharon lowered and started the twin 200hp outboards and the squad headed south at maximum speed. They had exited the town square undiscovered and easily evacuated the beach.

Within fifteen minutes of assassinating the four terrorists, the Israelis were riding at high speed back to Israeli waters. An Israeli naval patrol boat was assigned to watch over them, shadowing them offshore and providing cover in the event Hezbollah or Lebanese armed forces attempted to intercept them.

When Ari and his team returned to their base, there was a debriefing and congratulations from their commander, Captain Herschel Zimmerman.

"Nice clean op, Lazarus. The intelligence we're getting from across the border is that all four were about to be feted as heroes. Now the locals are all pissed that they are also martyrs. Apart from the usual trashy claims about the Zionist occupier and evil enemy, neither the Lebanese nor Hezbollah have a clue as to what actually happened. Well done."

Ari and his team were satisfied that they had sent a warning to future terrorists. The news out of Lebanon was that four heroes of the resistance had died while valiantly fighting off an overwhelming force of Zionist bandits who had attempted to occupy Lebanon. The four had easily fought the enemy before being overwhelmed by a much larger force of Zionist interlopers.

Naturally, the leaders of Hezbollah and the Palestinian Authority named the dead terrorists as martyrs of the occupation resistance, cried to the world about Israeli brutality, yet had not a shred of proof, since there were no witnesses.

As is the Israeli way, there were no celebrations or even declarations of Israeli participation in the assassinations. As far as Israel claimed, the terrorists had been killed in a tribal dispute.

Abu's very large family put on a week-long mourning event in the traditional grieving tent, garnering sympathy and condolences from far and wide. Of course, Israel was blamed, but strangely there was not a shred of hard evidence to connect to the Israeli commandos. There were no spent shells, only assumptions woven into the biased narrative of the anti-Israel media, which did not mention the butchered Israeli family.

For Ari and his squad of Mista'arvim, it was sickening to watch the anti-Israel media. At the UN, the EU Ambassador accused Israel of war crimes and completely ignored any mention of the beach attack and the murders of the innocent family. Even more repugnant was an op-ed in *The New York Times* calling for sanctions against Israel for war crimes. Joining the fray were two left-leaning congressmen, one from New York and the other from California, demanding that the United States cut off all aid to Israel and have the Prime Minister of Israel charged before the ICC in The Hague for Human Rights abuses.

If ever Ari needed a motivator for his later actions, it was these partisan attacks on his country and fellow Israelis.

CHAPTER 11

Montreal, Quebec, September 2002

After completing his tour of duty, Ari entered the Technion and excelled at all of his studies. After two years, at age 23, he elected to take a break and go to his mother's alma mater, McGill University in Montreal, Canada. Ari arrived in Montreal eager to explore and understand life in North America.

He entered McGill University in awe of the beautiful setting among the trees and the mountain, the dominant feature of the Montreal landscape. He stayed with his grandparents, Arnold and Rhoda Grantzman, who were happy to have him with them.

Ari studied French literature, since his French language skills, acquired from Sophie, were excellent, and he perfected his English while taking a philosophy and bioethics course. The philosophy course was one of the most sought-after classes on campus. The professor, Dr. Jackson Aronstein, was well renowned for his brilliance, but besides being a masterful lecturer and author, he was one of the funniest individuals Ari had ever met.

It was during his year under Dr. Aronstein's tutelage that Ari honed his analytical skills and power of reasoning. Dr. Aronstein, through the use of incredibly effective humour, drew Ari out and forced him to think about and debate any subject he turned his fertile mind to. The teacher and mentor was a unique character; an oenophile and a gourmet. Every session he taught usually began or ended with a quick funny commentary on a dinner he had enjoyed in a cozy little restaurant in Old Montreal or an incredible wine tasting he experienced in the Italian district.

At the end of one lecture, Dr. Aronstein asked Ari to remain behind. "So young Lazarus, I understand the Grantzmans are your grandparents and you live in Israel. Now that is a wonderful country! I've travelled there several times, always fascinated by the ever-changing demographics and culture; yet it always remains Jewish in a way we here in North America can never replicate. Tell me, besides getting to know your grandparents, why are you here taking my courses?"

Ari was a little taken aback by this direct and intriguing question. "Professor Aronstein…"

"Ari, when it's just us you can call me Jack."

"Professor… I mean, Jack, I heard of your course and felt it would help me reconcile my thoughts and actions from when I was in the military."

"Interesting. I do not believe I've ever had a student on active service in the military. You were in the Israeli Army, I gather?"

"Yes. I spent almost four years in the IDF. Killing has not traditionally been the Jewish way, but I have learned from you to settle my conscience. I am at peace with all I've done."

"How so?"

"If my country is attacked as it has been, from all sides, by countries intent on destroying us just because we are Jews, and even with international support, I cannot allow it to happen. So, Jack, you helped me determine that if a man kills another in the course of protecting his family and countrymen, he has the right to do so."

"Ari, did you enjoy taking those lives?"

"Not at all. In fact, the knowledge that I was going to have to kill sometimes made me sick to my stomach. I would lie awake the night before an action and debate if I really had any right to terminate another's life."

"So how did I help?"

"You were specific, and careful to describe essential differences between killing and murder. Your explanations made sense in the context of the commandment 'Thou shalt not murder.'"

"Interesting. Here you are in a McGill course, reconciling your actions on the battlefield with the impact of my teachings. I will not pry into where you were and what you did in your IDF, but let me assure you that the very fact we are discussing this here and now is a great testament to your character. I want to thank you for sharing your thoughts."

"Profess—I mean, Jack. Thank you, your support means a great deal."

"I'm glad. It's rare that I am able to have such a discussion with a student. Thank you, Ari. Now I have a rendezvous with a magnificent bottle of Pouilly-Fuissé and an exquisite sole meunière at my favourite establishment in Vieux-Montréal. We shall discuss again. Bonsoir, Lazarus."

"Goodnight, Jack. Enjoy."

As he made his way home, Ari reflected on his meeting with Dr. Aronstein, and for some reason felt more at peace with himself than he had in several months. His belief in his country and his contributions were reaffirmed.

One Shabbat evening not long after, at dinner, Arnold Grantzman asked Ari, "What do you think of Professor Aronstein?"

"Opa, without doubt this man is one of the most brilliant I have ever met."

"How so?"

"He gets a whole class of fifty-plus students in a lecture hall to hang on his every word while he lectures on philosophy. I've never experienced anything quite like it. There is no irritating background noise of paper or feet shuffling. No whispered side conversations. Just rapt silence and attention."

"You know he is very well known inside and outside of McGill. Within our social circle, there are several professionals who attended McGill, as well as their children, and they all speak of Jack Aronstein in glowing terms. As a matter of fact, a number of your grandmother's lady friends vie with each other to have him as a dinner guest. We have been at one such dinner and I have to grant you he is brilliant, but along with that sharp mind is an incredible sense of humour. We were rolling in the aisles listening to him, and after dinner on the way home, we discussed the most entertaining lecture we had received on bioethics that we didn't appreciate until we had departed.

"Indeed, Ari, you are most fortunate to be one of the lucky students to attend his classes."

"Opa, I know that. We all so look forward to his classes. The best part is that he knows every one of us by name, even our backgrounds, and is quite prepared to stay after his lecture and debate or counsel us. Always with a wonderful overriding sense of humour. He is an amazing man."

CHAPTER 12

After two years of the harsh Canadian winters, Ari returned to Tel Aviv in 2004. He was overjoyed to see that his grandparents were now living in a small apartment close to his parents.

Ari was not so sure of what he wanted to do now that he was back home, so he went back to the Technion for two years and finished a degree in electronic communications. After graduating at twenty-seven, he began a search for a job with one of the many new high-tech companies springing up all over Israel at that time. None of the companies or jobs really caught his interest until he joined a small start-up that was manufacturing software for the Air Force. They were taking anti-missile electronics out of the US-supplied fighter aircraft and reconfiguring the software; this would enable IAF pilots to identify and evade multiple missile threats with a greater degree of speed and accuracy.

As he was being shown around the facilities, he noticed a stunning young woman peering through an electro-microscope in one of the test labs. Later that day, he caught up to her in the commissary and introduced himself.

"Hi, I'm Ari Lazarus and I know you are Leah. Hi, Leah."

Taken aback, Leah ignored him. She was diffident, but since he had noticed her name on her ID tag, she knew he knew her name was Leah Friedman.

Following in his brazen, direct manner, Ari sat at her table and began a conversation, albeit one-sided. "So, beautiful Leah Friedman, you are being really cold toward me. That is totally unacceptable. I would suggest before you completely brush me off and send me on my way that you at least do me the honour of agreeing to a coffee date at a nice café. Then, if I am not your type, I will unhappily say goodbye and that will be the sum total of our relationship."

Leah could not believe the nerve of Mr. Ari Lazarus. She appraised him in silence for about a minute and then shocked herself by standing up, smiling, and saying, "Since you put it that way, yes, I'll have coffee with you. Tomorrow at six, at the Origem coffee house."

She turned on her heel and walked away, bothered by the effect he had on her. *Uhmm! He is certainly captivating.* Nevertheless, Leah was convinced she would have her coffee and then politely be on her way.

Things did not work out so simply. Ari's sophistication and good looks lowered her resistance. She was enthralled.

Ari stood when she approached his table. "Hi Leah, I half believed you wouldn't show up."

Conversation was easy. Time stood still for both of them and the quick coffee date became a two-and-a-half-hour discovery tour of each other. Leah finally had to go home to her parents for dinner, but not without exchanging phone numbers and addresses with Ari. When she arrived home, she described him to her parents, something she had never done before.

Ari and Leah began dating and shortly after, Leah invited him home for the first night of Passover. Ari had to plead his case to be excused by his parents, since Eli and Sophie always made a big Seder, which was very important to Ephraim and Miriam.

Ari also captivated Leah's parents. Her father, Max, had served with the Sayeret Matkal and immediately bonded with the young man, even though they both knew that they could not share stories about past missions. Leah's mother, Ruth, was smitten by Ari's demeanour and caring attention toward Leah. They had never before felt so connected to a stranger. It was obvious to both families that Ari and Leah were head-over-heels in love.

Ari's parents, especially Sophie, were constantly insisting that Leah visit at any time. As the relationship between the two families grew, the three women—Sophie, Ruth and Leah—would embark on shopping expeditions or charitable events at Hadassah Hospital together.

Six months after that first encounter in the commissary, a wedding was planned. For Eli and Sophie, it was a highlight of their lives. Ari's grandparents were beyond excited, never having imagined that they would have children, let alone grandchildren who were getting married.

Sophie's parents travelled from Canada and renewed their warm relationship with the Israeli families. Leah came from a small family, and only her parents, Max and Ruth, and Max's sister, Golda Silber, were in attendance. Of course, Ari's whole family welcomed Leah and her relatives with open arms. Ephraim and Miriam gently prodded Eli into making sure their friends Ariel and Yitzak Blum, their great friends from Kibbutz Yagur, were on the guest list. They had continued their special relationship through the years.

Miriam, Ephraim, Yitzak, and Ariel sat next to each other at the ceremony and all had tears in their eyes. They each knew that this joyous occasion was the result of their heroic efforts to survive a living hell and then their joint efforts to enable the Lazaruses to rebuild their lives in Israel.

Ariel's eyes said it all. They were sparkling with joy as she watched the young couple exchange their vows under the chuppah (wedding canopy). She leaned over and whispered to her husband, Yitzhak, "If it had not been for my chance meeting with Miriam and Ephraim on the dock in Haifa all those years ago, I honestly don't believe we would be witnessing this incredible simcha. We and they have been truly blessed to know each other and have had such an enduring friendship."

"*Amen*," her husband replied. "Darling, you worked your magic on Ephraim and Miriam, and since you first met, so much good has happened. Their repaired lives, their children and grandchildren getting married, the incredible success of the canning enterprise at Yagur. They all have stemmed from your adopting the Lazarus family. Even though you are from Brooklyn, you should be considered an Israeli national treasure!"

For that, he received a well-directed elbow jab in the ribs, delivered with a huge grin and sparkling adoring eyes.

CHAPTER 13

After the wedding, Ari realized that getting married was what he truly wanted. For the first time in his life, he had a purpose beyond the military, but he had no grounded career. In the months after he met Leah, he had resigned his position and joined another company, but he now came to recognize that corporate life was not for him. He had thrived during his tour with the Mista'arvim. He revelled in the sheer excitement of providing unparalleled security to his country and the thrill of the hunt in chasing down the radical Islamist terrorists whose only mission in life was to kill Israelis and Jews all over the world.

With Ari in command, his particular group had had significant success in eliminating several score of terrorists both inside Israel's borders and in neighbouring Jordan, Lebanon, Syria, and Gaza.

Ari and his colleagues vowed that one day the terrorists would have no cause to make brazen and cowardly statements of bravado.

Eventually, he discussed his situation with his father, Eli.

"Abba, we are both aware of my general duties in the army, which neither of us can discuss, but I must tell you I miss the purpose and the action."

"Ari, you are married now. Hopefully, please God, you and Leah will have children. You have served your country well; far beyond any expectations. Why would you want to place yourself in harm's way?"

"Abba, I have been on some operations I cannot forget. The hate and vile acts perpetrated on our little country cannot be forgotten or ignored. I know I am able to make a significant contribution to our security. Sitting in an office working up sales and marketing plans for some start-up electronics company doesn't excite me. I know, I know it is nice and secure and safe for Leah, and it makes you and Ima feel settled that I am not crawling around some shithole in an Arab terrorist camp or country. I get all of that. But I must do more for Israel. I will not stand aside while we are threatened every day."

"OK. I understand as a military man. Believe me, I get it completely. But as your Abba, I don't want to understand. The very thought of you in harm's way is difficult to bear. When you were in the Mista'arvim, your Ima worried every day; we knew you could be on a mission. We knew you were when we didn't hear from you for days on end. Your Ima and Nana Miriam sat and drank tea with each other all day. Occasionally they would ask me when I came home if I had heard about or from you. I can tell you it was not a good time. Now you want to put us through that again?"

Eli could discern from his son's body language how despondent he had become.

"OK, my boy, let me make some discreet enquiries. I'm not promising anything, but let me work on it for a week or so."

Eli recognized the talents Ari possessed; and even though he was reluctant at first, he agreed to search out some doors that might open for him. Eli Lazarus was a senior member of the IDF command structure and as such he had a lot of connections, including relationships with the some of the most influential people in the Israeli military and intelligence security establishments.

Eli quietly called on one of his connections, Retired Colonel Avram Kedar, who had fought with Eli on the Golan. Kedar had been an intelligence officer; he and Eli had struck up a collegial relationship. Colonel Kedar had been assigned to the Mossad immediately after the Yom Kippur War; he slowly worked his way up the ranks, so when Eli called him to discuss Ari's desire to get back into the security operations of his country, there was immediate interest. When the second intifada initiated by Arafat broke out in the aftermath of the Camp David Accords, Israel was rocked and stunned by suicide bombings, shootings, and stabbings that ultimately killed over one thousand Israeli civilians and several dozen foreigners.

Colonel Kedar took it upon himself to broach a radical and novel idea to the security cabinet. He proposed that they establish a deep clandestine organization that had no visibility to the Knesset, the press, or the general public, whose mandate would be to track down and kill any terrorists or terrorist leaders wherever they were in the world. All missions would be conducted under deep cover with no lines of accountability, communication or reporting, except to the Prime Minister and the Minister of Defense.

Kedar got his wish and immediately established 9.

"Eli, my old friend, let me pull his service record jacket and check him out."

Soon after, Ari received a call from the retired Colonel. Kedar, who was the director of the very secret and covert department adjunct to the Mossad, invited Ari to meet and discuss his future. The department was so undercover that it was only known as 9, a name based on an original address in Tel Aviv. Today, 9 is the department that focuses on counterterrorism and counterintelligence. It follows no rules of engagement. There are no PC guidelines to adhere to. There is no probing left-wing article from *Haaretz* about the politically incorrect and disproportionate actions of the organization. All activities conducted by 9 are off the reservation; no questions are asked, no answers expected.

Ari's interest was immediately piqued. He went for an initial interview with the colonel and two of his assistants. After the interview, Ari informed his father of the meeting.

"Ari, my son, Avrum Kedar is a very tough and demanding sonofabitch. I've seen him in action. Are you sure you want to be tied up with him? Even I am not sure what he really does, although I'm told it is something to do with Mossad."

"Abba, I just had one interview. He asked some questions. He kept rummaging through my service file and then said I might hear from him."

A week later, because of his broad academic and military skills, Ari was invited to join 9. Eli called Avrum Kedar to thank him and said a silent prayer for his son's safety. He dared not tell Sophie. Neither did Ari—not a word to his mother or Leah.

CHAPTER 14

For the next nine years, Ari travelled to most of the major European capitals, plus several in the Middle East, as the leader of a team of retribution operators. Based on intelligence gathered and provided by 9, team members, either in a group or sometimes solo, sought out the worst Islamic jihadi radical terrorists that were promoting hatred and inciting murder in Israel and against the Jewish people around the world. Their mandate was to remove the monsters and send them to live with seventy-two virgins in the nether world. Most of the operations entailed the use of a silenced handgun or a double-edged commando knife, and occasionally a serrated piano-wire garrote.

The "customers," as 9 referred to them, never knew what happened. Some were shot sitting on a bench in Central Park in New York or Hyde Park in London. Some were garroted standing outside their mosques in Paris or Malmö, while others were lured to building rooftops in Madrid and Montreal for clandestine meetings where, after their throats were slashed, they were left to bleed out and die.

One particularly difficult and dangerous mission involved Ari and a colleague, Alon Nuss. Macha, as the director of 9 was known, had tasked his two top operators with tracking down one Mohamar Al-Said Erekat. Erekat was a Hamas leader who had been responsible for several deadly attacks on Israeli civilians in Judea and Samaria. Erekat was also behind a heinous shooting of a young family—a husband, Gideon Shalit and his pregnant wife, Ruth, as well as their three-year old daughter, Judith. They had been waiting at a bus stop just outside Jerusalem. Ruth and her unborn child, as well as little innocent Judith, died in a hail of bullets fired by Erekat.

Erekat managed to elude the Shin Bet and the IDF despite a massive manhunt. Ultimately, the Shin Bet and Mossad picked up intelligence that Erekat, using false identity papers, had managed to travel to Greece and then obtained a cleverly forged passport. As a citizen of Cyprus, he had crossed the Atlantic Ocean to New York.

The Israeli authorities had the option of unmasking him to the FBI and the NYPD as a known terrorist. Instead, Macha gave the green light to Ari and Alon to follow Erekat to New York. By the time they identified their target, they discovered that he had been passed along through the radical Islamic network to the gritty area of Roxbury, just outside Boston. Ari and Alon drove to Boston and determined that Erekat had been given a menial and obscure job; he was assisting a Hamas sympathizer who owned a stall in the Faneuil Hall Marketplace downtown.

After conducting surveillance for five days, the two Israeli operators were familiar with Erekat's daily routine. He travelled by public transit to and from his rented room in Roxbury to work at the market. At lunch time each day he bought a sandwich at one of the market stalls and, weather permitting, went outside to eat on a bench in the square, ironically adjacent to the Boston Holocaust Memorial.

On the sixth day of their Boston stay, Ari and Alon watched Erekat buy his sandwich and a cold drink, then walk out to the square. He sat down and began to unwrap his sandwich, but before the paper was half off, Ari walked quickly behind the bench and in a single swift strike he plunged his double-edged combat knife into the nape of Erekat's neck, severing his spinal column and killing him instantly.

With Alon providing cover by rushing to Erekat's aid, pretending to believe it was a random medical emergency, Ari quickly disappeared into the Market Hall and exited out the other end, unobserved. Alon and other passersby quickly concluded that Mohomar Al-Said Erekat had been stabbed to death and summoned the Boston Police. By the time the first responders appeared, Alon had drifted away and jumped on a transit bus. When he was sure he was not being noticed or followed, he got off the bus and went back to the safe house he and Ari had rented.

By the time Alon entered the living room, Ari was packing up their equipment and bags, tuned into the local TV news station, which was blaring the news of what appeared to be a murder in broad daylight in Faneuil Square. The victim had just been identified as Mohomar Abbas, a recent immigrant from Lebanon.

Within fifteen minutes of the broadcast, Ari and Alon were driving up I-95 to Portland, Maine. There they dropped off their rental and booked into a Motel 6 under assumed names. Ari contacted 9 HQ in Tel Aviv and ascertained that so far there were no reliable clues, suspects, or motive in the Boston murder. Macha advised Ari and Alon to lay low in the motel for two days, then purchase tickets from Portland to Philadelphia on American Airlines. Once in Philadelphia, they were to go to a Mossad safe house and again lay low for two days, then again purchase tickets from Philadelphia to Paris on Icelandair.

Once they deplaned in Paris, they rented a car and drove across the French–German border to Frankfurt. They stayed for another two days in a Holiday Inn at the Frankfurt Airport and once again purchased tickets online to Tel Aviv under yet another set of aliases. By the time they checked into the 9 offices the day after their convoluted trip from Boston, the whole incident was quiet in the news. The Boston Police Department, not having any credible witnesses or clues, let the case fall by the wayside and announced that it was probably some sort of revenge killing from within the immigrant victim's community.

It was only after the NYPD received a heads-up from one of their contacts in Mossad that Erekat had travelled to the United States under the alias of Mohomar Abbas that they informed the FBI. The FBI consulted with the Boston Police and the case mysteriously closed.

CHAPTER 15

Vienna, July 2015

Ari and his family had just sat down and ordered their coffees and pastry selection. Leah and Esther were mesmerized by the bustling street scene of the Schottenring. Leah turned to Ari, "Sweetheart, why are you so down on the Austrians and Viennese? They look so happy and carefree."

Esther chimed in, "Yes, Abba you have always been so negative about Austria and this beautiful city. Just look at the architecture; everywhere you turn there is another magnificent site. And the music! Oh, Abba, the music it is so glorious!"

Ari indulged his wife and daughter with a smile. Valiantly, he tried to push his history in Vienna out of his mind and made a concerted effort to enjoy the time with them. They were so happy to be here.

"Esther, you know that not far from where we are sitting, my grandparents, your great-grandparents, used to live in a beautiful apartment? They were both highly respected members of the Jewish community. Both medical professionals who loved Vienna. Then the Nazis came and that all changed. This city became a dark, hateful place where culture and enlightenment died with most of Austria's Jews."

Leah and Esther both knew when to leave Ari to his thoughts. He sat there sullenly for a few moments, trying as hard as he could not to brood about the past.

CHAPTER 16

Vienna, May 2005

In May 2005, Ari got a tip from his friend Laurent Tremblay of the French DGSE that Ali-Ibrahim Yasser was living quite openly in a small suburb of Vienna. Yasser was a PLO mastermind behind a wave of suicide bombings that had devastated Israel for nearly fifteen years. Ari and three fellow 9 operatives made their way to the old city. They spent four weeks surveilling Yasser, following him on foot, and keeping his home under watch as he travelled in and around Vienna. They were impressed with their target. Unlike many terrorists who paraded around the European capitals with an entourage of bodyguards, Yasser was a solo operator. He was an unobtrusive individual who lived in a nondescript apartment building in the Leopoldstadt District, an area inhabited by young people and multiethnic immigrant groups. Yasser's thinking was probably that he would blend in and disappear among the crowd.

Leopoldstadt offered many choices for getting in and out of the city. Yasser always used different routes and methods of transportation to get around as he visited the various internet cafés he frequented.

Abu Yasser had been educated in Cairo and earned a degree in electrical engineering. While he was attending university, he became radicalized by the Muslim Brotherhood and for no reason at all developed a violent and vicious hatred for Israel, Jews, and Americans. He honed his engineering skills and his rage into a diabolical killing machine, developing several sophisticated bomb-making factories in Gaza, Judea and Samaria, Kabul, and Baghdad. His designs were built and given to misguided youths, who strapped them on to become suicide bombers. One of his wicked devices was responsible for killing several senior US military and CIA officers in Afghanistan, after the bomber, posing as an Afghani officer, gained access to a secure military installation and blew himself up. Abu Yasser was a high value target and Ari and 9 were determined to take him down.

Avrum Kedar was adamant that the action had to be clean; no collateral casualties, including the members of Yasser's family. He had a wife and two young children, a boy of five and a girl of three.

Each week, Yasser went to a different café, but unwittingly he had established a pattern. After each visit to one of his routine haunts, one of the three 9 operatives would enter the café and purchase time on the computer Yasser had just released. On every occasion, they found nothing, as Yasser scrupulously removed any evidence of emails or internet chats. Nevertheless, they persisted, and on the fourth Wednesday they hit pay dirt. Yasser had inadvertently not deleted all of his email trail.

Ari, wearing a disguise, entered the café at the same time as Yasser and purchased time on a computer. After working at the station for about twenty minutes, Yasser ended his session and left the café with Eli, also in disguise, following him. Ari walked out of the café a few minutes later, after he had managed to discretely download all the information from the terminal Yasser had just used.

As Noah picked him up at the curb, Ari had the look of a cat that finally caught the mouse.

"As they say in North America, *bingo*!" he exclaimed to Noah. Ari then sent a text message to Eli to abandon his watch on Yasser and meet them at the safe house.

Once they were all together, Eli downloaded the flash drive onto his encrypted laptop. Once he opened up the trail of emails, they could not believe how careless Yasser had been.

"Look at all this stuff. He is obviously establishing a network of assets with the intention of doing some major damage here in Europe."

Ari leaned over and read the screen. "He's coded all this, but the references to the princes and princesses can only mean the Royal Family in London. Here he is sending a message to one of his co-conspirators in Tehran that the biblical enemies of Muhammad will soon feel the wrath of Allah."

Noah injected his opinion. "This means an Iranian-funded attack somewhere on Israel or a major Jewish target in Europe. Perhaps the recently refurbished Great Synagogue in Berlin or the Jewish Museum in Berlin."

Eli sent an encrypted security email blast that would not even be detected by the NSA in Maryland or GHQ in Cheltenham, England. It contained all the information and was sent back to Netanya. Then they waited for 9 to respond.

Within a half day, Ari received a text. "You have an important customer awaiting service before next Thursday." It was signed M. Sales Department 9.

They had all the information they needed. Ari implemented their plan to terminate Yasser.

The following Wednesday, right on cue, the four Israelis followed Yasser to Café Babylon on Lindauergasse, another internet café he used. To their utter amazement, he still had had no contact with any other jihadis and appeared to have no protection. They had not only read his emails, received and sent, but 9 had deciphered some of the hidden codes they used. Most of the intended recipients and senders appeared to be Iranian Quds operatives and Europeans believed to be sleepers for the jihadis.

When Yasser was set up in front of his rented computer station, Noah entered the café and purchased half an hour of internet time in the seat next to him. Ari and Adam were in a rented Audi A4 across the street from the café. Eli was sitting at a table outside the café, sipping a coffee.

When Noah was almost through with his half hour, he stood and went to the men's room. It was through a door almost immediately in front of Yasser's desk, and with casual confidence he sauntered to the washroom.

On returning, with Eli observing him, Noah held his right hand down by his thigh, carrying a .22 calibre Beretta pistol. As he walked past, he shot Yasser twice in the left ear, killing him on the spot.

The dead terrorist unfortunately created a disturbance as he fell from his chair and toppled the computer he had been using. The small calibre rounds that were fired into his ear did little or no outward damage to Yasser's head; there was only a small amount of blood to identify his injury.

Within seconds, the café was in chaos. When Abu Yasser fell to the floor, it took a few seconds for the four other patrons and two staff members to process what had occurred. Then mayhem broke out, with people screaming and searching around as to what had happened. Noah quickly stepped out of the café onto Lindauergasse, unfortunately into the arms of a passing policeman who had heard the commotion.

Eli jumped from his seat and attempted to push the policeman to the ground so Noah could run. Noah took off, sprinting onto Ottakringerstrasse, where he was able to jump on a passing tram. The policeman was not giving up so easily, and now was grappling with Eli.

Both Ari and Adam left the car and ran to Eli's aid, with Adam finally incapacitating the police officer with a sharply administered blow to his ear, stunning him and causing him to collapse to the sidewalk. He would awaken moments later with a massive but nonthreatening headache after the Israelis had fled the scene.

People were starting to congregate around the entrance to the café and the scene outside. The team operators each went in separate directions. Eli quickly walked to Freedmangasse and eventually rode a tram for thirty minutes before retreating to the safe house per their emergency exit plan. Ari and Adam left the Audi where it was parked legally; it would gain little or no attention for at least three hours, until the rush hour commenced, when it would be removed by the traffic authorities. After riding on buses, trams, and the subway, they returned to the safe house. The Audi would be a mystery vehicle that no one would claim from the towing impound lot until long after the team had exited Austria.

Soon the news outlets were chattering about the assassination of a Middle Eastern businessman in broad daylight in an internet café. As the day progressed and his real identity became public knowledge, the Hezbollah–Hamas–PLO propaganda machine went into high gear, proclaiming Yasser's innocence as a devout Muslim and family man. All three groups vowed revenge on the Israeli oppressors who had probably killed their hero.

Of course, within a few days, his demise was old news and faded onto the back pages.

CHAPTER 17

Vienna, 2015

Ari was reflecting on his team's close call in Vienna during their last mission there, when he looked across the terrace and froze. A tall, rugged man had walked in and sat down at one of tables across from Ari and his family. There, sitting alone, was one of the most wanted and feared terrorists in the world, Ibrahim Al-Baghdadi.

Ari had only once seen a blurry picture of Al-Baghdadi, about nine years earlier when the United States was seeking Israel's cooperation in trying to capture him. Al-Baghdadi was responsible for hundreds of American and Canadian military deaths in both Iraq and Afghanistan since 2003. He designed nearly all the IED explosions that killed or maimed the Allied troops. He had trained in Iran and became one of the most feared bomb-makers and instructors in the world.

Al-Baghdadi was rarely, if ever, seen in public. The United States and Israel both had him at the top of their most-wanted lists. Ari and the teams from 9 always kept an eye out for him but never caught even a whiff of his scent. Now here he was in broad daylight, sitting larger than life in a Viennese café.

Why now, when I'm with my family?

With his photographic memory kicking in, Ari went from relaxed vacationer to 9 working mode. While he was observing and processing every detail of his target's appearance, body language, facial patterns, and anything else he could without being noticed for staring, Leah and Esther happily chatted about their plans for the day, especially the evening Strauss concert at the Salonorchester Alt Wien, perhaps the most famous concert hall in Europe.

As the waiter brought their orders, two unsavoury-looking characters joined Al-Baghdadi at his table. Ari did not recognize them, but he concluded they were probably Chechens or Bosnians.

Why are they in Vienna? Wherever Al-Baghdadi went, there was a heightened risk to nearby innocent citizens. He was believed by the Mossad to have been the mastermind behind the bus bombing of Israeli tourists in Bulgaria two years previously. While Leah knew that her husband worked on national security for a living, she never was aware of the extent of Ari's activities, the direct role he played in planning and executing covert missions, and the dangers his job presented.

Suddenly fearing for his wife and daughter, Ari asked them to hurry and finish their coffee and breakfast. At first Leah was about to protest; their food had just arrived! But once she saw the firm, cold expression in her husband's blue eyes and the set position of his jaw, Leah knew enough not to question him.

Ari got up and excused himself to go the men's room, and on his return, while appearing to be texting on his cell phone, he captured a picture of all three men. Aware that he would need assistance, Ari sent a copy of the pictures he had taken to his trusted contact in the French DGSE (Direction Générale de la Sécurité Extérieure), Laurent Tremblant. They had met when Ari was studying at McGill and Tremblant was there on a year's English language course. After college, both had coincidently travelled similar paths into the world of counterterror and covert operations.

Ari stood and kissed Leah and Esther goodbye, then loudly proclaimed in French that he would meet them for lunch back at the hotel. They both hurried away.

As he sat down again, his phone signalled an incoming call. It was Tremblant.

"Where are you exactly, and are they still in sight?"

Ari replied in French. "I am seated on the terrace of the Café Schottenring looking at three good customers." Ali-Baghdadi was still deep in conversation with his two companions.

"Bon! Stay there. You will meet two old friends from school, Jacques and Pierre, in five minutes. They are two of my best operators there in Vienna; they've been sitting on a couple of money launderers we think are tied to Islamic Jihad."

Within minutes, Jacques and Pierre arrived and Ari and the two DGSE operatives made a big fuss of renewing acquaintances. The two Frenchmen sat down and ordered espresso, all the time observing the three men at Al-Baghdadi's table by watching their reflection in the windows of the café.

Ari had gone against his better instincts and left his weapon in the hotel room safe. He had promised Leah that he would focus on their family time together and leave work behind… now, for the first time ever, he found himself unprepared. His training had taught him to always be ready, especially for an unexpected situation; yet he was currently at a disadvantage. Jacques and Pierre, however, had silenced Beretta pistols and one had a garrote, which he passed to Ari.

Always in French, Ari asked, "What the hell are these guys up to? They are sitting here as large as life and we have to know they are not on a vacation."

Pierre responded, "That fucker Baghdadi is a monster; he for sure cannot be up to any good."

"Oui, J'pense la même chose." Yes, I think the same thing.

Ari, Jacques, and Pierre concluded that Al-Baghdadi was in Vienna to carry out a bombing. They believed he had developed a plan and the other two thugs were strictly temporary muscle, there to provide security for him. If they encountered any opposition or trouble, those two assholes would be deemed expendable.

There were three potential venues for a high-casualty attack. First was the world-famous Spanish Riding School of Austria. The Duke and Duchess of Cambridge were invited guests of the Austrian president and were due to attend a performance at the school in two days. This sent cold shivers down Ari's spine; Esther was planning to take her parents on a tour the next day.

A second possible target was a working session of OPEC, which was a target of terrorists led by Carlos the Jackal in 1975. The OPEC session was being held at their headquarters in Vienna a week later. A third possible bomb location was a glittering event at the Vienna State Opera that same evening. All three were soft targets for Al-Baghdadi.

Ari was consumed with worry. To put himself in danger was one thing, but the idea of Leah and Esther anywhere near a possible Al-Baghdadi target was horrifying. He needed to focus and function as a professional, even though this suddenly affected him on a very personal level.

Ari, Jacques, and Pierre spoke in animated French about the political problems in France, the rise of the far right, and how it was impacting the French economy with uncertainty around the upcoming elections. Pierre, who was vociferous in his contempt for the current French president, got up and went to the washroom. When he returned, he told them that there was a back door leading to an alley behind the café.

Once Pierre returned to the table, they held a quick discussion, during which they agreed that Jacques and Pierre would shoot the two thugs and Ari would get behind Al-Baghdadi and finish him with the garrote.

There were still a few patrons in the café. Ari and the two DGSE agents concluded that they could be out the back door and away from the scene before anyone reacted to call the police. Pierre's biggest concern was the young barman/waiter; he was not that busy, and therefore he was paying attention to all the patrons and general activities inside the café. The single waiter was in and out, serving coffee and pushing the pastry cart; he would not be so quickly aware of anything untoward occurring.

They discussed the chance that the barman would be able to identify at least one of them—probably Ari, as he had arrived earlier and spent the most time in the café. After some cautious discussion, they agreed it was a risk they would have to take. None of the three operators, Ari and the two Frenchmen, wanted to harm the innocent man, but they were prepared to neutralize him if necessary.

Jacques and Pierre stood and said goodbye to Ari in French, then both went inside the café—one to pay the bill and the other to the restroom. They did this with a flourish; noticed and yet unheeded by the three terrorists as Pierre and Jacques walked by their table in a lively conversation. As they came alongside the two goons, they raised the silenced Berretta pistols from their right legs and shot each in the nape of the neck.

Ali-Baghdadi's eyes bulged in shock and he stood to investigate the sudden spurts of blood. He didn't notice as Ari slipped behind him and in one quick moment severed his carotid artery with the piano wire. All three kills took less than five seconds, and Ari, Jacques, and Pierre were out the back door of the café before anyone, even the barman, realized what had transpired.

The barman, poor fellow, was left to assess the situation—copious amounts of blood, three dead patrons, and several screaming, traumatized customers, including the waiter, who was rooted to the floor in shock. The barman was overwhelmed; he never even registered the three men who hastily exited through the rear of the café as he urgently called for emergency assistance.

When Leah and Esther met Ari for lunch, he seemed distant yet satisfied with himself. Taking another human being's life was not something he ever relished or enjoyed, but by eliminating a terrible threat, Ari and his two French companions had saved all three possible targets, and that was most satisfying. There was also a feeling of settling an old score for his grandparents, Ephraim and Miriam, whose lives had been ripped apart by the evil that had lived in this beautiful city only a few short years ago. To this day, neither his grandfather nor grandmother had ever discussed their time in Auschwitz. They never mentioned the hell they survived there or the subsequent death march in January 1945. Ari mentally noted this as he remained mindful of Dr. Aronstein's teachings at McGill.

Applying the rules of bioethics and philosophy was a challenge when confronted with taking another human life. Many was the time, and now was another, when Ari wrestled with whether any killing of his violated the Ten Commandments. Ironically, his grandfather Ephraim and Dr. Jackson Aronstein had each separately explained the rabbinical thoughts on this commandment.

"Thou shalt not murder" means that you shall not murder for gain or crime. As the ancient Hebrews were forced to kill to protect their families and lives, so were the modern-day Jews of Israel. Having settled that internal argument once again, Ari sat back to enjoy lunch with his family.

Jacques and Pierre checked in to DGSE headquarters two hours later, as they drove across the border into Germany. Laurent Tremblant, fully understanding Ari's situation, had advised the CIA, SIS, and the Mossad, who informed 9 of Al-Baghdadi's demise. The LVT (BVT)—Landesamt für Verfassungsschutz und Terrorismusbekämpfung (State Offices for the Protection of the Constitution and Counterterrorism)—quickly took over from the local police. The LVT commander, Joachim Voelpel, informed the media that the killings were part of a Serbian gang war and the perpetrators were probably professional assassins long gone from Austria. By assuming charge of the investigation, he took statements from the witnesses—the most credible being the barman, who had sorry little to offer as the incident had unfolded so fast.

"There were three men who spoke good French. I heard shots, they left in a hurry, but so did everyone else. Did the French guys kill him?"

"Could you identify them again?" questioned the inspector assisting Voelpel.

"No." The bartender was still shaking. "All I remember is that they were maybe in their thirties. No hair on their faces. Short dark hair—at least I think so. They were definitely French. I don't even know if they even did it—it all happened so fast. I think they ran out the door with everyone else, on Schottenring. I don't even remember what they were wearing! Everything happened so fast! I'm sorry I don't know more."

Voelpel had sidelined the local police investigation and shut down any further description of Ari and his DGSE colleagues being disseminated to local law enforcement. Quietly, he confirmed to his counterparts in SIS, the CIA, Mossad, and DGSE that Al-Baghdadi was indeed dead.

After an enjoyable lunch, Leah and Esther met up with Ari at the hotel and continued their vacation in Vienna. Ari for some reason now had a better feeling about the city. Leah and Esther were fascinated by the Leopold Art Museum. Esther particularly was a great fan of the famous Austrian artist Gustav Klimt and the Leopold museum housed the largest collection of Klimt's works.

That evening, they all went to the famous Vienna concert hall and were treated to a magnificent performance of Strauss. On the way back to their hotel in a taxi, Ari and his family passed by the restaurant where he had had his encounter with Al-Baghdadi. It was as if nothing had happened. There were no crime scene tapes and the restaurant was full of Viennese and tourists, enjoying their late evening coffees and Sucher tarts.

CHAPTER 18

Later, in their hotel room, Leah and Ari watched Euro News and BBC 1, both of which had a news item on a suspected assassination of one of the most-wanted terrorists in the world, Al-Baghdadi, in a Viennese café. BBC One was closest to the mark, saying that Austrian authorities were describing the killing as a hit between two rival drug- and arms-smuggling gangs. In fact, their informed sources were telling them that since Al-Baghdadi had been one of worst terrorists still at large and on many most-wanted lists for many years, the probability was that he had been assassinated by either the Israeli Mossad or one of the US intelligence agencies—perhaps the CIA or a Department of Defense retribution team.

Leah looked at Ari and their eyes met. His face was an expressionless mask.

"What do you think happened, Ari? Those three men in the café. Immediately after you saw them you froze and chased us back to the hotel. It was you!" She whispered. "What they are saying about an Israeli assassination squad, that was you, wasn't it? Ari, tell me!" Leah was careful not to raise her voice but did nothing to hide her shocked realization and frustration. "Oh, Ari! My God, this isn't anything new for you, is it? All these years, you've kept your job hidden from me. I get it now. I understand you had to keep this work secret, but I am so scared for you, Ari! For us. For Esther... My God, I married a killer!" With this she let a tiny laugh escape, a laugh from pure nerves. "I trust you, Ari. I have to trust you. I only wish you would have trusted me."

Ari sat immobile and said not a word. Finally, he stood up from the edge of the bed and walked around to Leah's side. As he leaned over her, he said, "We Israelis are alone in the world, my love. Most of the globe's population would be perfectly happy if one morning they woke up and there was no more Israel—no more Jews. I have fought for our beleaguered little nation as my father did before me. We can't stand with heads bowed or go quietly—not again. We have a right to safety, Leah. I could not watch that bastard kill more people, spouting that it is all for the sake of so-called Occupied Palestine—when it's just one more excuse to butcher our people. And the world won't raise a finger to protect us, and they will blame our country for all of it. The world shows over and over again that they won't save us. We have to protect ourselves.

"I will tell you just this once, Leah. There is no way I will ever allow anyone to hurt you, Esther, my family, or my country. I will not discuss this further, but just know when it is necessary, you have my word that I will ensure our safety."

Leah nodded as tears rolled down her cheeks. She had always suspected that Ari's involvement in the security of their country was more than a desk job. She had never asked, but now she knew. Taking a deep breath and pulling herself together, she looked at her husband and saw him as if for the first time. "Darling Ari, I understand. When I saw the look on your face this morning when those men came into the café, I knew something was terribly wrong. Even then, I was afraid to think about it, let alone ask questions. Now I know, and honestly on one hand, I wish I didn't, but on the other, I am so, so proud of you. Darling, you have my support and I know you do what you do for the good of all of us."

Ari walked back to his side of the bed and sighed. "Don't be concerned, Leah. You're safe, I promise. The people that have to be afraid are those terrorists. My friends and I know who they are and even where they live. In Ramallah or Damascus. In Beirut or Paris. Even Los Angeles or Buenos Aires. They need to be very afraid. Now, enough of this talk! We have a long day of sightseeing and museum tours Esther has arranged for tomorrow. I don't want her to be disappointed, and we need the rest. Let's get some sleep and have some fun tomorrow." Ari turned out the lights and shut off the TV. Soon he and Leah were fast asleep in each other's arms.

CHAPTER 19

Tel Aviv, one week later

Their Vienna vacation over, Ari, Leah, and Esther were back in Tel Aviv. The weather that day was stunning, with iris blue skies, a balmy temperature, and the vibrancy that is unique to Israel. Leah had prepared a traditional Israeli breakfast of shakshouka (a poached egg and tomato dish), Israeli salad (with cucumbers, tomato, and mint), fruit, hummus, cheese, lox, special thick yogourt, and of course, coffee.

"Ari, my dear husband, what are you plans for the day? Esther and I are going to take your mother for a girls' day out in Tel Aviv. We're going shopping and having lunch, then we'll visit the new exhibit at the art museum. It will be a nice excursion for Esther before she goes back to school."

Ari considered this news for a second or two. "I am going to meet one of my old army buddies for lunch, and then I hope to go back to his office and apply for a new position at his company." This surprised Leah; she did not know that Ari was considering changing jobs. "When did you decide to change your job?"

"After that episode in Vienna, the company suggested I come in from being a field sales consultant and take up a head office position responsible for training, but I really don't think I'm suited to the burdensome politics of office life. I realize how worried you are and it's time to make a change."

He knew he was only placating Leah. Ever since their hotel room conversation, he recognized that any time he had to go away on a business trip, she would fear for his safe return. He hoped this little subterfuge, letting her believe he was shifting to a desk role, would put her at ease.

Leah walked around the table and placed her hands on her husband's shoulders, whispering in his ear as she nuzzled him. "Ari, you have always been good at what you do. Whatever you decide, just be happy. I am sure you will find your feet in any new position."

Ari was thankful that Leah had abandoned any more discussion regarding the assassination in the Café Schottenring. Although he knew she wasn't taking his work lightly, she had quickly come to grips with his profession. With that encouragement and unconditional acceptance, Ari stood, hugged his beautiful wife, kissed Esther, and left for his meeting.

CHAPTER 20

The 9 building, Netanya, Israel

In reality, Ari was not going to have lunch with an old army buddy. His meeting was with the newly appointed director of 9, Benyamin Nadel. Nadel had been Director of the Military Intelligence Directorate, AMAN, until his retirement from the military two years ago. Recent changes in the senior ranks of Mossad and 9 had led to the surprise nomination of Nadel to the position of director.

Ari had received a coded message to come in for an important meeting. He was surprised, since once he came in from a mission, he was typically allowed to debrief and then take some time off. Because his vacation in Vienna had so suddenly turned into a full mission, he had immediately been debriefed when he returned two days before.

Being summoned so soon after his Vienna debriefing was not protocol. Ari figured there had to be a major operation in the planning stages that required his presence.

Within 9, the director was known simply as Macha. Ari was ushered into Macha's spartan office by an attractive young woman, Captain Netta Levi.

She acted as receptionist for the general office when in fact she was a first-class analyst. Netta's team was a group of five young men and women who gathered reams of raw data; under her leadership, they provided Macha and field operatives such as Ari with the most up to date intelligence available.

Also seated in front of Macha was David (Dov) Horowitz. David was a Sayeret Matkal commando senior officer, who had a reputation within the IDF secret forces for being a fearless leader. Horowitz was tall, 6'2", and powerfully built, with massive shoulders and forearms. He had successfully played American football at Ohio State University for two years and then had been keenly sought after by many NFL teams because of his speed and physicality. A few years later, he led his Sayeret command on a number of highly classified missions in Gaza, Iran, Lebanon, Syria, and Iraq. Each country was harbouring several less jihadi terrorists as a direct result of Dov's actions. Ari knew of Dov by reputation and had met him briefly several years before, when he and Dov had participated in a joint training exercise.

"Ari come sit down," suggested Director Nadel. "Major Horowitz and I wish to discuss a situation with you. As you know, the PM has been fierce in voicing his concerns surrounding Iranian nuclear ambitions. He is distressed over US reluctance to let us cut those ambitions short and angry at the duplicity of the American president for entering into secret negotiations with the Iranians. The nuclear deal cobbled together by the US and other powers this year, is still, in his opinion, a terrible deal—not only for Israel, but also for the world at large."

Macha looked to Dov and nodded for him to continue.

"Here is the thing, Lazarus, the reason we are here. Whether the Americans like it or not, we have no choice with all that is happening in the Middle East but to cut off, once and for all, Iran's path to the Bomb. The USA is getting a new president next year. If Iran remains free to build a viable nuclear bomb, however long it takes them, we know with Hamas, Hezbollah, and the Palestinians as their proxies they will use it on Israel and Saudi Arabia. We are in this; we don't have a choice."

Macha interjected, "The PM is horrified that the US president could even consider such an accommodation with the mullahs."

Dov continued, "PM Mendelsohn believes that the hubris and arrogance of the US leader is so great that he cares more for his immediate legacy and standing in the Muslim world than the safety and security of his own citizens, much less Israel and Europe. To me it is fucking incredible that he cannot understand how dangerous those pieces of shit in Tehran are. They have indoctrinated close to eighty million people against us and the US. They are trying to build nuclear weapons with the required delivery systems to reach us, and that eloquent, elitist prick in the White House wants to make nice and play patty-cake with them."

Ari could sense the rage and passion in every word Dov spoke.

"I have proposed an operation to Macha that I believe has a good chance of success," Dov said. "It will be as effective as our air ops that destroyed the Iraqi and Syrian nuclear facilities in the past."

Macha studied both men, paying close attention to Ari's face as he listened in respectful silence to Dov laying out the plan.

"Lazarus, I am convinced the Iranians are expecting us to hit them the way we did in Iraq and Syria at Oswirik and Kibar. They have beefed up their air defences with the aid of Russia and their guards are training constantly to be prepared for any kind of attack. We have done our due diligence and we believe that Israel has no alternative but to hit those bastards hard. We must obliterate their nuclear infrastructure and, more importantly, their seat of government. The Ayatollah and the Council of Clerics have got to go, before they can deploy their fucking bomb."

As he spoke, Dov was pacing furiously back and forth across Macha's office. Ari studied him with intensity that Macha noticed with concern, but he held back from making any comments.

Dov laid out the overall concept of his idea. "We will carry out a deception with air assets to get their attention in the wrong place. We can use ELINT assets of the IDF Air Force and Navy to shut down their military communications just as we did in Syria. At the same time, we insert my Sayeret Matkal Special Forces to destroy the nuclear facilities."

Dov continued the mission outline for another fifteen minutes, then sat back and stared at Ari, awaiting a response.

Slowly, Ari stood up walked over to the darkened window. All the windows had been painted with a sound-reflecting material that prevented any microphones from picking up conversations within the premises and any outside surveillance. Their current location was one of the most secret installations in Israel. Ari sipped his water slowly, then walked back to Macha's desk and placed his hands firmly on the surface. He leaned over the desk and focused his blue steely gaze first on Macha, then on Dov and back again.

"Is this a politically sanctioned op, or is it one of your off-the-books schemes?"

"It's sanctioned," Macha responded plainly.

"By whom?"

"That is above your pay grade for now. Just know that it is sanctioned. I have accepted the directive. You've heard the bones of the operation from Dov. Now I want the two of you to go away. For the next month, you are to plan this operation down to the last detail so the only conclusion will be no more nuclear threat from Iran. Is that clear? You can have any resources you require, but all requests for supplies, human resources, and special intelligence must be directed only to me. I will ensure that this office supports you by all means possible."

Ari remained standing, staring intently at the ceiling without moving. Finally, he turned to Dov and silently nodded his assent, and then said to Macha, "When do we commence?"

CHAPTER 21

Dov Horowitz's grandparents, Mayer and Ruth Horowitz, like Ephraim and Miriam, had survived the horrors of the Nazi extermination camps. In the Horowitz's case, they had been incarcerated in Stutthof, Poland. They also survived by sheer determination to bring the injustices of the Nazis in Poland to light. When the Russians had liberated Stutthof, Mayer realized that he and Ruth had to get as far away as they could from the Soviets. He quickly saw that the Russians were not too concerned about the health and welfare of several thousand starving Jews. They were much more concerned about conquering Poland and Germany.

Once they were able to leave the camp and before the Russians set up a new camp, Mayer and Ruth and other like-minded survivors quickly made their way to Gdansk. From there, they were able to gain humanitarian passage on a ferry provided by the Allies. Once in Hamburg, they were in the British sector of occupied Germany. There, the British Red Cross and military had established a displaced persons camp. The DP camps housed survivors of the extermination camps from Poland, who were fleeing from the Russians and the Poles.

Mayer and Ruth were eventually documented and processed into one of the camps near Menden, a small town not far from Dusseldorf. After spending almost two years in the Menden DP camp, they were able to leave and made their way to Palestine in 1947. Dov's grandfather, Mayer, was a giant among men, both physically and mentally. Recognizing that the Arab world was about to repeat another Holocaust, he had joined the nascent IDF and was soon selected for subsequent leadership roles. Because of his imposing size and razor-sharp intellect, Mayer attracted both support from his commanders and loyalty from the men he led.

During the heavy fighting in Jerusalem, Mayer was trying to prevent the Jordanians from capturing the whole city. It was because of his efforts in multiple locations that the Israelis were able to hold on to West Jerusalem. Without much food or water, and dwindling ammunition, Mayer exhorted his tiny group to attack. One of his biggest regrets was that he and the small but ferocious band of defenders of Jerusalem had to cede the Temple and the Kotel (Western Wall) to the Jordanians. The Jordanian occupation lasted for 19 years until Israeli troops chased the Jordanians back across the Jordan River in 1967, during the Six-Day War, liberating the occupied Old City of East Jerusalem, Judea and Samaria.

Mayer forever held a deep-seated animosity toward the British. Their Foreign Office had always been against the establishment of the State of Israel. The overt support they provided to the Jordanian military enraged him. Without armaments and the leadership of a rabid anti-Semitic British commanding officer known as Glubb Pasha, the Jordanians would never have taken East Jerusalem.

Soon the opposing forces began to recognize the "eimlaq" (giant) who was terrifying simple peasant Arab soldiers. When the cry was heard, "The Eimlaq is coming!" most turned and ran with good reason. Mayer gave no quarter and expected none. He was ruthless in his defence of his homeland, killing any Jordanian soldier he found on sight, often with a knife or his bare hands to conserve bullets. He refused to consider taking prisoners. Any Jordanian who surrendered to his group was killed.

On one occasion, Eimlaq caused quite a stir because his group captured two British officers assigned to Glubb Pasha's Army. If one of his senior commanders had not interceded, Mayer was prepared to execute them. Once he captured them, he couldn't help but despise them for their arrogance and venomous attitude that reeked of anti-Semitism.

The senior officer, a captain, addressed Mayer. "My dear fellow, you really cannot believe you and your ragtag band of mercenaries will succeed. I mean gosh, how could you?"

Mayer just glared at him. The English captain continued, "You do realize that this little brouhaha will all be over very soon. Of course, Whitehall will ignore that ridiculous UN resolution. We will have our chaps back here sorting you silly buggers out and putting you all in your place in no time. You Jews really have no rights here."

Mayer drew himself up to his full height and stood towering over the British captain. He spoke in a calm, low, raspy voice. "Listen to me, you arrogant piece of shit. The fucking Nazis didn't intimidate me. For damn sure a little pussy like you doesn't. I am waiting for orders regarding what to do with you. You are lucky, very lucky, that I was given a direct order not to shoot you instantly. Now with all respect, Captain, *shut the fuck up*." Mayer was seething, barely containing his lack of patience.

Both British officers visibly paled, and the junior lieutenant began to tremble as he realized his survival was hanging in the balance. He was well acquainted with the reputation of the legendary Eimlaq.

Fortunately for them, the other senior commanders of the IDF did not want to create an incident that might alienate many supporters of Israel. Reluctantly, Mayer turned them over to a security detail that placed them in the Acre prison, under guard for their own protection.

After hostilities ended, they were shipped back to Britain, where the captain eventually became a member of Parliament and whose distasteful anti-Semitism was always on display, especially when the issue of Israel was up for debate.

Mayer set an example for the troops who followed him without fear or question. Most were either teens from Israel or survivors of the camps in Europe. They had little or no military training, but like Mayer, they each had an iron will to defend their homeland against all comers.

Under Mayer's natural leadership, they quickly coalesced into a formidable fighting force. One legendary story about Mayer's exploits involved a skirmish that took place near French Hill. Early one morning, a company of Jordanians accompanied by two armoured cars, advanced on a small group of Israeli defenders who had dug in across from an area of destroyed homes and a burned synagogue. Mayer had heard that they were coming under fire from the armoured vehicles and immediately took his platoon, such as it was, and hurried down the rubble-strewn street to assist. As he turned a corner, he caught a glimpse of the two vehicles, stationed on a slight rise, firing down on the Israelis. Quickly assessing the situation, Mayer signalled to his men to follow him. Taking a route where they were not visible to the Jordanians, he circled out, around, and back behind the two armoured cars, killing any Arabs they encountered as they closed in.

Directing four of his men to slowly crawl under each of the armoured cars, he had them attach satchel explosives to the drive tracks and the latches of the bottom hatches. Scrambling back and away from the cars, the men made their way back to Mayer, who had deployed his small group to locations enabling them to provide cover fire in turn throughout the manoeuvre. When the explosives detonated, the Jordanian survivors who thrashed their way out of the burning cars came face-to-face with Mayer and his team. One of the Jordanian commanders attempted to draw his revolver as Mayer ran at him. Without missing a beat, Mayer wrapped his huge arms around the Jordanian's torso and threw him to the ground. He then grabbed the man's neck and broke it in one swift, powerful twist.

The other occupants who escaped the two burning vehicles tried to surrender to the formerly beleaguered Israelis, but once they saw the armoured cars neutralized, they killed all the Arab soldiers who tried to run away. As the day's fighting continued, the story of the Eimlaq's brutality reverberated among the troops, and more importantly, among the Jordanians. They were terrified to confront any Israeli posts where he was rumoured to be. Their British-trained officers, try as they might, could not exhort the infantry to advance or engage the Jewish forces, so frightening was Eimlaq's reputation.

CHAPTER 22

Once the War of Independence was over, Mayer and Ruth settled into a normal life. Mayer stayed on as a training officer in the burgeoning IDF; and he and Ruth were able to live in Tel Aviv in a nice apartment close to the beach. Ruth, whose education had been in economics before WWII, decided that she could start a home-based business to supplement Mayer's military income. She had met some other survivors and realized that they shared an impressive combined talent base. She started a small company buying art from some of her new artist friends. Through her social connections, she began advertising the art in Jewish publications around the Diaspora, and soon she was receiving orders from as far away as Canada, the United States, Australia, and South Africa.

Mayer and Ruth had two sons and a daughter: Avraham, Max, and Sarah. Avraham grew up and became a career army officer in the IDF logistics division. His brother, Max, moved to the United States after marrying an American girl, Gail Abrahams, whom he had met while she was at Bar-Ilan University on a year exchange program.

Sarah, Mayer and Ruth's third child and only daughter, married an Australian who had been on an Ulpan (Hebrew language immersion program). They met at a social gathering in Haifa. She and her husband, David Greenfeld, now lived in Melbourne, where they ran a successful national chain of electronics stores.

In 1980, Avraham married his childhood sweetheart, Rivka Solomon, much to the delight of Mayer and Ruth. Dov was born in 1981 and grew up to be a huge man just like his grandfather. When he completed high school and two years studying engineering at Technion, he was accepted at Ohio State in the United States, courtesy of his uncle Max's connections and, needless to say, the donations Max made to the school. There Dov studied a variety of engineering and science programs, and during his time at Ohio State he completed his Bachelor of Mechanical Engineering degree while playing fullback for the college football team. He gained a sterling reputation as a hardnosed player and was scouted by several NFL clubs.

Two years after graduation, Dov returned to Israel and immediately signed up with the IDF, where on completion of his basic training he was assigned to the Sayeret Matkal commandos. Because of his leadership skills and direct, no-nonsense style, he quickly rose through the ranks to a senior command position. He also came to the attention of 9, and Macha had on several occasions reached out to Major Horowitz and his Sayeret command when reinforcements were required for 9 operations.

CHAPTER 23

Tehran, July 7, 2011

Dov Horowitz arrived at Tehran's international airport from Germany. His papers and passport described him as Stefan Reisloh, a metallurgical engineer working for Mettalsgeschaft GMBH, Munich. He spoke fluent German.

Lining up at customs and immigration, he stood out because of his size and bearing. He had let his dark curly hair grow, and his casual clothes—expensive jeans and an Italian leather jacket—helped him portray a successful sales executive.

The immigration officer—a slight, bearded, surly Iranian with an officious attitude—questioned Dov about his intended stay.

"How many days do you plan on being in the Islamic Republic, Herr Reisloh?"

"My return ticket calls for me to leave in five days."

"Why five days?"

"I have two full days of appointments starting tomorrow morning, and I need to leave some time for follow-up meetings."

The bureaucratic little Iranian appraised Dov up and down for several seconds, then waved him through.

As soon as Dov exited the customs and immigration hall, the officer gave a sign to a secret service VEVAK agent who was standing off to one side of the booths. Dov had been identified as a person of interest.

Once he left the terminal building, he waited in line for a taxi to take him to the Hotel Homa in Tehran, aware that the immigration officer had alerted VEVAK. Dov was sure they now had him under surveillance. Any Iranian background check on his company would find him listed at the company's offices in Munich. Any calls to him would be received and a message taken by a youthful and vibrant receptionist. He was in Iran to develop high tensile steel sales and also evaluating opportunities for a new aluminum casting division his company had just purchased. His cover story rang true and any effort by the VEVAK to verify his credentials would prove him to be who he said he was. Even if they tailed him, they would only find him visiting bona fide clients.

Dov spent two days making calls on potential clients in Tehran. Each evening, he went back to the Homa Hotel. Three days after he arrived, two more German businessmen, from Siemens and Deutsche Bank, checked into the same hotel. Ulrich Meinster and Andreas Goetke were, in reality, fellow Sayeret Matkal operatives. Meinster was Uri Golman and Goetke was Avi Schiff. Golman and Schiff were veterans of the Yom Kippur War and of several highly classified Sayeryet operations in the Middle East. The three German businessmen met casually over breakfast on two occasions and one evening they met in the coffee bar of the hotel.

Dov had rented a Toyota Land Cruiser and Uri was using taxis. Avi had rented a small Mercedes B series. During the day, each of them would pass by, at different times, the home of Darioush Rezaeinejad, a senior Iranian nuclear scientist believed to be a key player in the development of Iran's nuclear bomb. Macha had coordinated with the Mossad and they sent three agents posing as Greek businessmen to Tehran two days after Dov's arrival. They deliberately gave the Iranians some cause for suspicion and then split up in three different directions, checking out municipal infrastructure and construction. This they did in a calculated, clumsy fashion to draw surveillance on to them and away from Dov and his business colleagues, but careful not to give the Iranians any cause to apprehend them.

On July 11, the operators had gathered enough information about their customer. They left their rentals in the hotel parking lot and with relative ease, liberated two motorcycles from a street near the hotel.

Uri rode one bike alone as a decoy. Avi rode the second bike with Dov riding pillion. Just before 5 p.m., as Rezaeinejad arrived, Avi and Dov rode by on their bike. As Rezaeinejad exited his SUV, Dov shot him five times. The wife, who had been waiting by the gate after she walked back from visiting a neighbour, chased the attackers, but they raced away. Uri rode at high speed in the opposite direction from his two partners, so it all happened quickly and there was much confusion as to what had initially happened. There were several witnesses, including Rezaeinejad's driver and bodyguard, but by the time they realized what had just taken place, both motorbikes had screamed out of sight, leaving a hysterical Mrs. Rezaeinejad keening over her husband's corpse and the bodyguard talking excitedly into a cell phone. Even the few bystanders present were unable to describe the killers. The SUV driver was wandering around in shock, surprised he was still alive, as two of the bullets fired had narrowly missed his head before they connected with the nuclear scientist.

During this time, the three supposed Greek businessmen were at the airport under surveillance by VEVAK and clearly could not have been implicated. Avi, Dov, and Uri rode the bikes to a quiet part of town and left them, walking to public transit and then taking separate taxis to the hotel.

They ate dinner in their hotel rooms and watched the news reports filtering in across the country. They checked out the next morning and had the concierge arrange transportation for them on the hotel airport shuttle. They left separately, at intervals. Dov flew on Air Berlin to Munich, then back to Tel Aviv via Rome. Uri flew to Frankfurt on Lufthansa and then to Heathrow from where he took a BA flight to Tel Aviv a day later. Avi left Tehran for Madrid on Iberia and stayed in a hotel near the airport for two days then flew back to Frankfurt and on to Tel Aviv.

CHAPTER 24

When they were in the passenger lounges, they followed the news networks, which were giving major coverage to the assassination. The American networks were running ticker tapes exclaiming how shocked and angry the American president was that a prominent and well-respected scientist should be so brutally murdered. He was vociferously denying any involvement by the United States while secretly he was aware that the Israelis were probably responsible, and from then on, he applied enormous pressure on the Israeli government to curb any further such missions.

At one point, the secretary of state, on orders from the president, had strongly admonished the Israeli prime minister. Some accounts of the phone discussion reported that it was extremely heated, with the PM loudly advising the secretary that it wasn't the States being threatened with annihilation, but tiny Israel. He also told the secretary that he didn't appreciate lectures from him or his boss.

"Mr. Secretary, you and the sycophant bastards that run your State Department are world renowned for their vicious anti-Semitism. It's been that way for a hundred years. We in Israel will never bow down to your distorted view of the Middle East."

The secretary was aghast. "Mr. Prime Minister, this is no way to conduct a diplomatic discussion. I am unable to even think about conveying this conversation to the president; he—"

Prime Minister Gershon Mendelsohn interrupted him, "You can convey to your boss, Mr. Secretary, that the State of Israel will never allow Jews anywhere to be threatened with annihilation, such as your fucking Iranian friends are proposing every chance they get. We will defend ourselves, up and to using physical force, to prevent that from ever happening again. Tell your boss from me, *never again!*" These last two words were shouted.

Backpedalling from the verbal assault, the secretary attempted to close off the discussion. "My dear Gershon, you need to cool down and understand that these negotiations are always more successful when they are conducted in a polite and cordial fashion."

The PM responded, "Israel will never again allow any regime or country to threaten its citizens — or Jews anywhere — with destruction. You need to clearly understand this, Mr. Secretary. We will hunt down and eliminate all those who incite the murder of Israelis or plan or carry out terrorist attacks. Iran is on a path to build a bomb. Who do you think they intend to use it on? Eh! Who, Mr. Secretary? Fiji? We both know, as does your boss, that Israel is the target. Trust me, we will not let it happen. We will remove any participating player. That includes any North Koreans and Russians. Tell your president that if he does not like it then he had better turn up the pressure on Iran with the sanctions we both know are not working. We will not have this discussion again, Mr. Secretary. Good night."

Later, it would be revealed that the US president and his close advisers didn't want their secret nuclear negotiations with Iran to be derailed. The assassination of Rezaeinejad had resulted in a series of furious phone calls and secret meetings between the US administration and the Iranians, who were essentially blackmailing the US president to have the Israelis halt the elimination program, or any negotiations around the future nuclear treaty would be abruptly cancelled.

CHAPTER 25

9 Headquarters, Netanya, Israel, August 2015

Ari and Dov were seated in the basement of 9, surrounded by dozens of maps and flip charts. Their plan was now condensed into a briefing book of 52 pages. It had been given a name: Operation Begin, in recognition of the famous Begin doctrine.

Macha introduced them to a third man, whom Ari instantly recognized; Colonel Eli Naftalin (Ret.). Naftalin was the newly appointed director of Mossad, known for being both ruthless and brilliant.

Prior to the meeting with Eli Naftalin, Dov and Ari had proposed to Macha that if the objective were to end terror once and for all, then the North Korean threats would also have to be removed.

Colonel Naftalin, before he was appointed head of Mossad, had already achieved an outstanding military career. He had joined the IDF immediately after graduating from Bar-Ilan University, where he had majored in Middle Eastern and Arabic studies. Naftalin was a superb linguist, fluent in Russian, Arabic, Mandarin, Farsi, and English. He had acquired these languages from an early age.

Eli's father, Alexander, was originally a refugee from Russia, and his mother, Nancy, was from Brisbane, Australia. Nancy's father had been born in Taiwan. Alexander's parents had escaped from Russia and the Shoah, landed originally in Shanghai, then moved to Taiwan ahead of the Mao-led Chinese communists.

Alexander Naftalin subscribed to the theory that one man speaking one language was just one man, but a man who could speak six languages had the value of six men. As a result, his son, Eli, learned six different languages as soon as he was able to speak and understand. Both parents encouraged him from an early age to not only speak all six languages, but to read and write in them also. Once he was in school, he delved deeply into his studies. His real loves were and remain Chinese and English.

On joining the IDF, Eli's talents were quickly recognized, and he was appointed to a secret department of intelligence within the Defense Department. There he was responsible for monitoring terrorists or governments who intended to murder Israelis or destroy Israel—many of them in Iran, Syria, and Gaza. As he determined to stay on as a professional soldier within the IDF, Eli Naftalin later became responsible for planning covert missions to protect Israel.

Before he retired in 2015, he was recognized by the prime minister for being responsible for setting up the under-the-radar relationship with Russia. Prime Minister Mendelsohn, because of Eli Naftalin's efforts, had a close and respectful relationship with President Vladimir Putin. This was proving invaluable during the Syrian Civil War, where Russia was fighting to rescue the Assad government.

Many people in the West were supremely critical of the friendship between Israel and President Putin. Nevertheless, both the Russians and the Israelis had ancient cultures and knew how to play the Great Game of global politics and power struggles. They easily and readily determined that for there to be any chance of stability in the Middle East, the two countries would have to work together to avoid a violent and uncontrollable conflagration which ultimately would lead to a military confrontation between NATO and the Russians. Many in the US State Department could not comprehend this.

It was soon after this that Col. Naftalin was appointed head of the Mossad. Immediately on taking office, he purged the organization of a number of senior bureaucrats who in his evaluation were not loyal to the government. They were being political in their decision-making, failing to understand that the role of Mossad was to protect

Israel from invasion and terrorism. The housecleaning was considered vicious and ruthless by the liberal Israeli press, who for a number of years had been critical of many operations taken on by Mossad. Naftalin brooked no deviation from his directive; Mossad was a secret intelligence organization and all of its operations would remain so. Those who broke ranks were immediately dismissed and he made sure that offenders were disgraced, making it impossible for them to find employment of any worth following their exit.

CHAPTER 26

After their initial meeting, Macha convened another with Ari and Dov.

"The PM has green-lighted our program to move ahead immediately. Col. Naftalin has also been charged with setting up a similar operation against North Korea. Mossad and the Defence Intelligence Department have a great deal of information that clearly indicates the two rogue nations of Iran and North Korea are working closely, way too closely, with each other. They are sharing technology and materials as well as exchanging personnel."

Ari and Dov listened intently as Macha expanded the scope of the mission. While they would be taking out the Iranian nuclear facilities and the Iranian seat of government, Col. Naftalin and the Mossad would be on a similar errand against the threat from North Korea.

For a decade or more, the Mossad had recognized North Korea as an existential threat to not only Israel, but also the world. In the past, the Mossad had been nurturing and developing long-term surveillance and espionage plans specific to the Kim regime. The Mossad had worked in close cooperation with the South Korean Intelligence Service, NIS. The NIS had a department exclusively focused on North Korea. As the Mossad/NIS relationship developed, the two agencies shared intelligence of mutual benefit between them.

The Mossad kept a wary eye on the many Iranians and North Koreans circulating in Germany, France, and the UK. These individuals had attempted to influence radical movements and to purchase restricted materials and equipment for missile and nuclear weapons development. Iran and North Korea furthermore had roaming assassination squads travelling around Europe who were tasked with killing dissidents and politicians who opposed their ugly regimes.

Because of Mossad and NIS efforts, many Iranian and North Korean hit squads were quietly eliminated or outed to the media. Most had been posing as attachés to their various delegations and consular offices. The NIS kept the Mossad informed of the activities of the two terrorist countries' activities in the Far East, especially in Pakistan and Japan, and the Mossad kept the NIS informed of activities in the rest of the world.

As a result of sophisticated surveillance techniques, Mossad had neutralized several Iranian hit squads, thwarting attempted assassinations of high-profile Iranian dissidents. These actions frustrated Iran, because the attempts were always made public and the perpetrators identified or terminated. Once their identities were leaked to UK, French, German, and US intelligence services, they were no longer clandestine or secretive and had to return to their homeland. Or they were neutralized.

CHAPTER 27

In 2012, Ari and Eli Gershon, part of the 9 team that eliminated Abu Yasser in Vienna a few years before, were sent to London to keep track of an Iranian Embassy staffer, Hussein Nasri, whose nickname was "The Messenger." Nasri appeared to be a third economic attaché at the Iranian Embassy, but in fact, he was a senior Islamic Quds hit man whose mandate was to search out Iranian dissidents and kill them. Both Mossad and 9 had been gathering intelligence on Nasri for about six months and were now ready to remove him.

The two 9 operatives were staying in a Mossad safe house near Wembley Park and travelled into West London on the underground transit system. They had observed Nasri regularly going for walks in Green Park not far from Buckingham Palace. Once they had clearance on his bona fide confirmation as a really good customer, they implemented their plan.

As per his habit, Nasri was seated on a bench watching birds and small rodents fight over the crumbs and broken remnants from his lunch. He usually absorbed himself in his smartphone or an Iranian newspaper.

With Eli covering his back, Ari simply walked past The Messenger and, as he drew level with him, without missing a step, shot him in the eye with a 22mm silenced Beretta. Nasri slumped over and appeared to be asleep. There were a few passersby and a pair of nannies pushing strollers, but no one paid any attention to the man seemingly dozing on the bench.

Ari and Eli unhurriedly exited the park, walked to the Green Park Tube station, and used their Oyster cards to take the Piccadilly Line to Acton Green. This tactic was part of their countersurveillance protocol, to ensure that they had not been acquired — identified — by any of the British or foreign security agencies. At Acton Green they exited the Tube and waited for another Piccadilly line train destined for Uxbridge. On leaving the Uxbridge station, they took a bus to Wembley Park, where they retrieved their rental car from in front of the safe house and drove directly to London Stansted Airport for a flight to Athens. From there they transited to Tel Aviv, Ben Gurion Airport, in Israel.

By the time they landed at Ben Gurion, the BBC was delivering a headline about an Iranian man attached to the Iranian Embassy who had been found dead in Green Park. There were no initial reports of the cause of death, but some sources—who wished to remain anonymous—believed him to be associated with several Iranian regime attempts to assassinate expatriate dissidents. Early assumptions were made that one of the anti-Regime organizations had managed to assassinate him.

Keen interest in anything Iranian in Europe and the Far East had allowed the Israelis and the NIS to compile a huge amount of intelligence on both Iran and North Korea. While US intelligence agencies relied mostly on electronic and satellite surveillance, the Mossad and the NIS went in on the ground and captured their intelligence directly from the sources they had spent years cultivating. Many Mossad agents were Farsi speakers and the NIS could infiltrate North Korean cells. Both agencies had been developing these skills over a long period of time, thus making their intelligence highly valuable and pertinent.

CHAPTER 28

Tel Aviv, July-August 2015

Dov and Ari used HUMINT from Tehran, Qom, and Bandar Abbas with information shared by Naftalin's Mossad to develop a radical and dangerous plan. The mission was to destroy the heavily fortified and guarded nuclear facilities and knock out the Iranian threat once and for all.

It was determined that any direct air raid on the nuclear installations would be unsuccessful; they were heavily protected by surface-to-air missile batteries and the entrances were blast- and bombproof. Several installations, especially Natanz and Fordow, were deep underground and impervious to an air bombardment. Dov and Ari believed that they had to introduce high explosives directly into the facilities and destroy them from below instead of from above. They asked their analysts at 9 and the IDF to provide as much detailed topographical information about the installations and their surroundings as possible.

The findings were surprising. The information they were able to decipher from satellite photographs and on-the-ground human intelligence was that the underground facilities were all using sophisticated air exchange systems to provide fresh air to each facility and to exhaust stale air back out. The most interesting observation was that all the breather systems had their ducts installed a distance from the perimeter walls and infrastructure of the facilities.

At first, the analysts and Macha's team didn't have an explanation for this anomaly. Finally, in a more in-depth review, one of the IAF pilots, Lt. Shimon Jacobitz, came up with a probable and plausible reason. The Iranians, prior to receiving the S-300 and S-400 surface-to-air missile defence systems, were concerned that the Israelis and/or the United States would initiate an air bombardment in an attempt to destroy the facilities. Jacobitz proposed, correctly, that the Iranians had been concerned that an air attack could block or knock out the air systems if they were located too close to the underground nuclear and missile plants. By locating the air-breathers a distance away from the main infrastructure, the Iranians minimized risk of the breather systems' being damaged or rendered inoperable.

For Dov, it was personal. His large family of ancestors—with the exception of his grandparents, Mayer and Ruth—had been destroyed in the Holocaust. Having been exposed to the rantings of the Iranian President Mahmoud Ahmadinejad, who had vowed on several occasions before and after the assassination of Darioush Rezaeinejad to wipe Israel off the map, Dov was emotional and passionate about doing everything in his power to prevent another Holocaust, regardless of what he or his team needed to do.

The plan was both bold and simple. It was fraught with risk and would need steely resolve for Ari, Dov, and their teams to succeed. The two commanders spent twelve to fourteen hours daily laying out a highly detailed plan and intense training program. Much of their information in planning for Iran was shared with Colonel Naftalin as he prepared and trained the Mossad teams for the North Korean operation.

Between the intelligence assets and data of both 9 and Mossad, the wealth of knowledge about Iran and North Korea's cooperation was much larger than many had originally considered. The more due diligence was carried out, the more apparent it became that both Iran and North Korea posed grave danger to the world in general and Israel in particular. The brutal leaders of both nations had previously shown many times that they had no compunction in murdering their perceived enemies or critics anywhere in the world.

Colonel Naftalin was adamant that no Mossad intelligence of his was to be shared with other Israeli or Allied agencies, specifically SIS and the CIA. He was still concerned that there were staff at Mossad who believed in clandestinely sharing future operations and plans. Some did it for self-aggrandizement, others for pure financial gain. The liberal media, such as *Haaretz* and *CNN–Middle East*, paid small fortunes to leakers. Their motives were simply to sell news regardless of whether or not it jeopardized national security.

Ari and Dov's plans required eight teams of special forces to infiltrate Iran and make their way to Bandar Abbas and the seven nuclear facilities: the Arak heavy water plant, the Bushehr and Fordow nuclear power plants, the Bonab and Tehran nuclear research centres, the Natanz enrichment plant, and the Parchin military complex. Ari and the 9 executives agreed with Dov and Lt. Jacbovitz that the underground nuclear facilities at Fordow, Bushehr, and Natanz would have to be attacked and destroyed via the breathers. The aboveground facilities and Bandar Abbas would require commando teams' breaching the security systems and barriers to infiltrate and destroy the plants and facilities.

Ari and Dov had no illusions about the risks and dangers inherent in their plan. The Iranians were a sophisticated people with a fanatical sense of pride in their technological achievements, which were considerable. The Iranian military was not third world; their defence systems were regarded as formidable.

After presenting their proposal to Macha, they were summoned to the office of the prime minister, Gershon Mendelsohn, who was joined by his Defense Minister, Yaakov Melnik. Both Mendelsohn and Melnik had been frustrated for the past eight years because of restraints placed on Israel by the US president, who had seemed more concerned with his standing in the Muslim world than the tangible threat from the Shi'ites in Iran to not only Israel, but the whole Sunni Arab world and even the Americas.

CHAPTER 29

Gershon Mendelsohn was a Sabra; he was born on Kibbutz Ein Gev, where his grandparents had settled after securing passage from Poland in 1936. Gershon's grandfather had read the tea leaves and believed that Nazi Germany would eventually go on a rampage across Europe. There was already open anti-Semitism in Poland, which the rise of Hitler and the Nazis only enabled and empowered. As a result, Menachem Mendelsohn, who had a successful wholesale jewellery business, sold all his assets to secure a circuitous journey through the Balkans and Turkey to reach eventually what was then Palestine. They became founding members of Ein Gev in 1937 and quickly settled into kibbutz life.

From the time of their arrival until after the Six-Day War thirty years later in 1967, life on Ein Gev was just an artillery shell away from the Syrian controlled Golan Heights. Menachem became a skilled banana plantation farmer, and he and his wife, Sarah, led a happy life. They had two children, Isaac and Nathan, who grew up through the early years of the State and were staunch Zionists. Nathan married a stunning Iraqi Jewess, Shoshana Shamash, whose parents had arrived at Ein Gev after they fled Iraq in 1948.

Nathan and Shoshana had three children: Naomi, born in 1951, Hannah in 1952, and then Gershon in 1954. Gershon was fascinated by politics and at the young age of eighteen he had already served a term on the kibbutz council. When he joined the IDF just in time for the 1973 Yom Kippur War, he distinguished himself in some of the heaviest fighting in the Sinai. After he mustered out in 1976, he ran as a MK for the district where Ein Gev was located. Easily elected, he soon became a star in the Knesset. He was considered extremely capable and built a solid reputation as a fair and dependable Knesset member.

During the time when Menachem Begin was prime minister, Gershon became a valuable aide to Begin. He was called on many times to be a spokesman for the PM. Begin was Gershon's hero and mentor, and as Gershon rose through the ranks of Likud and ultimately became prime minister himself, he always remembered the famous Begin doctrine, which stated, "*On no account shall we permit an enemy to develop weapons of mass destruction against the people of Israel. We shall defend the citizens of Israel in good time and with all means at our disposal.*"

Prime Minister Gershon Mendelsohn was a fierce defender of Israel and world Jewry; he would follow the Begin doctrine on many occasions. Previous plans had been developed by Israel to enter Iran with stealth aero technology and bomb the nuclear facilities as they had done in Iraq and Syria. Notwithstanding US reservations and the hate for Israel of some members of the US State Department, certain influential leaders within the IDF and the Cabinet were also unconvinced bombing would succeed. Even while negotiations regarding the nuclear pact with Iran were being carried out in great secrecy, members of the IDF and the Israeli Defense Ministry were in deep discussions with some of their counterparts at the Pentagon. US military professionals were terribly frustrated by the inertia of the White House and State Department vis-à-vis Iran. The Pentagon had already war gamed stealth bomber attacks on all the facilities in collaboration with the Israelis using the huge bunker-busting munitions.

Each time the Joint Chiefs pushed their plan up to the civilians at State and the White House, they were rebuffed with nebulous and obsequious excuses: "The timing isn't right," or, from the president to the chairman of the Joint Chiefs, "Haven't you got enough on your hands without another war in the Middle East? Good gracious, General, we will be a pariah among nations if we drop bombs haphazardly all over Iran or the Middle East or Asia just to demonstrate to that war hawk Mendelsohn in Israel that we have his back."

At a subsequent meeting in the Oval Office regarding the impending nuclear treaty with Iran, the secretary of state said, "Mr. President, if we pull this off with the Iranians, you will be up for a Nobel and so probably will my Iranian counterpart."

"You must understand that as my secretary of state who negotiated this deal, you for sure should also be eligible."

The secretary shared a broad smile. It was easy to see his ego grow as he preened on receiving encouragement from his boss.

CHAPTER 30

Macha proposed a radical addition to their plan. During their intelligence-gathering, 9 uncovered alarming information. The nuclear missile tests being carried out by the North Koreans were being made in tandem with the Iranians'. This information validated what some in the Israeli security and military had surmised for several years.

When Israel destroyed the Syrian nuclear reactor at al-Kibar in Northern Syria, there was little or no reaction or international condemnation. Based on intercepted communications between Syria, Iran, and North Korea, the Israelis determined that the three countries were coordinating their nuclear ambitions. Syria wanted a nuclear reactor and the ability to build a bomb and was leveraging its relationships with Iran and North Korea. The Iranians were providing technical and personnel assistance to North Korea on missile technology and fissionable material, and the North Koreans were aiding in the design of nuclear reactors and testing Iranian-designed nuclear bombs while aiding the Libyans and Syrians.

Macha and Eli Naftalin recognized that if the objectives were to end terror once and for all, then the North Korean threat would also have to be removed at the same time as the Iranian threat. Israel was in North Korea's crosshairs ever since a train loaded with plutonium fissile material destined for shipment to Syria had been destroyed in 2004 and both suspected Israel.

The train had been nearing the North Korean port of Namp'o carrying sealed wagons with suspected nuclear material. The train also held Syrian and Iranian technicians and scientists as well as some of their respective special forces. An anonymous commando attack sabotaged the train, killing most of the Syrian and Iranian scientists and many of their and North Korean special forces. The Mossad operators, aided by South Korean Special Forces, had planned the attack for weeks. The most difficult part of the operation was that they only had minutes to exit the area after they had triggered the bombs, destroying the train. The eight men – four Israelis and four South Koreans – had to immediately run to evade the massive North Korean manhunt that activated almost immediately. Hiding in rice paddies and small copses of trees by day, they finally reached their extraction point on the coast on the fourth night, escaping via a South Korean Navy operation. All of the team members were removed safely and without injury.

Israel had not taken official responsibility, but most understood that Israel was responsible. From this point on, Israel was a key focus of the North Koreans. They knew that the Israelis were keenly aware of their close cooperation with the Iranians.

Then in September 2007, Israeli fighter-bombers and fighter jets destroyed the Syrian facility at al-Kibar, for which the original shipment was intended. This Kibar facility was Iranian financed. They were estimated to have spent between one and three billion US dollars on the illicit project. The design was essentially a North Korean design constructed under North Korean supervision. The intended bomb was a hybrid of the Khan design, which was created by the Pakistani nuclear physicist, AQ Khan.

Khan was suspected of offering his designs to several rogue Islamic regimes besides Iran and North Korea, including Libya and Saudi Arabia. At least a dozen North Korean scientists and engineers and several Iranians were killed in the bombing raid on al-Kibar. Obviously, the North Koreans could not acknowledge this fact, but they were absolutely furious with Israel and determined to exact revenge. The loss of face felt among the Syrians, North Koreans, and Iranians was huge, but nowhere near the weight of the financial blow suffered by Iran and Syria.

In Iran, people were living in poor circumstances because the national treasury was being squandered on the nuclear program and the financing of arms for Hamas, Hezbollah, and other terrorist organizations. This was leading to serious discontent among the populace. The details of Operation Orchard had provided 9, Ari, and Dov with the keys to planning a successful attack on the Iranian nuclear facilities. Operation Orchard was carried out by eight IAF fighter-bomber F-15Is and F-16Is supported by an ELINT aircraft. The day prior to the air attack, elite teams of Sayeret Matkal Special Forces were involved in highlighting the target with laser designators, so the missiles and bombs deployed by the fighter-bombers landed with pinpoint accuracy on designated targets.

The ELINT aircraft pioneered the Israeli use of the electronic warfare techniques being developed by the IAF. These were able to take over control of Syrian air defence systems, providing false feeds during the period of time the Israeli jets were in Syrian airspace.

Since the early part of the 21st century, Israeli military and security forces were convinced that the Iranians and North Koreans were marching in lockstep to develop nuclear weapons. Iran had the funds and advanced engineering capabilities to build large banks of centrifuges. North Korea had vast supplies of uranium yellowcake that could be refined into plutonium. They also had other fissile materials required for nuclear weapons and significant knowledge and expertise in missile development and manufacturing. This they had acquired from close ties with Russian scientists who were looking to continue their work and be paid. Since the collapse of the Soviet Union in 1991, many scientists had been eking out a living by offering themselves to the highest bidder. Once Iran and North Korea were made aware of their value, they hired the Russians and they became a key element in the accelerated programs of both countries.

The whole upper echelon at 9—Macha, Ari, Major Dov Horowitz, Sayeret Matkal, plus Defense Minister Melnik and Col. Naftalin of the Mossad—were convinced that the two rogue countries were working closely together. Iran was regarded by most countries around the world as the leader and source of funds for major terrorist entities in the world: Hezbollah, Boko Haram, Hamas, Al-Shaheeb, and the Muslim Brotherhood. Once they had begun to conceive a plan to remove the Iranian nuclear threat, the conclusion was made that the other half of the terror axis would also have to be destroyed.

North Korea had for many years been terrorizing nations in the southern hemisphere and carried out some notoriously deadly strikes against South Korea, Japan, Australia, Malaysia, and Vietnam. Many were not recorded in Western Eurocentric media, yet they were a message sent by the Kim dynasty that they had worldwide reach and were willing to settle scores at any time and any place.

After prolonged debates and much heated discussion, it was determined that Israel would attempt to take out both the Iranian and North Korean threats, since the sclerotic and impotent governments of the EU and the US seemed incapable of making tough decisions. They only appeared to care about their re-elections, regardless of national security and the destabilizing force of a nuclear Iran, Syria, or North Korea.

In making the decision, the Prime Minister and Defense Minister were overwhelmed with the enormity of the task. There was no room for failure. The two combined operations would have to be like no other in the history of modern warfare. To lose would be catastrophic.

Sitting in the prime minister's living room, Gershon Mendelsohn and his friend, Defense Minister Yaakov Melnick, wondered aloud if they were making a tragic mistake. They spent hours discussing pros and cons until, finally, Prime Minister Mendelsohn made the fateful determination. "Yaakov, if we don't take any preemptive action, these two terror nations will try to destroy us. Everyone has heard them promise to destroy the State of Israel—and every Jew in the world—over and over. And no one will care. Anti-Semitism is rising all over Europe once again. Even supposed friends and allies will wring their hands but do nothing. If that bastard Corbyn, the British Labour leader, ever becomes PM, there will be a wave of open and rabid anti-Semitic attacks across the UK. He is playing to the Islamists that are gaining ground all over Britain. Make no mistake, the Islamists that have occupied the towns and hold a strong presence in Corbyn's party will ensure that. The UK will abandon us; so will the French, for the same reason. Politicians will cave to the Islamists because they are scared of them. With that prick in the White House lying and deceiving everyone including himself, we probably will not get any help from the US. Yaakov, we will be on our own again."

"Gershon, please, not so much drama. I understand your feelings, but we must be cautious in our decision-making."

"Yaakov!" shouted Gershon Mendelsohn at his friend, "I have decided! We will give the green light to Macha and 9 and Naftalin's Mossad. If we fail, all that we have done is hasten our own demise. We must be successful; we will surprise the world and possibly ourselves."

On that note, the meeting ended and Minister Melnick left to go home for what was probably his last night of uninterrupted sleep for many weeks. The next morning, he called Macha and Eli Naftalin to his offices and the wheels began to turn.

CHAPTER 31

Rosh Pinah, September 2015

Dov was promoted to colonel in the Sayeret and Ari was reappointed to an active commission as a colonel in the IDF; they began the task of strategizing and implementing their plan.

During their intelligence-gathering, Ari had uncovered the fact that his unexpected run-in in Vienna with Al-Baghdadi and his companions had a direct influence on the mission. The Islamic Revolutionary Guards (IRGC) leadership, under the direction of General Hussein Soleimani, had recruited Al-Baghdadi to begin a Hezbollah-executed reign of terror in Europe and the United States. Answering to the Quds Force and Soleimani, they would spread out across the planet, attacking soft but strategic targets. They had already been successful in Khobar, Saudi Arabia, where Hezbollah under Iranian command attacked the US Air Force barracks.

After Kim Jong-un, General Soleimani was possibly the most dangerous man in the world. He commanded the overseas operations of the Quds Force and was the second most senior commander for all the IRGC. He was also fabulously wealthy because he was skimming a percentage of all revenues generated by arms sales to Hezbollah, Hamas, and others; plus, he garnered illicit funds from many businesses and companies controlled by the Guards in Iran. Moreover, he was known to be the kingpin in Hezbollah drug enterprises and maintained close ties to the South American and Mexican cartels.

US authorities began to investigate as a result of information passed to them by Mossad. They planned a major assault on

Hezbollah's worldwide operations in armament smuggling, money laundering, and drug running. Assigned the code name Project Cassandra, various US agencies including the CIA and DEA assisted by the FBI and Special Forces, planned a massive interdiction of Hezbollah's worldwide terror support activities. They hoped to bring Soleimani and his network down and expose Iran and Hezbollah for what they were—murderers.

Tragically, because of the obsession of the US president and secretary of state with securing the Iran nuclear deal, the investigations were shut down because of a direct request from Iran's foreign minister to the secretary of state to back off. This demand was a core condition of achieving the nuclear deal to which the administration acceded.

Al-Baghdadi's demise at the hands of Ari and his French pals had significantly, almost as an act from heaven, derailed these plans. Al-Baghdadi was the leader and his shortened time on earth had caused a pause in the IRGC's plans.

Led by General Hussein Soleimani, who was stationed with Hezbollah in Lebanon and Syria, Al-Baghdadi and the IRGC had been planning a series of spectacular and devastating raids on northern Israel and Jewish institutions in England and the United States. It was only after planning began that Israel and the IDF learned how fortunate the timing of Abu's assassination in Vienna had been. Soleimani was thrown off balance when Ari and his French colleagues removed the key leader of his operational proxies.

The Mossad and 9 picked up multiple clues and general chatter that Soleimani was insane with anger and wanted immediate revenge. Two of his targets were the Duke and Duchess of Cambridge. President Rouhani and his foreign minister placed heavy restraints on the general that any attacks on the Royals were off limits and made it clear that no attacks on any of the nuclear pact participants were to be carried out. Israel was fair game, but no other countries.

The Israelis had had Soleimani in their sights for several years; on at least one occasion they had an assassination attempt planned and ready to go when the US president instructed his secretary of state to inform the Iranians. Once they were aware of this, the Israelis cancelled the plan. Prime Minister Mendelsohn had never forgiven the US president for this betrayal.

General Soleimani, as head of the Quds Force, was the mastermind of many of Iran's terrorist activities. His fingerprints were all over the attacks Israel suffered from Hamas, Hezbollah, and Islamic Jihad. Soleimani was a smart and audacious individual who was both feared and respected in Iran and totally feared elsewhere. His IRGC units stationed in Lebanon and Syria were training Hezbollah-armed units into a cohesive and formidable fighting force. Prior to General Soleimani's leadership, they had been an undisciplined group of fanatical Islamists without any real sense of purpose other than to hate Jews. After being conscripted to fight on behalf of the Syrian regime of Bashar Assad, these Hezbollah irregulars had developed into a well-trained and disciplined fighting force.

There had been several Hezbollah-led attacks on northern Israel from across the Lebanon border; and now that Suleiman had committed his forces—Iranian and Hezbollah—to combat in Assad's Syrian Civil War, these forces of evil were now stationed near the Golan Heights on Israel's northern border. On the Lebanese border with Israel, Hezbollah threatened the very existence of Israel with over 120,000 missiles and rockets. Soleimani was a marked man, and during their planning at 9 headquarters, Ari, Dov, and Macha had Soleimani targeted and there was a plan to take him down.

Of even more concern was some of the anecdotal street intelligence acquired by the Israeli security agencies indicating that Soleimani was gradually pulling all the threads of the worldwide terror groups into one global organization with himself as its undisputed leader. Some reports even filtered out of Iran that the mullahs were concerned about his ruthless consolidation of power. There were fears that if he carried out a military coup, the ruthless regime of the mullahs would be overturned and replaced by an even more fanatical one-man rule with hegemonic designs on all of the Middle East, Afghanistan, Iraq, and North Africa in an attempt to re-create a great Persian Empire.

Soleimani fancied himself as a modern-day Darius who would govern this great empire, which until 2,344 years ago was the dominant power in the known world, until Alexander the Great defeated Darius at the Battle of Gaugamela in 331 BCE. Soleimani wanted the Persian Empire back, and the nuclear program was vital to his plans. He was adamant with his masters in Tehran that Iran must have a credible nuclear weapon. He had contemplated many times using such a weapon on Israel but was pragmatic enough to recognize that the collateral damage to Israel's neighbours would be too great. His plan was to acquire the means to build and deliver several nuclear weapons simultaneously. He would then unleash a three-front war against Israel. Hamas would invade from Gaza in the South, at the same time launching terror attacks from Judea and Samaria; Hezbollah and Iranian troops would invade from Lebanon and Syria; and Iraqi and Iranian troops would invade from the east through Jordan.

The Iran nuclear threat would be levelled at any European or NATO country that might contemplate going to aid Israel. As far as the United States was concerned, he planned to initiate spectacular terror attacks carried out by the many Hezbollah sleeper cells he had infiltrated into the continent. He had little or no concern for collateral damage in infidel countries. He would deliver a direct message to the American and Canadian governments that any interference with the Iranian attack on Israel would be met with unprecedented retaliation—now with nuclear weapons. He calculated that in light of this news, none of Israel's allies would lift a finger to repel the Iranian invasions.

Macha and Naftalin set the capture or elimination of Soleimani as one of the operation's top priorities. There was no question that his removal from the control of the terror networks would severely curtail their activities and above all, derail his maniacal plans.

CHAPTER 32

Training Rosh Pina and Port of Haifa

A secret training facility was set up for the missions at the Rosh Pina military air base in central Israel.

On this day, there were some 450 men and women assembled from all the Israeli Special Forces outfits: Navy underwater demolition experts, paratroopers, deep penetration Sayeret, and female commandos—elite practitioners of the fearsome martial art of Krav Maga. There were IAF helicopter, fighter, gunship, transport and tanker pilots.

For the Mossad operation against the North Korean nuclear facilities, four teams of twenty special forces soldiers consisted solely of second- and third-generation Vietnamese Chinese whose parents had been admitted to Israel as refugees during June 1977. Many of their parents had fled the repressive Communist regime of Vietnam because, as ethnic Chinese, they were deemed second-class citizens. They had embarked on unseaworthy fishing boats chartered to them by unscrupulous captains. Once on the China seas, they were subjected to attacks by pirates and many of the boats sank with no survivors. Some experienced vicious attacks and barely managed to survive. Many attempted to gain entry to Hong Kong and other South Asian ports but were turned away. Two such craft had been refused by the British authorities in Hong Kong and denied landing in Taiwan. A passing Israeli Zim container ship rescued them from almost certain death by drowning as their boats were on the verge of capsizing. After attempting to disembark them in Hong Kong, the victims were once again refused. The Zim vessel was instructed by the Israeli government to "bring them home." Once in Israel, the government offered the desperate souls asylum and, eventually, citizenship. As citizens of Israel, they completed their service in the IDF and some had continued in the Sayeret Matkal, where they were recognized as being some of the detachment's fiercest and most proficient warriors.

For the current operation, South Korean US Navy Seal–trained special forces teams joined the training at Rosh Pina. Now they were going to be deployed into North Korea. Their objectives were the nuclear plants and underground missile factories as well as the capture and dismantling of the Kim dynasty.

In the meantime, the Mossad had already run several clandestine operations inside North Korea. Several years prior, Mossad agents had entered North Korea and derailed a train that was carrying vital Iranian nuclear material from the Musudan-ri missile facility. Their agents had learned of a cargo ship that was going to be loaded with sophisticated missiles and armaments in a North Korean port with a final destination in the Sudan. From Sudan, the cargo would be smuggled into Gaza. Once the freighter left the North Korean port, it was shadowed by Mossad and Israeli Navy assets until it entered the Red Sea. Israeli and US Navy forces stopped and boarded the ship and uncovered a huge cache of missiles, arms, and ammunition that would have been unloaded at a Sudanese port and then destined for Hamas and ISIS.

CHAPTER 33

Jerusalem

Seated in the prime minister's office, Dov, Ari, and Col. Naftalin presented their plans while Macha observed like a proud father. The Defense Minister had briefed the prime minister about both Ari and Dov, in particular Dov's mission in Tehran and Ari's recent success in Vienna. Dov detailed their plan for over an hour. When he completed his presentation, Eli Naftalin laid out the intended Mossad operation in North Korea. The Israeli Vietnamese Chinese citizens who had been recruited from the military into the Mossad would infiltrate into North Korea posing as Chinese scientists and observers. After the groups' training at Rosh Pina, they would be deployed into North Korea along with the Mossad teams.

The Iranian operation ground force was divided into eight twenty-person teams under the direct command of Ari and Dov, and seven six-person Sayeryet deep penetration teams. The Navy and Air Force groups were assigned special targets and objectives. A ninth special forces team was to specifically target and, if possible, capture General Soleimani in Lebanon.

The Mossad teams were stationed at Rosh Pina at the commencement of their training, but after a short period they were dispatched to practice in the inhospitable mountains of northern Greece. Since their objectives and strategies were different and separate from those of Ari and Dov, it was determined that exposure to the harsh conditions of the Greek terrain would be essential to their training, as it was similar to the landscape and climate of North Korea.

The prime minister, as was his wont, sat as still as a sphinx and listened while his hooded eagle-like eyes bore into Eli, Ari, and Dov. Minister Melnik occasionally interrupted to ask for clarification on a specific point. Once they were finished, the Prime Minister and Defense Minister quietly thanked the two men from 9 and Naftalin from Mossad. They were dismissed.

Prime Minister Mendelsohn sat at his desk in deep thought for several minutes, then turned to his Defense Minister and said, "Yaakov, those brave young men have conceived of a very daring plan that I believe will put a stop to this Iranian–North Korean nexus of terror and bombs. We must keep this strictly covert and absolutely we cannot share it with the Americans."

Minister Melnik looked askance at his boss and friend, "Gershon, don't you think we need to gain the support of the US?"

"My dear Yaakov, the last time we consulted with the US when we planned to bomb the nuclear plants, the president went ballistic and applied so much pressure we had to cancel. It will not happen again. I don't trust the US president, nor do I trust his secretary of state. The president will as always stay high and mighty, but the secretary will tip off all the people we don't want to know. For sure the Turks and the Russians will get wind of our plan and then so will the Iranians."

Melnik appraised his friend and saw in his eyes an anger and resolve he had never seen before.

"All right, Gershon. We'll do it your way. You realize if we don't succeed, the US will be a very angry ally, and even if those three young men do pull it off and successfully eliminate the Iranian and North Korean nuclear facilities and destroy their terrorist leaders, the US president will still be furious on two counts. One, we didn't advise them in advance, and two, we will have destroyed his administration's grand plan for the Middle East. Furthermore, the US State Department will be apoplectic when they find out we have done an end run around them in North Korea. They believe that the US holds all the cards when it comes to dealing with the Kim regime."

"Fuck them, Yaakov! As far as I am concerned, Menachem Begin got it right when he once stated, '*The world only respects Israel when they fear us, and by God, they will fear us.*'"

"Yes, I know, Gershon, but we will also have to deal with the Arabists in the UK Foreign office and the US State Department, as well as the histrionics from Erdoğan."

"I don't give a damn. For too long we've had to hide in the shadows and kiss every diplomatic ass that parades around the UN and EU in New York, Geneva, and Brussels. We will take these bastards down once and for all, and perhaps we can succeed. If we can't end terror entirely, we can at least destroy the roots and thus eventually the tree."

Yaakov Melnik had never seen his friend so emotional and enraged. Prime Minister Mendelsohn had always been the epitome of restraint and calm, but he continued, "Yaakov, as far as that Muslim ass-kisser in the White House is concerned, we know he is no friend of ours and I don't give a shit what he and his sycophant secretary of state think. I'm done playing their games. The Palestinians will never agree to a two-state solution or any peace deals. That *momser* Abbas can also go fuck himself. Let the White House suck-ups kiss his ass. I intend to kick it and take his damn sponsors in Iran down. If we don't, they will try to destroy us sooner than later."

Minister Melnik knew that the full weight of the Israeli leadership would be behind 9 and the Mossad and that the prime minister would encounter no opposition in the War Cabinet when he detailed the plans to them.

After Eli, Ari, and Dov left the office of the prime minister and the defense minister recovered from Gershon Mendelsohn's furious outburst, he made a flurry of calls to various departments of the IDF, instructing them to give top priority to a secret mission being prepared by 9. The plan was hotly debated and fine-tuned over a period of weeks by the master planners at IDF headquarters. Countless meetings were held to consider every detail, to ensure that every resource required was made available. Prime Minister Mendelsohn had given strict instructions that he was to be informed every step of the way and on many occasions demanded more clarity and confirmation about key aspects of the planned operations.

After much prolonged and heated discussion, it was agreed that Israel would attempt to take out both the Iranian and North Korean threats. The enormity of this commitment was not lost on the players. All understood that their tiny nation was once again forced to stand alone. The geopolitics surrounding their decision were almost insurmountable.

Prime Minister Mendelsohn, despite some powerful opposition from within his own cabinet and the IDF leadership, was adamant that not a word was to be leaked to the United States. He did not trust the American leader who had shown an anti-Israel face in his agenda and dealings with Israel. The Iranian nuclear threat especially, and the subsequent nuclear treaty were continuing to irk Prime Minister Mendelsohn. The US president and his secretary of state were trying to score a political victory for themselves in attempting to also negotiate a nuclear treaty with North Korea, regardless of the several insulting rebuffs proffered by Kim Jong-un. Therefore, he was irrevocably opposed to enlisting US support or even alerting them as to his intentions.

CHAPTER 34

Training Rosh Pinah and Port of Haifa, September

Ari and Dov immediately established a rigorous and relentless training program for their ground force teams. These teams would be small and highly mobile, executing precision attacks on the heart of the Iranian nuclear program, their military, and the IRGC. The plans were designed for speed and surprise. They would stun the Iranians on the immediate commencement of their attacks and provide the Israeli commandos with overwhelming ground superiority to knock out or manipulate the Iranian communication centres. For this, they would rely on the IDF naval force and IDF Air Force to destroy or jam the communication centres at Bandar Abbas, in Qom, and in Tehran, as well as the Iranian airfields. The key was to jam the S-300 and S-400 surface-to-air missile sites using high-altitude AWAC aircraft circling the perimeter of Iranian air space. If knocking out the missile sites should prove impossible, destroying or jamming their communications was paramount.

Mossad HQ had received intelligence from an NIS asset in Pyongyang that Kim Jong-un had ordered an atmospheric test of a hydrogen bomb mounted on an intercontinental missile. Kim's objective was to intimidate the United States into sitting down to negotiate on his terms. First, he wanted acknowledgement that North Korea was the final victor in the Korean conflict that ceased in 1953. Second, he demanded that as a result of the North's being the ultimate victor, South Korea be reunited under the Communist regime immediately. Third, the United States and NATO would be required to withdraw completely from the Pacific theatre of operations.

The very idea of Kim's exploding a nuclear bomb above the Pacific was beyond imagination. The resulting chaos and damage to shipping and aircraft operations would be horrific. The US leadership was still convinced that through negotiation they could come to terms with the North Koreans as they had with the Iranians in their nuclear pact. What the US president and secretary of state didn't understand was the fact that Kim held them in utter contempt and considered them cowards. The Israelis knew that if terror and nuclear blackmail was to end, they would have to be the force that decapitated the two countries responsible for worldwide terror—especially since the tiny Middle Eastern country was the catalyst for most of the terrorist acts in the world. From a terrorist's standpoint, if there is no Israel and no Jews, no need for bombs, stabbings, and all-around terror. Just peace and light.

CHAPTER 35

The Mossad groups under Eli Naftalin's supervision would have an equally dangerous and difficult insertion into North Korea. The Mossad and South Korean teams would have to enter North Korea from the sea in small groups. The key for them was to escape detection in the early stages of the insertion and to be able to exfiltrate safely after their operations.

The North Korean Navy aggressively patrolled their coastlines using helicopters and high-speed patrol craft. The only way the commandos could gain entry to the hinterland behind the coastline was to approach via silenced electric Zodiacs that were made with a grey material instead of the typical black rubber, so as to blend better into the seascape. This was another patented Israeli invention.

Once ashore, the teams would be challenged by the harsh conditions of the terrain of the North Korean peninsula, which was at best difficult to navigate and inhospitable. Rugged mountains and rice paddies dominated much of the landscape. Roads were few and far between, and always heavily patrolled by the militia.

The local peasantry was heavily indoctrinated by the Kim regime and terrified of appearing anything but totally loyal—since the regime put whole families into gulags, where they were brutally murdered, even the children. The teams recognized that there would be no assistance from local farmers and villagers. Leaning on the experience of the South Korean joint special forces, they would enter North Korea, having trained to blend into the countryside, and appear to be simple peasant farmers. Their most immediate concern was to land undetected and travel quickly inland, then get organized and move north to their assigned targets.

Their weakness was their physical appearance. The North Korean peasantry was by and large malnourished and stunted in growth. Colonel Naftalin and his team commanders were concerned that if their teams were in any way challenged by the militia or even the police, their physiques would be a dead giveaway. The South Korean Special Forces, led by a formidable individual, Captain Sung Hi Mok, allayed some of their fears. Captain Mok had a long-simmering loathing of the Kim regime going back to the current Dear Leader's grandfather.

Mok's maternal grandmother had been trapped in North Korea ever since the Armistice was declared in 1953. His grandfather had fought alongside the Allied forces. Badly wounded at the Battle of Chosin Reservoir, he was evacuated back to the South and eventually Japan for medical attention. His young wife, having been informed of his whereabouts, elected to stay with her family and sadly was caught up in the chaos after the Armistice was signed. Despite being trapped in North Korea, an uncle managed to spirit her two children away to the South, one of whom was Captain Mok's father.

Captain Mok's mother died in childbirth when Mok's younger sister was born. Captain Mok's grandfather never remarried and stayed loyal to his wife until she finally passed away in 2005. Only once in that 50-year period was she able to meet her husband and her two grandchildren at a propaganda reunification event organized by the South and North at the Panmunjeom border in 2002.

Captain Sung Mok had led several previous covert missions into the Hermit Kingdom and explained to the Israelis that when they had faced a challenge from the North Korean authorities, they used overwhelming force and removed the threat, hiding the bodies in fields or rice paddies. The bodies were only discovered long after the South Koreans had departed the scene.

The North Korean leadership, from senior military officers to senior noncommissioned officers, were usually faithful to the regime. The South Koreans perceived this as a structural weakness, since they believed that once an officer or noncommissioned rank was eliminated, the rest of the ordinary soldiers became paralyzed with fear.

The rank and file risked their own safety on two counts: 1) the potential deadly outcome at the hands of the enemy; and 2) making a decision that might fail or be contrary to the regime. Some had witnessed terrible punishments: whole families thrown into pits with wild dogs to be savaged to bloody shreds or when the victim was tied to a post and then shot by a heavy calibre anti-aircraft gun. The result was the poor victim was pulverized. Then the man's family was ordered to clean up the mess of flesh and bone. Immediately after, they were sentenced to be imprisoned in one of the forced labour camps for a minimum period of seven years.

Knowing all of this, the South Korean Seals always targeted the officers and noncommissioned leaders immediately when confronted by them. The North Korean troops, especially the local militia, became leaderless and totally inept. Nine times out of ten, they surrendered to await their fate at the hands of the enemy. Since the missions were top secret, they were not to take any prisoners. Unfortunately, the North Koreans were all eliminated.

Having convinced their Israeli comrades that this was the only way to avoid widespread detection, Eli and Macha accepted the rules of engagement.

CHAPTER 36

The special forces under Captain Sarah Holtzman's command would be charged with neutralizing the Basij militia. This group was feared and loathed by the Iranian citizenry on account of their vicious and brutal behaviour toward the dress codes of ordinary citizens. Thugs would ride around the major cities—Tehran in particular—on motorcycles, enforcing their interpretation of Islam. Men were required to have beards and women had to be veiled and covered. Any person they deemed to be dressed inappropriately or not growing a beard was brutally beaten in the street and, in some cases, taken for interrogation and imprisoned.

For Sarah, this operation held great personal importance. Her family had arrived in Palestine from Germany in 1934. Almost all of her relatives had been involved in secret security missions inside and outside Israel over the years. Her great-grandfather, Yitzak Holzman, had been an ardent Zionist. Having observed the Nazis under Hitler's dictatorship escalating violence against the Jews, Yitzak had managed to have one of his cousins in England provide funds so that he could leave Germany and emigrate to Palestine. As with any endeavour to escape a brutal dictatorship, all that was required was the lubricant of money. Yitzak's cousin, Jacob Holzman, greased the wheels (through some intermediaries) and made it possible for Yitzak and his family to leave Germany with relative ease via the Netherlands and Portugal.

The Holzman family that arrived in Palestine in October 1934 was a proud and ebullient group. The whole contingent, led by Yitzak and his wife, Sharon, consisted of his parents, Avrum and Talia Holzman; his aging grandfather, Marcus; his in-laws, Joseph and

Mina Nimowitz; two of his brothers, Micha and Schlomo; and his two children, Alon and Shoshanna.

All of the Holzmans were immediately drawn to the Zionist cause. Yitzak's son, Alon, signed up when the British formed the Jewish Brigade in defence of Palestine. He was quickly promoted, finally finishing World War II as a major. By 1948, he was a senior officer in the nascent IDF. By 1946, he had married and had his own children, Faigi and David. David was Sarah's father. Sarah was born in 1996.

Sarah continued the family's ardent involvement in the Zionist cause. There was no question about her joining the IDF and volunteering for the hardest missions. One of her uncles on her mother's side, Oscar Cohen, a brave man who had volunteered for the intelligence services when he was just twenty-two years old, had moved to Iran, posing as a Lebanese businessman importing machine tools and precision instruments. In fact, he was a deep cover Mossad agent and for over thirty years after the 1979 Revolution, he sent prolific information about the Iranian missile program back to Israel.

Oscar's successful machine tool and instrument business allowed him access to many influential regime officials and ministries. His expertise in sourcing specific products was eagerly sought after, particularly by the Revolutionary Guards, who were spearheading the missile and nuclear programs. On many occasions, Oscar travelled to Germany, Austria, Sweden, and the UK to negotiate purchases on behalf of the Iranian regime. Occasionally, he would meet one of his Mossad handlers while visiting a trade show in Frankfurt or London.

Oscar needed to exercise extreme caution, since he was well aware that the VEVAK and Quds Force across Europe were on the lookout for Iranian citizens whom they considered "enemies of the State." If he needed to deliver critical information to Mossad, he would book a trip to visit a supplier and always stay at a specific hotel in Frankfurt, London, or Stockholm. Mossad had agents in these cities and covertly had access to hotel reservations. When Oscar stayed over, he always stayed a minimum of two nights. On the second day, he would order breakfast to his room. When the dishes were cleared from his room, a microfilm or flash drive would be found concealed under some unfinished eggs. Mossad knew his room number and would have an agent retrieve them before the breakfast trolley moved off the floor. Oscar never met his contacts or handlers. If they wanted to communicate with him, they would leave a message on his room telephone. The message was simple and straightforward.

"Hello Oscar, it's Brian at Delta Machine and Tools. Please call me back. We need two more days to present our offer on the high-speed lathes discussed on Wednesday."

When he received this message, Oscar knew that the two days referred to Friday and he would travel out to Delta Machine and Tools, where he would receive a proposal package. Within the package would be specific instructions from Mossad. Unbeknownst to Oscar, Delta Machine and Tools was owned by a former Mossad agent. The company did in fact manufacture high-quality products that were in great demand, and even though Oscar imported products from many suppliers, he always visited with Delta, since they had branch companies in Frankfurt and Stockholm.

The information Oscar provided to Israel regarding the Iranian missile and nuclear programs was invaluable. All parties recognized the dangerous game he was playing and did everything in their power to protect his true identity.

Then, suddenly, Oscar's information and contacts ceased. One day in 2010, there was a large public execution in Tehran's Tanzim Square, where some fifteen homosexuals and enemies of the state were hung from cranes. The Iranian news media were obligated to show the gory details and as the TV cameras panned in on each of the victims, Mossad personnel saw Oscar before a black hood was placed over his head. He was about to be hung from a crane.

The Iranians never admitted they had been compromised, and as far as Oscar's crimes were concerned, they were never revealed. He was simply executed as an enemy of the state.

As is often the case, a small mistake had cost Oscar his life. While in Stockholm on one of his visits, VEVAK had decided to watch his activities in a routine check to see if he was who he purported to be.

Oscar was in the hotel bar one evening, waiting to dine with one of his suppliers. The owner of the supplier came with two colleagues, one of whom was an Israeli. Oscar recognized his accent and made the mistake of conversing briefly with him in Hebrew. The VEVAK agents were sitting at the bar, keeping a routine watch on Oscar and overheard him speaking Hebrew.

Inadvertently, Oscar Cohen had signed his own death warrant. As soon as he returned to Tehran, he was arrested, tried, and incarcerated, and probably tortured before his execution.

Sarah's large extended family had grieved Oscar's ignominious death, but for obvious reasons the details were kept secret. His body was disposed of along with the other fourteen victims in unmarked graves.

CHAPTER 37

As Sarah grew up and joined the IDF, she harboured a burning desire to seek revenge on the twisted, hateful Iranian mullahs and their repressive autocratic regime. Even though she was a young teenager at the beginning, she felt a terrible sense of loss. Over time in the IDF, she became a well-regarded officer and leader. She was a ferocious practitioner of the unique Israeli unarmed combat technique of Krav Maga. She and her fellow commandos were all trained in the fierce martial art so that even the smallest, slightest woman had the skills to kill a man twice her size.

Sarah relentlessly drove her command to practice and practice yet again. Her skills and those of her troops in the art of Krav Maga were legendary within the elite forces. She was incredibly protective of her charges and strove every hour to make them better warriors. Her biggest fear—and the content of her nightmares prior to a mission— was losing one of her personnel. The thought of having to face the deceased's loved ones was dreadful.

The seven Sayeret Deep Penetration Teams would each target the nuclear plants. The facilities at Fordow and Natanz in particular were fifty to seventy-five metres underground, impervious even to bunker-busting bombs. Ari and Dov had quickly determined that any kind of conventional air assault would be fruitless.

Dov had studied these facilities for a long time, and based on the intelligence gleaned, he recognized one key weakness in the design of the underground sites. They all needed air. He had identified cleverly concealed air vents and breathers surrounding each location.

The Mossad recruited a dissident Iranian professor, Nader Ruhani, who lectured at a college near the Natanz nuclear plants.

He had been an ardent but secret supporter of the opposition Green movement that was brutally suppressed after the rigged presidential elections in 2009. Ruhani had a passionate desire to aid any agency in bringing down the regime. He was a sleeper asset of Mossad and believed Israel could be that agent of change. The professor was unknowingly introduced to 9 when his handler and contact with Mossad changed. His new handler or control was one of Macha's 9 personnel.

Macha sent one of Ari's protégé operators, Nahum Gilwasser, into Iran. Gilwasser's remit was to meet Professor Ruhani and learn about the topography surrounding the facilities. Nahum provided Nader with some highly classified spy equipment, the most important being miniature drones that carried infrared sensing devices with miniature cameras and GPS instruments. The drones were not much larger than a car key fob and impossible to identify once they were five hundred feet above ground. Nahum instructed the professor in their use.

"Nader, never fly these during the day. The risks are too great. These little guys are robust and can stay airborne on a battery charge for at least twelve hours. Dispatch them in ever widening asymmetrical loops just before dawn. The chances of you being seen are greatly reduced at that hour. Plan to retrieve them after dark so you are not compromised."

Professor Ruhani was relieved at this news. "That will make the task less dangerous and there will be less of a chance of my being discovered."

Nahum also showed Nader a small electronic key-sized device that to the casual observer was nothing more than a Nissan key fob. In fact, it was a self-destruct trigger. If Nader felt compromised and the drone was in danger of being intercepted or captured, he could depress the trunk latch symbol on the key fob and a very small explosive, one gram of Semtex and an ounce of phosphorus, would destroy the drone in midair, leaving only a small pile of ash with scorched and twisted metal. The source of the destructive trigger would be impossible to identify.

Ruhani was also instructed to send the pictures and infrared data back to Israel via a highly compressed data burst over a secure 9 cell phone. Again, if this was somehow seized, it would appear to be just as an ordinary cell phone. The addresses within the contact list would all be innocuous names and businesses that regardless of how hard the secret security forces investigated, there would be no suspicions raised. Professor Ruhani would check out as just another harmless middle-class educator.

CHAPTER 38

Ari and Dov rehearsed with Sarah every day how they would deal with the Basij. Their headquarters was in a compound in the centre of Tehran. Their objectives were to storm the buildings once the armoured trucks had breached the gates and walls. Once inside the compound, they were to enter and seize or destroy the command structure. In particular they were to take the Basij commander, Gholamhossein Gheybparvar, into custody along with any commanders or senior officers of the Ansar-e-Hezbollah, an even more militant and cruel militia associated with Basij. All of these special militia forces were ultimately commanded by General Hussein Soleimani of the Islamic Revolutionary Guards.

Sarah pushed her sections as hard as possible. After the armoured trucks broke through the gates, the alighting commandos would have less than thirty seconds to enter the buildings. Any longer and they would run the risk of being caught out in the open and subject to withering fire from both groups of militants. Once they gained entrance to the buildings, rooting out any opposition would be much simpler.

While the squad leaders charged with seizing the commanders and evacuating them from the buildings were searching office by office and room by room, their compatriots would restrict the Basij from escaping the compound. In this effort they were to be aided and protected, hopefully, by the IDF Air Force circling overhead.

The armoured trucks were Israeli-modified Russian GAZ Ural-M drop-sided vehicles. The Russian GAZ standard product is regarded as one of the most rugged and reliable transport trucks; they are a common sight on Iranian roads. The Israeli modifications were not visible from the exterior. The straight in line ten-cylinder, heavy-duty diesel engines were upgraded with superchargers; and the chassis were strengthened and stiffened to withstand their battering-ram role when they crashed the compound gates. The drop sides allowed the teams to travel without being seen, yet they could easily and quickly dismount and execute entry into target buildings.

At Rosh Pinah, the teams practised for many hours driving at the posted speed limit along mocked-up city streets on the air base until they were drawing level with the entrance gates to the Basij and IRGC Headquarter buildings. Their drivers then had to be able to swing almost at ninety degrees across the roadway and accelerate as fast as possible into the gates. The Israeli military engineers had calculated that the sheer weight and relative speed and momentum of the trucks would carry them, with a relatively short accelerating run, through the gates. Once inside the compounds, the trucks would drive as close to the entry facades and the troops would be exiting over the sides covering each other as they leapfrogged into the buildings.

While the land teams were training at Rosh Pina, the naval team practised in and around the Port of Haifa. They always did this at night to avoid prying eyes. The most critical issue was disembarking unobserved from their mother-ship submarine, which would have crept into the Persian Gulf two days before. The biggest risk would be getting through the Straits of Hormuz. At its narrowest, the Straits were only twenty-one miles across, heavily patrolled and monitored by the IRGC. They always had at least thirty small high-speed craft circulating through and around the Straits, monitoring all surface—and they hoped—under surface craft. The Israeli Navy commandos would have to leave the sub and board their Zodiacs, then travel approximately two miles to the harbour at Bandar Abbas, on the eastern mouth of the Straits.

CHAPTER 39

Rosh Pinah and Azerbaijan, October

After thirty days of intense training, the mission was cleared by the prime minister and the IDF Supreme Command, and the groups assembled to execute their assignments.

The Air Force deployed eighteen F-16I fighter-bombers to Azerbaijan with which Israel, surprisingly, had a strong bond and relationship. Also deployed were three C-130 Hercules transporters, which made four trips delivering the eight converted CH-53 Yasur helicopters. They had secret access to a former Soviet air base, which was inherited from the Soviet adventures in the 1980s in Afghanistan. The helicopters were disassembled and, although a tight fit, two were able to be carried in the Hercules. Another transport plane flew in mechanics and ground crew for the fighter-bombers and the helicopters.

Macha, Ari and Dov concluded that the IRGC, mullahs, and ayatollahs would be expecting an air assault on the nuclear facilities, all of which were hardened with defences that were difficult to penetrate successfully, including the latest surface-to-air S-300 and S-400 Russian anti-aircraft missile technology. It was one of these that had brought down a Malaysian Airlines Boeing 777 over Ukraine in July 2014, with 298 passengers aboard, none of whom survived. While the whole world knew who was responsible for the heinous crime, the Russians never accepted responsibility.

The Sayeret and the female commandos had one of the hardest and riskiest assignments. Under Ari's and Dov's leadership, they were to infiltrate into Tehran, where the headquarters of the IRGC were located, and Qom where the ayatollahs and mullahs resided, and the Council of Clerics assembled.

The other deep penetration teams would fly from Azerbaijan and await the jump-off signal from Macha in Tel Aviv. Some Sayeret commandos were of Persian Jewish heritage, fluent in Farsi, so they could deal with any questions or problems from local farmers and villagers as they worked their way toward the nuclear plants. Others would drive the Israeli-modified GAZ trucks. The CH-53 helicopters would be reassembled at the Azerbaijan air base, then remain on standby until alerted by the AWACs to go. On command, they would fly the Sayeret teams close to their assigned nuclear site targets.

CHAPTER 40

Qom and Tehran, Iran

Dov went over his group's plans in one final review.

"Our arms and munitions have been driven in from Azerbaijan to a warehouse near where we are staying. The Persians running the warehouse are only to receive the trucks. If they are for whatever reason investigated and arrested by the IRGC, they will be charged as enemies of the State. They are not aware of us and our location, so there is no chance of them identifying us. Their instructions are to receive the trucks into the warehouse across from our hostel. We will watch for three days to see if anyone is curious. Then we will collect the material. Any questions?"

In Tehran, Ari reviewed the plans for his and Sarah's teams one final time, with five-person groups meeting in their hotel rooms. To ensure security, Ari had a tech team sweep the rooms for listening devices and the meetings were conducted with water running, thus rendering it almost impossible for anyone to record their discussions.

As determined in Rosh Pinah, the crux of the plan was to cause disruption among the IRGC and the ruling clerics so the eight special teams targeting the nuclear plants and Bandar Abbas could complete their missions without being compromised or hindered.

If all went according to plan, three C-130 Hercules aircraft would fly to Imam Khomeini International Airport from Azerbaijan, while the teams drove to the airport. Two would land at the airport while the third, a "Spooky" gunship, would provide overwatch if necessary. The Spooky is considered one of the deadliest air gunships ever deployed. The armaments on a Spooky were able to deliver a devastating rain of fire and lead accurately on any ground target, either from a height of 1,000 feet or a low level of 150 feet. Armed with five-barrel Gatling cannons and a M102 mm howitzer cannon as well as 40 mm Bofors machine guns, Spooky was capable of totally destroying armoured vehicles, including tanks. If they were unable to execute the exfil, then the teams would drive to a location where the C-130s would land on a straight section of highway and pick them up. Plan B would be determined by the AWACS command crew. In addition to Spooky, this site would also be provided cover by the fighter planes if necessary.

Sarah and her group of commandos would attack the headquarters of the Basij, the vicious and brutal civilian militia that carried out daily beatings and harassment of ordinary Iranian citizens while providing support to the IRGC. Sarah's objective was to destroy the Basij communications and prevent them from aiding the IRGC, plus capturing the commander, Gholamhossein Gheybparvar, who was on a terrorist watch list. Gheybparvar was responsible for crimes against humanity; he had been indicted by the International Court in The Hague. Sarah and her teams were also to prevent the Basij from organizing and threatening ordinary Iranian citizens.

The five teams under Ari's command were to destroy the Guard's ability to communicate with the Army and Air Force. Shutting down IRGC communications would render the Iranian military totally blind and deaf. This would allow the seven other commando teams to operate with a degree of impunity and avoid detection. The disruptions and chaos in Bandar Abbas, Tehran, and Qom would keep the Iranian Guards and military focused on the three centres and not the nuclear plants.

In the meantime, the Navy demolition teams would silently disembark from a submarine off the harbour of Bandar Abbas. Their task was to infiltrate the naval facilities and oil storage tank farms, and at a coordinated time with their fellow teams in Tehran and Qom, they would set off charges and demolitions that would render the Iranian armed forces useless for months. At the same time, they would restrict gasoline and oil distribution to the general Iranian public, thus severely crippling the economy even more than sanctions had done. This was a critical component of the plan, as the Iranian Republican Guard's Naval forces had been charged with closing the Straits of Hormuz in the event of an attack on the rogue nation.

There would also be two Israeli Dolphin-II class submarines: *Tanin* (Crocodile) and *Rahav* (Splendour) stealthily approaching predetermined locations forty kilometres off the Iranian coast. They would coordinate with the fighter planes coming in from Azerbaijan, and each fire thirty-six Israeli-designed cruise missiles at the command and control centres of the Iranian military in Tehran and the Air Force control centres at the major air bases. The guidance technology was a closely guarded Israeli secret not shared with any allies. The missiles were so accurate they could be programmed to enter a specific window or door in a building even when fired from eight hundred miles away. They were guided by an ultrasensitive opton-electronic, photo radar guidance system designed by Elbit Systems, able to identify and home in on a target as small as six inches square. They would be programmed to destroy the communication buildings and do so with little or no collateral damage to civilians.

The Iranians would be unprepared and confused as to the main targets. The Israeli second salvo of thirty-six missiles would be targeted on the control centres and runways of the Iranian Air Force bases, hopefully destroying any Iranian Air Force planes as they readied to defend against the F-16I bombers. The Israeli fighter-bombers would destroy the air bases and any related infrastructure such as fuel depots and remaining radar and communication centres. This action would be reminiscent of the destruction of almost the entire Egyptian Air Force in 1967 during the Six-Day War by the IAF.

Another two flights of Israeli F-15I fighter-bombers would take off from Israel to coordinate an attack on the Kharg Island oil facilities. These were the main source of hard currency income for Iran. The Kharg Island facilities were a terminal for their substantial oil exports. The effect on the Iranian economy with the destruction of the Kharg Island facilities would be crippling, essentially forcing the Iranian government to its knees. If the Israeli attacks on Kharg Island, the nuclear facilities, and the IRGC communication infrastructure proved successful, Iran would no longer be the Shi'ite hegemony threatening the whole of the Middle East and North Africa. Their plans for regional domination would be destroyed and the Iranian people would have to depend on sympathetic nations aiding them in rebuilding a free and democratic country that would be recognized within the community of nations—not as a pariah, but as an equal.

The ninth team of Sayeret troops would infiltrate Lebanon, where General Soleimani was training and organizing Hezbollah shock troops to invade Israel. With Soleimani the second most senior commander in the IRGC and feared head of the Quds Force, the Sayeret mission was to kidnap him and several Hezbollah commanders. They would bring them back to Israel to stand trial for war crimes in Syria and terrorism in Israel.

General Soleimani was a formidable opponent. He had trained and shaped the ragtag bands of Hezbollah almost single-handedly into a highly disciplined and effective fighting force. This was proven in 2006 when Israel invaded Lebanon to engage Hezbollah and were completely caught off guard by their tenacity and discipline. Since then, the general had been improving and honing the terrorist force into a fierce adversary. He had insisted they join the Syrian dictator Assad and his cause in the Syrian Civil War, and it was their training and expertise, along with Russian air power, that had swung the war in Assad's favour.

It was an open secret that Lebanon and Syria were basically under the military control of Iran. Soleimani brooked no opposition. Regardless of where opposition to Iranian influence came from, he immediately and ruthlessly eliminated them, many times personally. He was an arrogant and bombastic individual, who had been in the cross hairs of the Israelis for many years. Capturing him and his senior Hezbollah commanders was key to the 9 plans to eliminate terror from the region.

For over six years, General Soleimani had been consolidating his power base in Lebanon and Syria with his shock troops from the IRGC and Hezbollah. The incredibly strong force he developed had aided Bashar Assad in his fight to maintain control of Syria. General Soleimani was essentially the power behind the throne in Syria. He controlled Assad and his government ostensibly on behalf of the Mullahs in Iran. In reality, the general conducted his affairs as he saw fit with little or no direction from Tehran.

The Israelis had gathered an enormous amount of intelligence on Soleimani. They were concerned that he was developing a strategic plan to occupy the Golan Heights and draw Israel into a two-front war with Hezbollah in the North and Hamas in Gaza. He was using the brutal civil war in Syria to import large numbers of Iranian Guards and Shi'ite mercenaries into Syria. The Mossad and 9 were firmly of the opinion that if Soleimani was removed from his position of power, the whole plan he was developing would collapse.

Soleimani held the Lebanese and Syrian governments in absolute contempt. They either did his bidding and carried out directions or they would be removed. He had shown a great ability to engineer this in Lebanon, where the legitimate civilian government was completely subservient to Hezbollah under his leadership. There had been many mysterious accidents and killings in both Syria and Lebanon that removed vocal critics of Iran in general and the IRGC and Soleimani in particular. His arrogance was deemed to be his major weakness. He had a wife and family back in Tehran, but openly and publicly flaunted his relationship with a Lebanese TV personality. When he was not in the field, he would have her visit him at his headquarters and stay overnight or he would visit her lavish home just outside Beirut.

CHAPTER 41

Tehran

After they arrived in Tehran, Ari and Sarah, posing as Kazakh tourists, would stroll to the retail area near their hotel and observe who was walking on the street or in parked and moving vehicles. At one point, Sarah gave Ari's arm an imperceptible tug and drew his attention across the street from where they were walking. There was a dark green, older Mercedes 190 diesel four-door sedan parked with two sinister characters sitting in the front seats. Both were burly and angry looking, with thick black beards. Ari spoke in Russian to Sarah, "I think they are the religious police, waiting to pounce on some unfortunate women and men who are not dressed or bearded to their satisfaction."

Sarah shuddered and pulled her head covering more tightly around her head. The religious police were mostly radical Islamists, brutal in their enforcement of religious protocols, regardless of who the women were. Ari was glad he and the other male team members had let their beards grow. The thugs usually enforced rules using vicious punishment in the form of beatings in the street on anyone who disobeyed their religious laws.

Sarah put on a good act, laughing in a demure way and steering Ari up to the second level of the retail complex. They purchased some souvenirs and sampled offerings from various food stalls.

Ari froze as one of the thugs exited the Mercedes, came into the centre, and took the escalator up to the second level. Had they been targeted?

Again, Ari spoke in Russian. "Sarah, if he confronts either of us, be prepared to incapacitate him."

Sarah nodded, but then asked, "Why?"

"Because he will make a loud scene and attract other security, which will be very bad for us. Silence him if he confronts us!"

For Sarah this was easy; she was skilled Krav Maga. Within a few minutes, they relaxed. Religious Thug One had just come into the centre to use the men's room. Ari relaxed a bit when he realized they would not be interrogated after all. Instead the religious police agent stopped at a stall and bought some food for himself and his partner, then exited and returned to the Mercedes.

Ari and Sarah continued their tourist sightseeing routine for another hour. They strolled in and out of various stores in the complex, lingering over women's fashions and in some cases with Sarah trying on a coat or shoes. All the time, Ari was maintaining a close watch to see if they were under any kind of surveillance by the secret police or militia. There was none, so finally, they exited the mall and returned to their hotel.

The teams sent out couples during the day and evening to conduct surveillance, then reported back that the trucks were of no special interest to anyone. Macha's special friends had been routinely parking the trucks there ever since the plan was conceived. The weapons were hidden under boxes of nuts and dates set for delivery to local stores and markets. A closer examination of the trucks would have shown that they were cleverly disguised and armoured with thick, heavy plate steel that would protect the occupants from small arms and mortar fire. They also had a heavily reinforced front end that would drive straight through the IRGC and Basij compound gates and fortifications. Essentially, they were tanks without tracks. The trucks were driven by Mossad and Iranian opposition operatives across the border at Astara. This crossing was unique in that Astara, Azerbaijan and Astara, Iran are one town with a border separating the two parts. It is relatively relaxed and the guards on both sides are easily bribed to look the other way.

Once in Iran, the trucks were slowly driven to Tehran and Qom, where they were parked awaiting the teams from Israel. This part of the operation was the one with the most risk; Ari and Macha had decided that the Iranian opposition members were going to have to be relied on. They had agreed that this was the only way to get the teams and their equipment into Iran undetected. They had studied the disastrous American Desert One operations of 1980, when US Special Forces under Commander Colonel Beckwith had flown into Iran to free fifty-two American hostages being held at the US Embassy in Tehran. Unfortunately, they had been compromised by poor intelligence and bad weather.

CHAPTER 42

Tehran

Ari expected the "go" signal from Macha at 0001 hours. At 2200 hours, with the trucks having remained undetected and undisturbed, the teams quietly made their way to the warehouse and prepared for their mission. They commenced by putting on their battle dress and checking all of their weapons. The weapons chosen by all the teams were HK suppressed machine pistols with magazines of thirty high-velocity rounds, Glock 17 silenced automatic handguns, and a uniquely Israeli weapon known affectionately as the "Shaveh-ka" or Equalizer.

During the Gaza wars and various incursions into Lebanon, one of the deadliest weapons used by Hamas and Hezbollah terrorists with devastating results was the rocket-propelled grenade (RPG) launcher. Israeli munitions experts had created the Shaveh-ka, a stealth technology radar-driven deflector, which identified an RPG as soon as it launched from its tube. Each team member wore a ceramic breast and back plate, inside of which was a saucer-shaped disk powered by two AA rechargeable lithium batteries. When activated, the radar waves would lock on to incoming RPGs and a high intensity laser beam would fix the warhead to explode the munition instantly, literally as it left the launch tube. The intent was to explode the warhead well before it reached its target and if possible, eliminate the shooter.

Each team member, in addition to their HK suppressed weapon, also carried a piano-wire garrote; a two-sided, serrated black-bladed commando combat knife—again a uniquely Israeli weapon; four flash bang grenades; two smoke grenades; and two half-kilo blocks of Semtex and pencil fuses.

CHAPTER 43.

Qom, the same day

Dov's teams were staying in third-class hotels that were well known in the young traveller communities from Eastern Europe and Turkey. His four teams, totalling eighty combatants, had arrived in Qom over a period of several days from Sofia, Bulgaria, and Astana, Kazakhstan, posing as Kazakhs and Bulgarians. Macha's special friends had driven what outwardly appeared to be beat-up old farm trucks from Astara to a service area a few hundred metres from the hotel.

As in Tehran, they attracted no attention, since they had been there off and on for several days. The teams' weapons and battle uniforms were hidden in false compartments in the beds of the trucks. Earlier that day, the trucks had been driven to an abandoned industrial plant warehouse and the teams had made their way there during the afternoon and evening. As had Ari's teams, they dressed in their uniforms with Equalizer protectors and checked all their weapons.

While transporting via public transit or taxis to the area where the trucks had been stored, one pair of team members had a narrow escape. Sergeant Yoni Nuss and Trooper Yigal Teichman had been dropped off by taxi a few hundred metres from the warehouse. They were walking diffidently toward the entrance to the industrial plant when Teichman stepped in some dog shit. Involuntarily, he let out an expletive in Hebrew just as a group of militia men were walking by. The leader of the Iranian patrol quickly halted his group.

"Did you hear what that young guy over there said?"

One of the other militia men replied, "No, what did he say?"

"To me it didn't sound like Arabic or Farsi, but maybe Hebrew—too guttural."

Speaking to his colleagues in Farsi, he said, "Let's check them out. They look like two pieces of tourist shit from Turkey or Romania."

Switching to English, he shouted at Yigal, "Hey you, asshole! Yes, you, cleaning the dog shit off your boot. Get over here."

Private Teichman, his heart pounding, slowly walked over to the Iranian militia men. As he came within six feet of them, two circled behind and grabbed his arms while the leader—large, and muscular—demanded Yigal's ID papers. Yoni Nuss maintained a careful eye on his teammate, but since they were not carrying any concealed weapons, he was powerless to intervene. Yigal handed over his ID papers, verifying him as a Bulgarian student on a tourist visa. Big Muscles examined them and then punched him in the stomach.

"That's for being a fucking idiot, stepping in dog shit! When you did that you swore. What language was that?"

Teichman looked up, gasping for breath and explained in deliberately feigned poor English, "German, German! My father was German, and he was always swearing in German. I picked up his bad habits."

The thuggish militia man held his gaze on Yigal for what seemed an eternity, and then with a hard shove, shouted in his face, "Watch out, you useless fucking unbeliever. Take your dog shit and get out of our sight. We don't look kindly on your lazy asses traipsing around our country, looking down your snot noses at us. Now git, you piece of infidel shit!"

Yoni Nuss heaved a silent sigh of relief as Teichman quickly crossed the street and then continued to clean off his boot with leaves and grass he found in a mini park nearby.

"That was close." The four militia men continued to observe Yoni and Yigal, and for a moment, Yoni was sure they were going to summon them again, but just then, Big Muscles's collar-attached radio squawked. By his body language, Yoni and Yigal concluded they had been summoned to a more important assignment. The quartet hurriedly rounded the corner and moments later, the two Israelis saw them drive away in a 4x4 truck.

According to protocol, they continued past the plant and hailed another taxi to take them to a subway station. There, they boarded a bus that eventually stopped across from the plant, which was next to a wholesale fruit and produce market. After wandering through the market, Yigal and Yoni quickly slipped through the gates of the industrial plant and joined their comrades.

At 0001hrs, Macha and the IDF command leadership sent the "Go" signal to an AWACS plane circling the Caspian Sea. Dov and Ari received clearance via the AWACS to commence the mission, and Operation Begin was given the green light. There was no turning back. Ari's call sign was Macha 1 and Dov's, Macha 2.

CHAPTER 44.

Bandar Abbas, 0300 hrs

IDF Navy special forces Captain Levi Einhorn and his complement of demolition sailors were carried by the Israeli Navy's submarine *Tekumah* (Revival), commanded by Rav Seren (Captain) Saul Issa. They were taken to an insertion point 3.2 kilometres from Bandar Abbas. As they had determined in training at Haifa, this was as close as the submarine could safely go undetected.

Captain Issa slowly brought the *Tekumah* up to hover 35 feet just below the surface as they had practised. The *Tekumah* had been sitting on the bottom of the Persian Gulf across from Bandar Abbas for eighteen hours. So far, he had avoided sonar detection from any surface patrols. The Israelis were aware that the Iranian Guards had sonar on some of their surface patrol craft, but their greater fear was if the Guards had deployed any submarines into the area across from Banda Abbas. This was a delicate and precarious part of the operation. It was imperative that the submarine not be detected this close to shore, so they had to creep in at a speed of less than two knots to avoid leaving an underwater wake that may have been spotted from the surface or air.

The waters were shallow at this part of the Gulf, less than 240 feet deep. After Captains Issa and Einhorn verified the signal to deploy and confirmed their coordinates yet again, Issa clutched Einhorn's left shoulder and gripped his right hand. "Einhorn, my orders were to get you here safely on target. My direct orders to you are to return safely with all your men. Israel needs you. Be'ezrat Hashem (with God's help)."

With that exhortation, Levi Einhorn and his men, watched apprehensively by some of the submarine's crew, silently exited through the escape hatch and corralled their three electric-powered Zodiacs. The powerful electric motors had been stored in waterproof containers inside the Zodiacs, along with weapons and explosives. Once they surfaced, the commandos had to remove the containers, install the motors to the sterns of the Zodiacs, and check the weapons and the explosives. They had practised this in training countless times and achieved a 100% success rate in deploying the cargo. Each craft held ten highly trained naval commandos who, under the cover of darkness, silently motored toward their objective, Bandar Abbas harbour. Their mission was to destroy the oil containers in and around the harbour as well as to knock out the Iranian naval installations and communications centre.

They arrived undetected and secured and hid their Zodiacs under the wharves. Then they clung to the pilings around the wharves of the naval base awaiting the final "go" signal. Captain Einhorn quietly checked in with IDF command headquarters via the second high-altitude AWACS aircraft circling over the Red Sea. His arrival status was passed on immediately to Ari and Dov, who were awaiting word from 9 that Major Benyamin Avigold, who led the team that was tasked with capturing General Soleimani in Lebanon, was in place and ready. At 0012 hours, Ari, Dov, Sarah, Captain Einhorn, and Major Avigold received the signal to go.

Captain Einhorn and his three teams forming the naval force silently climbed up on to the dockside. Each had been outfitted with a wetsuit which was dull grey instead of the usual black. Grey blended into backgrounds better than black at night. Once on the huge dock, two of the three teams quickly headed for the oil storage tanks located at the northern end of the maritime facility. The tanks, at least thirty of them, were enormous; each held approximately a million litres of refined oil, gasoline, diesel, and aviation fuel.

As Team Aleph, led by Senior Sergeant Moses Meyers, began their dash to the oil tanks, the leader of Bet team, Sergeant Benny Marcus, spoke into the universal comms throat microphone that communicated with all of the operators, quickly alerting him a four-man guard patrol was coming his way. Meyers and his men sank into prone positions on the broad expanse of wharf and held their breath. The new grey wetsuits earned their keep. It would be disastrous if the alarm was raised before they reached their targets.

"Bet to Aleph; four guards will be rounding the space to the east of the tanks between the first two huts in thirty seconds."

"Aleph to Bet; Copy that."

Working their way slowly behind the guards as they came out into the open, Moses and his men slit their throats.

Moses Meyers' Aleph team quickly deployed to the fence surrounding the tank reservoirs. After quietly cutting through the wire fencing, the commandos made their way to the massive storage tanks while Bet team covered them.

Captain Einhorn and Gimel team were able to stay concealed. As other security guards patrolled, they left their concealment and silently eliminated them with garrotes and commando knives.

Aleph team, under Moses Myers' direction, set timed explosive charges that would detonate in forty-five minutes at the bases of the thirty huge oil storage containers, each holding hundreds of thousands of litres of fuel—oil for the Iranian Navy, aviation fuel for the Air Force, and gasoline and diesel fuel for domestic use. The base of each tank was surrounded by an earthen berm designed to contain any leaks. This demolition was a sophisticated one that they had practised extensively in Rosh Pina.

Blowing up a tank containing diesel oil—or just plain oil—was not as simple as many would believe. Myers and his team had noted what petroleum products were in each tank and, as planned, created a small explosion that would fracture the base of the heavy tanks. This would cause them to leak onto the ground, creating a pool of oil within the containment berm surrounding the tanks. Those pools would aid the combustion when the gas and high-octane fuel tanks exploded. The heavier oil products would cook off on the ground and eventually turn the whole tank farm into a blazing inferno. It would easily take two years to repair and rebuild.

Meyers had a reputation as a fearless leader. At less than a metre and half tall (just under five feet tall), he was a legend in the IDF Navy, the go-to person for teaching and instructing in the art of elimination—whether with a garrote, knife, or Krav Maga. He was also an instructor in sabotage techniques with explosives of all kinds.

Once the guard patrols were neutralized, Einhorn and his men hurried over to the administration and communications buildings in the centre of the facility, where they set more charges. Bet and Gimel teams forced their way into the communication centre, eliminating two sleepy guards. There they placed Semtex plastic explosive blocks in and around all the control consoles and computer banks. Captain Einhorn's team also carried several satchel charges with them. Those they had brought along in the event they saw other targets of opportunity.

Incredibly, none of guards had been able to alert the Iranian sailors and IRGC contingents who were still sleeping in their barracks, such was the speed and expertise of the Israeli commando teams. The explosive charges were timed to coincide with the charges set on the tanks earlier. The charges were set in and around the buildings housing the radio communications of the Iranian Navy. Once the explosions began, the anticipation was that disarray and panic would overwhelm the Iranian guards and their Navy counterparts so that their situation would be unmanageable for at least two hours, thus allowing the three boat teams to exit unseen.

As quietly as they had landed on the docks, they carefully worked their way back to the water and the pilings. There they boarded their Zodiacs and prepared to slip out of the harbour. As they were passing the end of the furthermost jetty, Moses Meyer identified two targets—the Russian built Kilo class submarine *Yunes* and the newly launched destroyer *Persian Gulf*. After a brief consult, Captain Einhorn ordered Aleph and Bet teams to continue to the evacuation submarine. Einhorn then detoured toward the moored craft and deployed four satchel charges just at the waterline on the sides of the two vessels. Then he sped away just as some lookouts on the destroyer sounded the alarm.

As they raced out to sea to rendezvous with the waiting Tekumah, the administration and communication buildings exploded. A minute later, the oil storage tanks blasted in a devastating pyrotechnical display. The firestorm of burning oil and munitions was observed from space by both Israeli and US satellites circling the earth.

Once all three teams were back safely on board, the Israeli submarine silently submerged to a depth of fifty metres and crept out to the Straits of Hormuz and back to Israel.

Two lesser explosions rocked the two moored warships back in the harbour, causing the destroyer to begin sinking immediately. The *Yunes* split apart at the waterline and sank within minutes.

The naval commandos had silently eluded or eliminated the Iranian guards and placed explosives and wireless activated flashbang devices designed to sow mass confusion and terror in the enemy. The added destruction of the submarine and the locally constructed destroyer, the pride of the Iranian Navy, was a huge bonus and would soon be a demoralizer for the Iranian military brass.

As the IRGC realized the base was under attack, they began quickly assembling and searching out the attackers. The wirelessly activated explosives were causing total panic and pandemonium among the Iranian forces. Eventually, after an hour of chaos, one of the Guard officers was able to get the alarm out by driving to a public telephone land line at a small retail grocery store two miles from the base. He notified the IRGC headquarters in Tehran and the Quds Force headquarters located in the former US embassy, as well as the Council of Clerics, who were all roused from their sleep by aides and junior clerics. All this telephone activity was monitored by the Israeli AWAC planes, confirming to the IDF command and 9 headquarters that the plans to take down the Iranian communication systems at Bandar Abbas had been successful.

CHAPTER 45

Qom and Tehran, 0500 hrs

A hastily convened telephone conference was held between Qom and Tehran, during which it was decided, exactly as Ari and Dov had expected, that the Ayatollah and his most senior advisers and mullahs should immediately travel to Tehran. Israeli communication and IT specialists intercepted and redirected instructions for all the clerics and senior officials to assemble at the Council of Clerics headquarters. With the communication centres destroyed or compromised, the Israelis controlled all communications to and from the various Iranian military groups.

Dov and his teams struck hard and fast during the shock and confusion surrounding the reports from Bandar Abbas. The Israeli commandos forced their way into the IRGC and Quds Force headquarters in Qom, taking the guards and those troops that were awake totally by surprise. The IRGC were considered elite troops and soon showed their skills. Although caught off guard by the intensity of the Israeli attack and penetration of their buildings, under the command of some seasoned veteran officers from the Syrian campaign, they soon recovered and fought back with fury and determination. The Israeli Special Forces were challenged for over an hour as the IRGC troops were expert fighters, well trained and coordinated. Their ability to react to sudden actions and organize among themselves via walkie-talkies instead of radios and cell phones impressed Dov. This was unexpected and Dov and his teams had to at times take defensive actions themselves. Several Sayeret were injured and evacuated to the aid station they had established for exactly that purpose.

Eventually, the Israelis overpowered the Iranians and either killed or wounded them to the point where they were removed from the fighting. Dov and Deborah Grunwalder and their commandos then began a floor-by-floor and room-by-room clearing action. They had to disarm IRGC communications so the Iranian commanders would be unable to communicate with any of their forces.

After the spirited firefight put up by the IRGC, the Israelis had suffered several casualties, two received serious and extensive wounds, although both would survive, and several others suffered minor wounds.

With the IRGC forces out of the picture, Dov and Deborah retreated down to the building where the Council of Clerics offices were situated. There they removed any threats from the small contingent of Quds Force providing security for the clerics. Those guards had no appetite for aggressive defence after they had witnessed or heard what happened to their former colleagues at the headquarters.

What surprised Dov and his teams was the complete absence of regular Iranian armed forces. He concluded that either the jamming and destruction of the communication systems was the cause or that the professional generals were smart enough to understand that the events happening all around them were designed to end the rule of the mullahs and clerics. Those soldiers were loyal to the state but disillusioned, as was the civilian population of Iran, with the stifling and corrupt rule of religious extremists and their thuggish Revolutionary Guards, Quds.

The AWAC planes circling the skies around Iran and the Lebanon-Syrian border picked up some early attempts from the IRGC to question the sudden poor communications. They also captured recordings of frantic radio and cell phone transmissions from IRGC headquarters to Soleimani's bunker in Syria. Because the transmissions were being blocked by the Israeli aircraft jamming all signals, Soleimani never understood what was happening. He eventually left the command bunker and returned to Beirut to spend the night with his paramour, the TV hostess and announcer who was his long-term mistress.

At first, the clerics and mullahs believed that the soldiers gathering them together were Iranian, so great was their shock. They were not able to process what was happening. The Sayeret quickly bound the mullahs and clerics in plastic tie handcuffs and herded them out to the waiting trucks.

"What has happened? Who are these sons of apes?" shouted one of the clerics.

"We are infidels from Israel. We are here to end your sick, depraved rule. Now shut up." This response was administered with the light tap of a rifle to the knee, accompanied by a smile from an Israeli commando.

The assembled and bound mullahs and clerics were in a complete state of denial. "Where are the Islamic Guards? Why are these infidels even here?"

Finally, after several bound prisoners were roughly pushed toward the trucks and manhandled up inside, the remainder began to quiet down when they realized there were no rescuers coming to save them.

Once Dov was certain he had the majority of the religious leadership captured, the Israelis having loaded them into the trucks provided by, as Dov put it "our Friends in Persia," they were driven at high speed back to Vasidieh, where an awaiting C-130 Hercules had swept in low under the radar in time to meet the trucks and their precious cargo.

CHAPTER 46

Natanz Nuclear Plant perimeter, 0230 hrs

Captain Leo Moscver, who was leading the Sayeret team charged with destroying the Natanz facility, quietly assembled his men and informed them that the Israeli plan to disrupt and degrade all the Iranian communications had been successful.

Captain Moscver was an elite among elites. Out of uniform, he was unassuming and quiet, with the air of a studious academic. He lived in the suburbs of Jerusalem with his wife, Gila, and their two young boys, Daniel and Benyamin. Gila obviously understood that her husband was in some group of special forces, but she could only guess what he was doing when he was away on a business trip, as she explained to the boys and her mother.

Once he was on a mission, Leo was all business. His troops held him in the highest regard, since Leo never asked anything of them that he wouldn't do himself. Within the ranks of the Sayeret, Leo was respected as one of very best. He never shied away from an action and always planned cautiously. His greatest fear in all of the eight years he had been in Sayeret was to lose one of his men. Leo believed that meticulous planning and incessant training down to the smallest detail resulted in a successful mission without men being lost. It was this careful focus that endeared him to his men and earned him the admiration of his commanders at operation headquarters in Tel Aviv.

None of the Iranian military command centres was operable; the airfields had been removed from any action. The Israeli fighter planes had destroyed the entire telecommunication infrastructure in the country, so no cell or land line phones were working.

Before they departed from Azerbaijan on the CH-53 Yas'ur helicopter that had carried them to their insertion point, Moscver personally checked all the equipment on each of his men. He had already drilled them to run their own equipment checks but he checked each of them again anyway. It was this attention to detail that Leo believed saved lives.

The helicopter deposited them 2.5 km from the nuclear site. They had received real-time intel from the AWACS that all Iranian communications were immobilized or scrambled. The radar stations surrounding Natanz had been rendered inactive, so the team was dropped without incident. Their biggest test now ensued. They had to advance on the breathers unseen and unheard.

All team members were equipped with night-vision goggles and Tavor CTAR-21 Bullpup assault rifles. One soldier, Lev Solomon, also carried a Barrett M82A semiautomatic suppressed sniper rifle.

Moscver led his team to one of the two areas their drone had identified as containing the air-breather ducts. The terrain was rough, coarse sand and hardscrabble rock—not easy to navigate at night.

Solomon was tasked with setting up on a small promontory overlooking the rocky outcrop, which the drone had precisely identified as protecting one of the air-breathers from sight. Moscver had reviewed all the photos and live feeds from the drone he had launched an hour ago and selected this breather as the easiest to reach without discovery.

Lev Solomon had one simple set of instructions: Eliminate any vehicle or person that approached the rest of the team as they inched their way to the breather.

Accessing the air duct was no easy task for Moscver and his team. All the digital and HUMINT intelligence they pored over during their planning exercises had indicated that the Iranians built very sophisticated defences around all their nuclear facilities, but none more so than Natanz. This was the facility they had attempted to conceal from the IAEA when they were constructing it. It was also believed to be where Iran transferred major technology from the Fordow plant after Fordow was discovered by the British Secret Service SIS and CIA intelligence agencies.

There was some solid anecdotal evidence that the relationship with North Korea had developed after the attack on the Syrian nuclear plant. Western intelligence services, mostly SIS and the CIA, with assistance and input from the Saudis and Jordanians, were very much convinced that there was a strong contingent of North Korean scientists and technicians, as well as some Russians, working alongside the Iranians in the centrifuge facility and the laboratories and weapons assembly area.

Imagery obtained by American and Israeli spy satellites had identified large covered trucks leaving the plant. Those trucks had been tracked to the naval side of Bandar Abbas port, where their contents were transferred to cargo vessels that changed flags and modified their superstructure. Those vessels also turned off their identification transponders so as to avoid detection as they sailed to North Korea. While no definite proof was established, the consensus was that the cargo consisted of missiles and the electronic gear required to fire them. Kim Jong-un had been boastful of his ICBM missile technology. The Western intelligence services and others did not believe he had the know-how or funds required to develop such sophisticated and highly technical equipment.

In the reverse, traffic captured by the intelligence services was a firm suspicion that Iranian cargo planes were bringing North Korean nuclear bomb technology back to Iran. There had been sightings of large cargo planes landing at Sari Dasht-e Naz International Airport near the Caspian Sea at night. The planes were quickly unloaded and would take off and fly to Isfahan International Airport or Tehran Imam Khomeini International Airport. No hard evidence could be gathered, but the dots seemed to connect.

Natanz was protected from air assault by a ring of surface-to-air missile sites, some of which were now the deadly Russian SA-300 and SA-400 systems. Because of its design and construction, even if bombers or cruise missiles could defeat the air defences, they would do little or no damage to the facility. Intelligence reviews by both Israel and the United States had determined that even the massive bunker-busting bombs the United States had made available would not be able to damage the installations.

The Natanz nuclear plant was constructed ninety feet underground and consisted of approximately one million square feet of underground buildings. Two large 250,000-square-foot halls housed the centrifuges and the enrichment activities. Another 500,000 square feet consisted of underground support buildings for the scientists and guards. Around the perimeter was a six-meter-high concrete wall, eight feet thick, which was in turn protected by an outer wall five feet thick. The design of the facility was considered to make it impregnable to attack from air or land. Any heavy assault vehicles, such as tanks or other armoured vehicles, would have to break through the outer wall, only to be hung up against the very thick inner wall. This would leave them vulnerable to deadly anti-tank fire.

Dov and the analysts at Rosh Pina had determined in evaluating the intelligence photos that the breathers were for reasons of security located outside the two perimeter walls. During their preparation at Rosh Pina, this had been confirmed by an IAF pilot who studied all the photo intelligence from the Keyhole US satellites and the Israeli Army satellite. One of their HUMINT agents had provided information that said there were sensors and cleverly concealed trip wires, plus antipersonnel mines haphazardly located around any direct path to the breather duct.

As a standard, the Iranian military used antipersonnel mines originally developed by the Germans in the 1930s. This mine had a small cylindrical housing with a telescoping trigger about the size of a soda can, which when activated by the pressure of a soldier's foot would catapult up to about waist level before detonating and unleashing a ten-foot cone of deadly ball bearings and shrapnel. Any victim within range of the mine's explosive force was literally eviscerated and quite often cut in half. During WWII it was one of the most feared weapons deployed by the Nazis against Allied troops, who referred to it as "Bouncing Betty."

Being aware of all this, Moscver had his men keep a distance of thirty feet from each other. Once they were within a thousand yards of the breather location, he had the whole team slowly lie flat on their stomachs and hold position for five minutes. This was to test if any ground-based sensors had picked up their presence. He figured that if they did set off a sensor alarm, only a small patrol would come out to check. If a patrol showed up, Lev Solomon and his MA-82 would bid them goodbye.

After five minutes, Leo had the first man crawl very slowly and gingerly forward, using the length of his body to check for the inverted tripod of a mine trigger. After they had gone about five hundred yards without detecting any mines, the lead commando, Benjamin Taber, a twenty-six-year-old father of two, suddenly froze and whispered into his communication device for everyone to also freeze in position. As he was inching forward, searching the ground in front of him and to each side with his AID goggles, he had identified the trigger of a mine less than four inches from his chin. Thankfully, the Sayeret had trained for this eventuality. Taber carefully removed his combat knife from the scabbard strapped on his left thigh and carefully began excavating around the mine. He started digging in a circle about a yard from the trigger and worked his way in until the knife made contact with the body of the mine. His whole nervous system was on high alert. Even though the night air was cold, his body was drenched in sweat. The fear of being eviscerated by the deadly Bouncing Betty and the stress of knowing that his failure now would end their whole operation weighed heavily on the young soldier.

After he had fully excavated around it, a process that took about twenty minutes, Taber slowly lifted the mine out of the sand it was buried in. Once he had it in his hands, another team member, Zachary Nussfeld, slowly slid up to him from behind and handed him a nine-inch threaded rod and nut. Corporal Taber then inserted the small rod into a hole on the telescoping trigger and carefully secured it with the nut. Thus secured, the trigger and the mine were inoperable.

Taber had served three years in the IDF infantry and then had been accepted into the Sayeryet five years ago. His grandparents and those of his wife, Mira, were survivors from Poland and Hungary, respectively. Mira's grandparents had escaped the SS and the Arrow Cross in Budapest by obtaining papers stating they were Swiss citizens from the Swiss Consul Carl Lutz. Lutz had risked his life to save as many Jews as he could from Adolph Eichmann's death trains and camps. At the war's end, they recognized that staying in Budapest under the communists and Soviet rule was not safe, so they managed to find their way to Austria and eventually Italy.

Benjamin Taber's father, Herschel, had been born at Kibbutz Yagur, where his grandparents first settled in 1953 after fleeing Hungary and the DP Camps. Later they moved to Tel Aviv, where Herschel and his father grew a small fledgling electronics store into a burgeoning empire. Benjamin wasn't interested in commerce; he was a dedicated soldier in the IDF. His grandparents and Ari Lazarus's grandparents were close friends who had met when they were all staying on Yagur in Israel's early days.

It was while he was completing his basic tour in the infantry that Benjamin had met and married Mira.

As he was searching for mines, his only other thoughts were of his beautiful young wife and children. Each time he went out on a mission, especially one as dangerous as this, he always knew that fate could cause something to go wrong, yet he had complete faith in Leo Moscver, his commander, and knew in his heart of hearts that as long as he followed Leo's orders they would all be safe.

Once the first mine was secure, Corporal Taber settled his nerves and continued his slow and careful search. Even though he and Zachary Nussfeld had trained for this eventuality, once Corporal Taber knew there was no allowance for any error, he focused on the task at hand like he had never focused before. He was sweating profusely even though the nighttime temperature was only in the midthirties Fahrenheit. The slightest misjudgment or wrong move would wreak disaster on the whole mission.

Bouncing Betty mines were a deadly, fearsome weapon. Once they were uncovered and identified, Moscver was wary of what other defences the Iranians had set to protect the bomb being developed at Natanz. He more than anyone on his team understood the enormity of their task. He did not underestimate the Iranians. The IRGC in particular had unlimited resources and were technologically advanced. He knew their attention to the security of Natanz would be first class and difficult to circumvent.

Zachary Nussfeld, whose grandfather fought the Nazis when he was in the Polish resistance, thought it somewhat ironic that the Iranians were employing the same nasty weapons as the Nazis. Both regimes had sworn policy statements to wipe the Jews off the earth.

After two hours of slow, stressful, and tedious crawling and excavating, the team reached the little escarpment where the breather was located. They had uncovered ten of the deadly mines, which had been set in concentric circles around the access to the breather. Once those were located and deactivated, they all relaxed slightly from the tension. Once Moscver and his six troopers arrived at the breather they had selected, they each began to implement the tasks that they had trained for with Dov's supervision in Rosh Pinah. Three of the Sayeret commandos carried packs holding five gallons of liquid PLX (nitromethane) in thick plastic containers. Two others each carried another five-gallon container of EDA (ethylene diamine). Once they were close on top of the breather, Zachary Nussfeld carefully examined the entrance, searching for tripwires and booby traps. After a painstakingly slow examination revealed no wires or surprise packages, they removed the grates and camouflage for open access to the duct. They assumed that the Iranians believed the mines were enough to surprise and eliminate any intruder.

Moscver and another trooper, Amos Geitner, carefully removed the containers and slowly proceeded to mix the two liquids together. Separated, the liquids were pretty much nonvolatile, but when mixed together, they became extremely potent, with an explosive value one-and-a-half times that of an equivalent amount of TNT.

Once the two liquids were thoroughly mixed, a small amount of gel was added to provide a more viscous consistency to the mixture. The objective was for the team to pour the contents down the breather pipe so that it slowly slid down without alerting anyone below. They correctly had figured out the duct was exhausting and exchanging air via a large air circulation plant located somewhere below the duct.

The Israelis correctly assumed that the equipment would be in a machine room not closely monitored by any occupants, especially at night. The scientists back in Israel had calculated that the mixture would take about five minutes to slide down the ninety feet into the large underground cavern. Once inserted underground, the explosive mixture would have the effect of a half kiloton of TNT when detonated. The detonation of that much explosives in the enclosed subterranean chamber would be catastrophic to the structural integrity of the other underground chambers.

The armourers had designed a special spherical detonator housed in rubber to avoid making any noise when it landed in the machinery cavern. This was set to detonate a half hour after being inserted. If their calculations were correct, the force of the explosions would collapse a large portion of the underground structures, thus totally destroying the facility and its infrastructure.

As they were gently pouring the mixture down the duct, Lev Solomon whispered into their headsets that he saw a small jeep driving up the escarpment toward the breather duct.

"Overwatch to Leader, three tangos in a jeep coming your way. Clear to remove?"

"Leader to Overwatch, Affirmative," replied Leo.

The suppressed M82 coughed four times in quick succession. The first .50 calibre round disabled the engine of the approaching jeep and, as the Iranian guards climbed out to examine their problem, Solomon neatly eliminated each one with a carefully aimed body-mass shot. The M82 .50 calibre rounds at a range of 500 yards totally destroyed the internal organs of the soldiers. In one case, the .50 calibre bullet cut the man in half; such was the destructive power of the shell. The speed and suddenness of the shooting had not allowed the Iranians to respond.

"Overwatch to Leader, threat removed. No communication after they dismounted from their vehicle."

Moscver and his team quickly withdrew along the path they had cleared earlier and headed for the extraction location two kilometres northeast of the plant. The plan was for the team to make their way to the exfil point without discovery. Once there they would signal to the AWAC aircraft and the CH-53 Yasur 2025 which had carried them in from Azerbaijan. The helicopter's range was limited to about 800 miles; however, the Yasur carried two external fuel tanks that extended its range to 1200 miles. The tanks were protected from damage from small arms fire thanks to a uniquely Israeli technical solution. During the Second World War, the Royal Air Force had developed a self-sealing technology for fuel tanks on their Spitfire and Hurricane fighters. An Israeli company had refined and modernized the technology and it was now utilized on many of their air assets.

This was an extremely risky play, because the external tanks added weight and reduced the aerodynamic efficiency, significantly slowing the airspeed down from 150 mph to 125 mph, but it was necessary for the helicopters to return to Azerbaijan without risk of fuel shortage in the event of any required evasive action. The round trip was just over 1,500 kilometres. Their biggest concern was the small IRGC security patrols circling the area. Typically, such patrols would be armed with at least one RPG launcher and a truck-mounted .50 calibre machine gun. Similar equipment was used by ISIS fighters in Iraq and the Taliban in Afghanistan, many times to great effect. Both weapons had the range and speed to take down a low-flying helicopter with deadly efficiency.

The helicopter would come in hot and the rear ramp would be lowering as it touched down. The team would race up the ramp and the Yasur would immediately go vertical, then race forward at high speed out of the area. Two IAF gunners would be manning chain Gatling guns on each side of the aircraft so that, if required, they could lay down withering fire on any enemy threats.

When the Sayeret team reached their extraction point, they soon heard the familiar whine of the CH-53 Yasur's turbine engines. Since they had not called off the mission, the AWAC crew following their progress via radio signals dispatched the Yasur to coincide with their arrival at the extraction location. After dropping the team off to begin their mission on Natanz, the helicopter flew to a deserted area about forty kilometres from the insertion point. There it waited until notified that the team was conducting an exfil. It immediately took off and raced for the exfil location.

Shortly after leaving the area, the crew and Sayeret team witnessed a massive explosion that rocked the Sikorsky CH-53 Yasur even though it was some two kilometres from the plant. It was obvious that the Israeli deep penetration team had achieved their objective.

Before the explosion, unbeknownst to the Israelis, their carefully planned mission was almost foiled. A maintenance worker had entered the machinery room where the detonator and explosives had been inserted. Fortunately, he missed seeing the detonator, but had observed the liquid explosives. Believing something was amiss, he ran out of the room in search of his supervisor. When he reached the maintenance office, the supervisor was in a discussion with the head of security for the facility, Rez Pahlev. Once they heard the concerns of the anxious worker, they instinctively realized a disaster was about to occur.

Pahlev ran from the office to call his team on a walkie-talkie and urge them to get to the machinery room as fast as possible. He then activated an alarm to alert the inhabitants of the facility that they were about to be attacked. Most of the civilian employees and scientists were frozen in shock.

One of the scientists responsible for the centrifuge facility was a huge Russian—Gregor Tartarov. Tartarov urged all his teams to make for the elevators and escape to the surface. Within a half-minute of the alarm sounding, there was total pandemonium. Men and women rushed in panic mode for the elevators. Tartarov was bullying his way to the elevator complex, shouting at people to get out of his way. Just as he and several other Russians and North

Korean workers made it into an elevator, the undiscovered detonator triggered a massive explosion. Concussion waves reverberated throughout the underground complex, destroying people, machinery, and infrastructure. Then a massive fireball raced through the halls, incinerating everything in its path. Close to five hundred workers had been below ground at Natanz. There were no survivors.

Moscver high-fived Alon Nuss and Geitner, exclaiming, "Scratch one nuclear plant."

As they continued on to the air base in Azerbaijan, they received news via the AWAC that the other teams had achieved similar success at Fordow and Arak.

CHAPTER 47

By 0800 hours, the C-130 carrying Dov and the clerics had departed Vasidieh and was landing in Rosh Pinah. At this time, there was still no noise coming from Iran about the abductions. There had been early news reports of a massive explosion at Natanz, but no details were being provided.

During the flight, the Ayatollah Khamenei sat in restraints, glaring at his Israeli captors. Dov engaged him in Farsi, "Khameini, we Jews aren't going anywhere. We aren't going to let anyone wipe us out. You will be treated with the humanity and respect we show to our prisoners. But you're no longer in control of Iran."

Khamenei sat there in shock. How dare this son of Little Satan address me this way. I am the Supreme Leader!

Finally, he responded by spitting at Dov. He missed. Dov, as much as he wanted to slap the Ayatollah, controlled his emotions and just smiled at him.

"If that is all you have, Ali my friend, then it is a great day for Persia. Your people are probably celebrating already."

"The invincible IRGC will follow you to the ends of the earth and we will have a special crane chosen for you. How dare you insult the glorious revolutionary regime of Iran," snarled the humiliated Ayatollah.

Dov offered a riposte, "Once we land, you will be transported to an Israeli detention jail reserved just for terrorists. There you will be interrogated and then charged with encouraging and funding worldwide terrorism, crimes against Israel and Israelis, and human rights violations. You will also be charged for participating in the Syrian genocide and then transported to the International Court at The Hague, where you will stand trial and inevitably be sentenced."

Several of the other leadership became restive and concerned when suddenly they saw their leader as a frightened old man.

One mullah, Nasir Adriahi, voiced his thoughts aloud. "I have always feared this day. We never listened to the young people. We believed we could prosecute them and then the internet gave them access to the world. We tried to inoculate them against corrupt Western life. I always believed we would lose the battle for their minds. They abandoned us in 2009 after the murder of Neda Agha-Soltan in the streets during the Green protests."

Another mullah, Nasir Adjiminedad, chastised Adriahi. "Silence!! You dare to speak with this despicable infidel scum? Our Islamic Revolution is leading the worshippers of Allah to glorious victory. Our Islamic Guards will destroy the crusaders. We will follow them to their homeland and destroy them there! Our valiant Soleimani has his Hezbollah in place. The wrath of Allah, blessed be he, will destroy the sons of the two Satans."

One of Deborah Grunwalder's female Sayeret commandos slapped him hard across the face. The very idea that he had been struck by a woman, an Israeli at that, so shocked him and the others that there was total silence from the prisoners. None of them could believe the predicament they were in.

Further back in the fuselage sat President Rouhani and Foreign Minister Muhammad Javad Zarif. Both had been considered in the West and the liberal media as moderates, men of stature within Iran who could be reasonable. Nothing was further from the truth. Rouhani was as deceitful and corrupt as the other leaders and Zarif was a duplicitous double-talker with a serpent's tongue. Rouhani was in great distress on two counts. First, his boss, the Ayatollah Khamenei was already blaming him for this calamity. It was both Rouhani's and Zarif's initiative that had led to the so-called Nuclear Agreement, an agreement Khamenei had totally opposed. He had been supported in his opposition by General Soleimani, the leadership of the Republican Guards, and the Quds Force. Secondly, Rouhani instinctively knew that the thin veneer of likeability he had earned in the West was about to be stripped away once he stood trial and the world found out about his fiendish hatred for Israel and the United States.

Dov looked at them with total disdain and ceased any more discussion. Under their rule, Iran engaged in hanging gays and dissenters, jailing journalists and opposition speakers, all in the name of protecting the Revolution.

He turned, speaking in Hebrew to Captain Deborah Grunwalder, the leader of the female commando team on his mission. "Look at these sorry sacks of shit now. Already plotting how they can throw each other to the wolves. If we didn't have orders to treat them like delicate china, I would pitch them out for the sharks in the Red Sea. Once we get them on the stand in the tribunals, watch how they will abandon each other to save their own sorry skins. These sons of bitches never ever had any intention of abiding by the so-called agreement."

Deborah placed her hand on Dov's arm and said softly, "Our personal feelings are not equal to the relief in the world capitals once these monsters are brought to justice. Dov, think about it, we are part of history. We are cleansing the Stygian stable of terrorists. Is there any word on Ari's mission?"

Dov smiled and relayed the news he had heard over the secure comms in the cockpit.

CHAPTER 48

Tehran

The Tehran teams led by Ari and Sarah Holtzman had assaulted the headquarters of the IRGC and the Quds Force. Just as they had planned and trained for it to unfold, they had destroyed Iranian communication capabilities. As the ground attacks were in full swing, the fighter jets that had appeared to be targeting Natanz changed course and flew in low over Tehran, bombing the other IRGC facilities, several of which ringed the city.

The eighteen enhanced two-seater F-16I fighter-bombers had probably the riskiest mission of all. They flew into Iran from Azerbaijan. The air group leader was Colonel (Alam) Uri Lieberman and his second in command was Major (Rasan) Jonatan Rogowski. Seated behind Col. Lieberman was his weapons operator, Captain Leon Megerov, and behind Major Rogowski, Lieutenant Ben Mischoff. Ostensibly they would be seen by the Iranian defense forces as targeting the Natanz or other nuclear facilities. Once Ari and Dov were able to knock out the communications, Lieberman and eight pilots would change course and head for Tehran while the remaining nine commanded by Major Rogowski would target the Iranian air bases at Bushehr, Hamadan, Tabriz, and Maherberad and destroy the Iranian air assets on the ground.

Colonel Lieberman knew his team's survival depended on their ability to fly below the Iranian radar through the mountainous border undetected, and also it was critical that their fellow combatants in Bandas Abbas and Tehran were able to completely destroy all Iranian military communications. This would allow Lieberman to enter Iranian airspace around Tehran and destroy the IRGC facilities without being targeted by the Russian-supplied S-300 and S-400 surface-to-air missiles, the greatest threat to the Israeli aircraft. All eighteen air crews knew there was a fifty-fifty chance that they would be blasted out of the sky by the deadly accurate missiles.

The prime targets in Tehran were the headquarters of the IRGC and the Basij militia. Devoid of communications and leadership, militia forces would be neutralized and no longer a threat to the regime's opposition groups. With the IRGC unable to communicate and still in shock, the combat nerve centres of Iran would be shut down and inoperable.

The hope was that the Iranian military and security surrounding the nuclear plants would see these assaults on their leadership as the main event. In fact, they provided a diversion to allow the seven Sayeret Deep Penetration Teams time to carry out their missions unimpeded.

The other six teams had similar targets at the other nuclear plants. The strict rules of engagement given to the IDF Command and Macha by the prime minister were for there to be few or no civilian casualties.

CHAPTER 49

Azerbaijan Air Base

The eighteen F-16I fighter planes had arrived in Azerbaijan and were now fully fuelled and armed, with each plane carrying different weaponry. Some were armed with air-to-surface missiles and five thousand rounds of .50 calibre bullets for the Gatling machine guns. Others had four wing-mounted 500-pound laser-guided bombs and one thousand rounds of 100 mm cannon shells for the two nose-mounted cannons. The remainder were loaded with four air to ground missiles and four thousand rounds of 100 mm cannon shells for the nose guns.

The crews were on standby, awaiting the *"Zanek! Zanek!"* (scramble scramble) call from headquarters in Israel. Even though all crew members were seasoned pilots and experienced operators, their tension in the ready room was palpable. More than any fear, there was the nerve-wracking and seemingly infinite waiting for the "go" signal.

Some were quietly discussing key points of their flights into Iran among themselves. They were reviewing all the critical data on speed and altitude, possible points where they could be threatened by anti-aircraft missiles, and of course, their designated targets. Others were resting on the floor or on one of several couches around the room. Some stepped out onto the hardstand to conduct checks of their aircraft with the ground crews even though they had already checked at least twice in the past three hours.

At 0330hrs, the call came through and all eighteen pilots and their weapons operators headed for their planes. The ground crews who had accompanied them from Israel in three C-130 Hercules aircraft now ensured all their gear was secured, their helmets and oxygen fully operational, and their secure comms were working.

The Russian-designed missile systems were state-of-the-art, almost impossible to evade once they locked on to their targets. It was no wonder that as the pilots closed their canopies, they received symbolic salutes and sorrowful smiles from their ground crews. This was the first time since the Yom Kippur War of 1973 that IAF crews would fly against extremely tough odds and opponents. Finally, with the massive engines spooling up, the pilots made one final systems check and began their taxi in line to the main runway.

In groups of three, with their engines roaring, the fighter aircraft thundered down the runway and hurled themselves into the sky.

At 0345hrs, Colonel Lieberman, call sign Khihl (blue) and Major Rogowski, call sign Hashmal (amber) crossed from the Azerbaijan base into Iranian airspace.

"Hashmal, we are radio silence here on in," Lieberman instructed his second in command.

Lieberman and Rogowski, along with thirty-four other pilots and navigators, were hooked into the special communications network established by the AWAC C-130 flying over the Red Sea. They were able to monitor the actions and movements of the naval and ground forces in Iran. They would gauge their chances of mission success by the success or failure of the ground actions.

Colonel Lieberman's two other wings tucked in behind his leading wing as did the two behind Major Rogowski. Each pilot belonged to the elite group of Israeli fighter pilots, who many in other air forces considered some of the finest in the world. The crews led by Lieberman and Rogowski were the best of the best; not one of them would shy away from their duty.

Colonel Lieberman was a veteran fighter pilot who had engaged in many missions during an illustrious career. He had led several raids on Iranian and Hezbollah targets in Lebanon and Syria. He thrived on the adrenaline rush of flying a supersonic fighter at Mach 2 speeds. The best part of the F-16I for Major Rogowski was the fact that it was the most superior fighter in the world, based on successful missions destroying both air and ground targets. The US manufacturers, Lockheed and General Dynamics, had developed and built a formidable aircraft; but once the IAF took delivery, they enhanced its weapons and electronics, making the F-16I one of the finest weapons in the Israeli arsenal. Pilots such as Colonel Lieberman and Major Rogowski were almost as one with their aircraft. They felt that they wore the aircraft and it responded to their slightest hint of a touch on the controls. Once the S-300 and S-400 batteries were neutralized, the Iranians would have no defences against the F-16I in the hands of these elite pilots.

CHAPTER 50

Heavy water plant, Arak, Iran, 0300 hrs

Two Sayeret teams consisting of fifty troopers were flown in by two CH-53 Yasur helicopters and landed two miles from the plant. Their incursion was undetected by Iranian radar and surveillance security systems, which had been either disabled or blinded by the IAF electronic jamming efforts.

The teams were led by a seasoned veteran of Sayeret, Captain Yohan Bar-Issan. Along with his team of 24 troopers, Captain Bar-Issan was to advance along the main road leading to the reactor plant. The other team, led by Lieutenant Yoni Berkovitz, manoeuvred around to the far side of the facility. Their targets were the industrial plant and plutonium storage.

Yohan and his team had accomplished about 75% of their journey when they observed a flurry of activity around the main gate. Since they had been on the road, there had been no traffic going in or out of the plant. Now, after leaving the road and taking cover in a low ditch, they saw several trucks and vehicles assembling just inside the main gate.

Yohan tasked one of his troopers, Ami Balevi, with getting closer to observe and report what they were doing. After ten tense minutes, Balevi returned and informed his captain that the Iranians were loading the trucks with some type of material and preparing to drive off. He also noted a sense of panic and urgency around what was happening. Bar-Issan speculated that word had reached them somehow of suspected attacks; they were removing some critical components from the plant—probably plutonium for the other nuclear facilities.

The original mission plan had called for the commandos to basically barge straight in through the front door and destroy as much of the plant infrastructure as possible. Their HUMINT intelligence had given them enough data to know the plant was lightly guarded by a security force of sixty to eighty IRGC and some forty regular soldiers. The Sayeret commandos were also aware that the IRGC divided the watches into three, so at most there might be twenty to twenty-five guards on patrol. The rest would be sleeping or off duty. They knew that the soldiers were basically labour and not frontline troops.

Bar-Issan and Berkovitz's commandos were all armed with suppressed IWI Tavor x95 Bullpup assault rifles and Glock 19 handguns. They also carried an assortment of sophisticated explosives, satchel charges, and a large stock of C4 as well as six Claymore mines. Two troopers on each team were equipped with light machine guns.

Bar-Issan deployed two troopers, Mordechai Levin and Motti Glasbon, who were armed with the machine guns, to the side of the road and set up two Claymore mines facing the direction the trucks would be coming from. Then, taking his remaining troop, Yohan moved on the main gate, surprisingly unchallenged. As they arrived, the convoy of five trucks left the reactor plant. Within minutes, the front two trucks set off the Claymores and the resulting explosions damaged them severely. As the soldiers dismounted, the two machine gunners opened fire, catching most of them before they could begin to react. There were only a handful of disoriented survivors.

Levi and Glasbon then retreated into the brush to provide overwatch for the others when they exited the plant.

Captain Bar-Issan and his men rushed the gate and headed directly for the main reactor and the heavy water facility. They met some sporadic resistance from the Islamic Revolutionary Guard Corps (IRGC), but they were quickly subdued. Many of the awakened guards had rushed down the road to aid the survivors of the attacks on the trucks.

Once Bar-Issan and his troops gained access to the main component of the plant, they planted Semtex and C4 charges on the equipment consoles in the control room. As it was early morning, there was only a handful of technicians in the control centre, civilians that the Israelis quickly herded out of harm's way, into an office area and into restraints.

When they reached the massive domed reactor and heavy water processing facility, they once again placed explosive charges in such a way that the components would be destroyed for the foreseeable future.

Yohan wanted to be in and out of the plant within a thirty-minute window. As they were setting the charges around the dome and its relevant infrastructure, they came under fire from some of the returning IRGC. The Guards had realized that the destruction of the trucks was part of a larger attack on the facility and hastened back to protect it. They were led by a seasoned IRGC commander, Major Ali Sul-Manihavi, who had seen action in Iraq fighting ISIS and also served with Hezbollah aiding the Syrian Assad forces. He had quickly ascertained what was happening as the control centre blew up and rushed thirty of his men toward the dome and the reactor.

Bar-Issan was able to move just in time as a hail of fully automatic fire pinned the Israelis down as they began their exfiltration. Two of his troops sustained non-life-threatening wounds. Trooper Nathan Assam was hit in the arm, and Trooper Hal Gutman received a flesh wound in his thigh. Both received preliminary field medical attention and could stay in the fight.

Retreating back inside the administrative centre of the reactor, Bar-Issan deployed two more Claymores in the walkway leading to the main entrance. He hoped to draw the rest of the IRGC toward his squad. After a quick consultation with his team, he scattered them inside the building and had them fire at random. His plan was to give the IRGC the impression that he and his men had suffered severe losses, prompting them to rush the entrance.

"Leader Bar to troop, hold your fire until I give the order. We will let them think we are badly disorganized, with many dead and wounded. Let them come to us."

Major Sul-Manihavi gathered his thirty men and had them prepare to rush the building. "These monkeys and pigs are almost out of the fight. On my command, rush the entrance hall in groups of five. You in the first five will move quickly on the steps to the doors."

Pointing to another group, he continued, "You will then leapfrog the first five through the doors while they provide covering fire."

Turning to the remaining nineteen men, he tasked them with covering the first two teams. "On my mark, fire at anything that moves," Sul-Manihavi ordered.

"Three, two, one, *go!*"

Ten Iranians rushed up the path to the main entrance in two groups, and as they approached the final five yards, Bar-Issan triggered the first Claymore. All ten IRG soldiers were killed instantly. Sul-Manihavi was so enraged that he and his men had fallen for such a simple tactic that he didn't consider that there would be another mine set up. Jumping to his feet, he urged his remaining men forward, but it was too late. He saw the other Claymore only milliseconds before it detonated, eviscerating him and two of his guardsmen.

Bar-Issan rounded up his men and ascertained that the two wounded troopers could still make it back out of the facility. They jogged back down the road toward the destroyed Iranian trucks and linked up with their comrades.

While Captain Bar-Issan was engaged at the reactor plant, Lt. Berkovitz led his team into the industrial plant. Once inside, they set charges and explosives on the strategic components of the plant: control rooms, the exhaust stacks and piping systems that delivered the heavy water, the isotope storage facilities, and the administrative offices. They were virtually unopposed as Ali Sul-Manihavi had not realized that both facilities were under simultaneous attack; he had concentrated his IRGC soldiers at the reactor plant.

It was only after one of his senior NCOs realized that there was an equally large force of attackers at the industrial plant that he quickly assembled a group of twenty fighters to repel the Israelis. Lt. Berkovitz had gamed this eventuality at Rosh Pina and was well prepared. The huge structures of the industrial plant provided secure cover for the Sayeret team. They took up concealed positions as the IRGC, led by Sergeant Mustafa Adminejad, rushed to defend the facility. The Israeli commandos picked his team off to the last man, but not before four Sayeret were wounded. Ami Shiller and Motti Vogel suffered serious wounds from small arms fire and exploding grenades; they had to be carried out, and two others received minor shrapnel wounds from grenades thrown by the Iranians.

Once their exfiltration was secured, the teams hustled back to their insertion point carrying the wounded men and sent a signal to the AWACS that they were heading for the pickup point.

Just as they left the road and began to cross the fields, the first of several heavy explosions went off, lighting up the sky all around the heavy water plant. They had no doubt they had been successful in destroying it beyond repair. And yet great care had been taken to avoid any damage to the reactor cores. The teams had strict orders not to release harmful radiation into the atmosphere. Their objective had been to take out only infrastructure and operations.

Within fifteen minutes of the teams' exiting the plant, the CH-53s swooped in and they rapidly boarded the helicopters. During this time, the medics applied emergency aid to the two seriously wounded. They hooked them to plasma bottles and applied more tourniquets to the leg of Trooper Schiller. There was concern that he would lose the leg, which was essentially shredded just above the knee. Motti Vogel had been hit in his upper body and suffered two devastating wounds—one to his right shoulder and another to the side of his head. He was unconscious and losing a great amount of blood. The medics and doctor on board were doing their best to stabilize him. Once they could get him to Azerbaijan, he would be placed on a C-130 transport that had been converted to an airborne hospital and flown to Israel along with the other wounded from the various operations.

As they began the flight back to Azerbaijan, Captain Bar-Issan communicated to the AWAC that both teams had safely returned with six injuries that were being treated by the medics in-flight, informing the hospital plane that there were two serious casualties on the way.

Fifteen minutes into the flight, the copilot called Bar-Issan forward to the cockpit and handed him a headset. "Captain, this is Minister Melnik. I've been monitoring your activity and want to congratulate you on behalf of a grateful country. Our intelligence has confirmed that the Arak heavy water plant is totally out of commission for at least two to three years. Well done, a superb action. Time to bring your boys home."

Yohan was surprised to be speaking directly to the Defense Minister. He handed the headset back to a grinning copilot, who had been listening to the conversation. "I guess you are very important, that you speak directly to Minister Melnik. Since you are such a big-time hot shot I wouldn't be surprised if the prime minister will be inviting you to his house for tea!" teased the pilot.

Yohan gave him a digital salute with his middle finger, then went aft into the main cabin to join his men and deliver the minister's congratulations. Communication between the pilots of the two Yasur helicopters confirmed that Lt. Berkovitz had received a similar call from the Defense Minister.

CHAPTER 51

Near Yongbyon Nuclear Site, North Korea, four days before the Iran attacks

As these scenarios in Iran were unfolding, the Mossad teams in North Korea were wreaking havoc on Kim Jong-un's nuclear enterprise. Their targets were the research centre at Yeongjeo-ri, the Yongdeok-dong high-explosive site, and the Yongbyon Nuclear Scientific Research Centre, as well as at the Musudan-ri missile launch site on the East Coast.

The Mossad operators, led by a brilliant young Vietnamese Israeli commander, Tron Duc Phonam, and the South Korean Seal teams landed at three separate locations on the North Korean coast, then spread out across the northern districts of the country. At the Yongbyon Scientific Centre, approximately one hundred miles north of the capital, Pyongyang, Tron Duc's agents had spent a week posing as visiting Chinese scientists. This deception had been planned and gamed by the Mossad for a number of years. The Israeli intelligence organization had been monitoring the activities of the Chinese and their involvement with the North Korean nuclear program. What they had learned was that the Chinese government was understandably concerned about the rise of an unstable nuclear nation on their border.

The Beijing government had determined to acquire as much knowledge as possible about the joint North Korean and Iranian program. Surprisingly, although outward diplomatic relations between the United States and China were cool and somewhat reserved due to the political posturing of both sides concerning

Chinese activities in the South China Sea, there were good communications between some of the Chinese military and their counterparts in the Pentagon. The Chinese were equally concerned about the reckless and unpredictable North Korean government. As a result, they wanted to keep a watchful eye on Kim Jong-un and his bizarre, dangerous nuclear activities. Whenever they identified suspicious activities taking place in North Korea, especially with regard to their nuclear weapons program, the Chinese brass quietly shared the information—not necessarily all of it—with their contacts in the Pentagon. The Pentagon routinely shared the intel with their counterparts in Australia, Japan, the UK, Canada, and Israel.

Regardless of political posturing, the professional military on both sides of the Pacific were not anxious for Kim Jong-un and his murderous regime to have an arsenal of nuclear weapons. It was this rationale that caused the Chinese, acting as the only real friend and ally of North Korea, to send scientific teams to foster friendship and share knowledge. They capitalized on the fact that the North Koreans would never jeopardize their relations with Beijing by denying them access to the nuclear research and fabrication sites.

Beijing sent a delegation of five top nuclear missile engineers and scientists to North Korea to learn as much as they could about a planned test of a new intercontinental missile believed to have a range in excess of four thousand miles. There were also rumours that Kim was going to test a nuclear warhead on top of this missile.

When the group departed Beijing for Pyongyang, they were trailed by five Mossad Vietnamese Israelis. The NIS had been monitoring telecommunications between China and North Korea and alerted the Mossad that the Chinese delegation was soon departing to Pyongyang. The Mossad team, which had been in Beijing for several days as part of an agricultural team sharing the latest tech advances in rice cultivation with the Chinese agricultural ministry, travelled to Beijing Capital International Airport and followed the delegation to North Korea on a later flight. After the Chinese scientists landed at Pyongyang, they were greeted by officials from the army and the scientific community. The Mossad team arrived an hour later, posing as Chinese, cleared through immigration and border security. They were warmly welcomed by their North Korean hosts, who believed they were junior members of the delegation.

The Mossad operators were taken to a reception and dinner at a luxurious hotel in the city of Pyongyang. The next morning, the Chinese group transferred to a convoy for the two-hour drive to Yongbyon. The convoy the Chinese were travelling in consisted of two Mercedes GL 350 diesel SUVs that the Chinese were riding in, and their escort of fourteen North Korean soldiers who were travelling in front and behind in two soft-sided, canvas-covered trucks. Each truck had a driver and officer up front and five soldiers in the back.

Six miles from the research facility, there was a stretch of highway where the mountainous terrain caused the road to twist and turn as it descended down to Yongbyon. Earlier that day, the Vietnamese Israelis had convinced their North Korean escorts that they needed to go on ahead of their bosses. The route had previously been scouted by the South Koreans and Tron Duc knew that at one point the vehicles would have to slow down to less than fifteen kilometres per hour. They had driven up earlier in the morning and, after overpowering their escorts, they hid one of their vehicles in a shallow ravine and waited in ambush for the convoy to arrive. Tron Duc positioned the other vehicle across the road to give the appearance of an accident or a blown tire.

As the convoy approached and slowed down, two Israeli agents disabled the front truck by shooting out a tire and incapacitating the North Korean driver and officer in the cab with gas grenades and then, tossing gas grenades into the back of the truck, they neutralized the other soldiers.

Two more Israelis repeated the exercise on the rear truck. The drivers of the SUVs were not military, merely North Korean Security minders who surrendered peacefully to Tron's men without any opposition and before they could send any radio or phone communication. The highway to Yongbyon was mostly empty with the exception of occasional farm carts or slow-moving local vehicles. One of the Mossad operators drove their other truck down to the ravine and then quickly hustled the North Koreans into the hidden trucks, where they were bound, gagged, and forced to lie down in the bed of the trucks.

The paradox of the responses of the soldiers versus the two officers was interesting, to say the least. The two officers, both captains in their thirties, were raging with hate. Initially immobilized by the gas grenades, they had quickly recovered and struggled as they were being manhandled down to the hidden trucks. They were incensed, snarling threats and intimidation not only at their captors, but at their own soldiers. Their soldiers were for the most part docile and complied with all the orders given by the commandos. The two officers knew that, ultimately, they would be held responsible for the attack and charged with neglect of duty, an offence that could carry a death sentence. If the soldiers in their charge were interrogated by the officers' senior commanders and described their capture, their chances of survival were slim at best.

The Israelis had no intention of causing an international incident between Israel and China and thus had arranged to hold the legitimate scientists in a safe, comfortable location until the operation was over. Through their shared intelligence contacts with the South Koreans, Tron had arranged a safe house on a vegetable farm away from the highway and prying eyes. Tron and his men drove the SUVs to the farmhouse accompanied by one of the North Korean military trucks after his men had changed the shot-out tire. The Chinese scientists were told that they were not in any danger and that they would be well cared for the next four days.

Tron invited the Chinese delegation leader, Wyun Hi Lee, to share tea with him while he explained that he and his crew were assuming the Chinese men's identity. Speaking in Chinese to Lee, Tron assured him that they would be unharmed and eventually returned to China. Lee was skeptical at first, but when he finally deduced what was happening, he became quite calm and meditative.

The Israelis acquired the Chinese scientists' identities and some of them changed into the North Korean uniforms. This presented a challenge to the Mossad operators. The North Koreans have hygiene and cleanliness low on their priorities, so the uniforms they had to change into were grossly rank with severe body odour. One of the agents, Dudi Hon Luc, vehemently objected to wearing a North Korean uniform until Tron emphasized that it was necessary.

"Dudi, do you think that the other North Koreans we have to meet at the facility will appreciate your walking by them with some fancy men's cologne and deodorant on your ugly little body? Now get into that uniform! We are running late and if we don't get back on the highway soon, the people at the research centre will become concerned as to where we are."

The Israeli operators, after assuming the identities of the Chinese, drove to Yongbyon. They were met at the gates and greeted warmly by the administration staff.

Tron and his team had spent four days posing as the Chinese scientists and were hosted and detailed around the Yongbyon Scientific Centre. What they observed was an operation far more advanced and sophisticated than any of the intelligence acquired over the years had led them to believe. The innovative equipment, all of top-quality European and Russian manufacture simply proved that the UN- and US-imposed sanctions had been completely ineffective. Tron and his team also observed Caucasian scientists in white coats and masks working alongside the North Koreans. They eventually were introduced to them, albeit briefly, and Tron ascertained that they were Russians and Iranians, with two standout exceptions. One of the scientists who appeared to be in charge was a large, surly German who completely ignored the visitors. The other exception was a Pakistani whom Tron recognized as Ali Imra Khan, one of the original team of Pakistani nuclear engineers who had developed the Pakistani nuclear arsenal. This was certainly an eye-opener.

Here was the absolute conclusive proof that the Iranians and North Koreans were still very committed to developing a nuclear weapon and advancing those efforts all the time. All the denials and sanctions along with the 2015 treaty were nothing more than window-dressing. The two rogue nations were aligned with each other, sharing expertise and equipment, aided and abetted by some very bad people.

Tron and his crew were able to maintain their false identities for the four days. During that time, the North Koreans, assuming they were Chinese, willingly showed them around the complete installation.

On their fourth day, the Israelis requested to view the massive control centre one more time. They had been able to bring some sophisticated destructive devices in their luggage. The devices were in some cases ultrasonic, so when activated, they discharged an ultrahigh-density signal. When the devices were placed on or near computers and other communications equipment, they would totally destroy all the memory and RAM when activated. This top-secret Israeli technology was not available to any other nation. It was one of the most closely guarded secrets in the Israeli arsenal.

The Mossad team strategically stood around the key communication and engineering equipment, engaging the plant operators in discussions about their duties and the specifics of the controls. Valuable information was willingly shared. In the course of these ad hoc meetings, they casually left the devices stuck to the underside of consoles and workstations to be activated by a satellite-transmitted signal once the bogus Chinese visitors had departed.

Throughout their four days at the centre, they were treated as honoured and exalted guests. After thanking their North Korean hosts, Tron Duc and his team of imposters departed the centre. Dudi and his compatriots had to be evasive and skillful during the stay. Typically, they would have been billeted with the other guards at the centre, but they were able to convince the North Koreans that their trucks needed some repairs and they would take them back down the highway to a small village that had a service centre. Prior to the operation, the Mossad had gleaned some intelligence from the South Koreans that because of parts and skilled labour shortages, the village repair centre was the only place near the research centre for such repairs. Dudi and his companions took the trucks down to the shop and received clearance to stay for the four days. The South Korean secret service had taken over the repair shop and prepared with the Israelis for this event. The Mossad team, still in their stinking uniforms, were housed and fed in rooms next to the repair shop and basically remained out of sight most of the time.

CHAPTER 52

On departing the centre with effusive smiles and handshakes all around, Tron and his team headed for the farmhouse where they had detained the Chinese delegation. They were now being escorted by some new North Korean soldiers. Dudi and his men discreetly followed the convoy to provide cover in case of any unforeseen challenges. When they reached the cutoff for the farmhouse, Tron had his SUV pull over to the side of the road. The soldiers stopped also and, as they approached the SUV, Tron was now standing outside on the roadway. While Tron engaged the senior officer, two of his team used Krav Maga techniques to disable the other five. So great was the total surprise of the Koreans that Tron decided to spare their lives. There was no need to kill them. The soldiers in the second truck quickly surrendered to Dudi and his men. The Koreans were made to remove their uniforms and boots, then bound and gagged and placed in the back of one of their transport trucks, which was then driven off the road and hidden in a small copse of trees.

When Tron arrived at the farmhouse, the Chinese were at first very apprehensive because they did not trust the Koreans. Soon they realized that this was the Mossad team dressed in North Korean uniforms. Tron explained to them that they meant them no harm and would happily escort them back to Pyongyang or leave them vehicles for their own use to return.

The head of the Chinese delegation, Wyun Hi Lee, had quickly determined what the Mossad operation was about. Philosophically, he supported any attempt to cut down Kim's nuclear ambitions. As part of his directive from Beijing, he had been asked to identify any ways that the Chinese could either abort or at least quietly delay the program.

Tron Duc and the Mossad offered Lee and his colleagues transit out of North Korea if they so wished. Lee accepted the offer and his group accompanied the Israelis to the coast, where they were to catch up with the other teams charged with disabling and destroying Yeongjeo-ri and Yongdeok. The team whose mission was Musudan-ri would exfiltrate to the East Coast and await a rendezvous with a fishing trawler supported by the South Koreans.

Early in the morning that Yongbyon was hosting its "Chinese" delegation, a second team gained access to the Yeongjeo-ri research centre posing as a high-level security inspection team. Led by a Mossad officer, Lin Pho Duc, who had conducted many classified missions to countries unfriendly to the State of Israel, the team arrived unannounced in two S-Class Mercedes sedans. The NIS had liberated the cars from a hotel parking garage in Pyongyang.

The first indication the facility managers had that they were in some serious trouble was when they were alerted to the arrival of the sedans. These were the preferred ride of the top leadership of North Korea, a rare sight anywhere. When they did show up, the people they came to see were almost always brutalized.

The facility director, Dr. Hook Lee Dong, and his chief technology officer, Dr. Ban Jee Noon, were transfixed watching the sedans arrive and disgorge four senior military officers and four state security men.

Both Dong and Noon hurried down to the main reception lobby to greet their surprise visitors. Both men were civilian scientists, deathly afraid of the military and the Kim regime.

Once they were admitted to the main entrance of the facility, leaving one lower-ranked soldier at each car as a driver and guard, Lin Pho Duc began shouting orders to the submissive officials. Lin was well-built, and when he wore an angry face, he was intimidating. "*Who's in charge here?*"

The portly Dr. Hook stepped forward and introduced himself. "Dr. Hook Lee Dong, I am the general manager of this research centre." He was shaking and sweating before who he thought were high-level North Korean state security officers.

Addressing Dr. Hook, Lin frightened the assembled scientists even more. "We are here to examine your security. Our informants within the US and the traitorous regime to the South tell us that your security is lax and has been compromised, *mignuk nom*! (American bastard)."

Dr. Hook quailed at this worst of insults.

"Secrets from this facility are, as we speak, being evaluated by the warmongers in the US. The Dear Leader is most infuriated that this should happen, and you all know the results if indeed this is true. Dr. Hook, take me to your offices so we can immediately conduct a review of your documentation and computers. Anyone trying to hide or change anything will be taken to the courtyard and immediately shot!"

Lin then put Lee in an arm-bar and shoved him to the main offices.

Dr. Hook and his team were terrified. They immediately shot looks of rage at Captain Do Ro Lik, who was the NK Army intelligence officer overseeing security at the centre. Lik was shaking and almost in tears as he contemplated his fate if any security breach was discovered. Uppermost on his mind was the fate of his wife and two sons, his parents and grandparents, and his wife's parents. If the Dear Leader was made aware of any transgression, he would be summarily executed by being thrown to a pack of wild, starving dogs while his extended family would be forced to watch. Then after his barbaric execution, they would disappear into a forced labour camp until they died of malnutrition, multiple daily rapes, and frequent brutal beatings from the camp guards. Captain Lik felt like throwing up.

Lin had his team interrogate computer and equipment operators at random. This was done imitating North Korean senior officials who always intimidated the unfortunate people with much shouting and threats. As Lin bullied his way around the centre, his associates were following him and further terrorizing the civilian personnel.

Lin and his team worked their way around the facility constantly prodding Dr. Hook forward to all the areas they wanted to observe.

Lik trailed abjectly behind. At every station where the Mossad team halted and perused the documentation or programs, Captain Lik almost lost control of his bladder and bowels.

As they circulated and created chaos in their search for phantom security breaches, Lin's team deployed the ultrasonic destruction devices on any piece of equipment they identified as critical to the facility. These were synchronized to detonate at the same time as those in the Yongbyon facilities, when a specifically designated satellite would pass over North Korea and activate the devices after the teams had managed their exfiltration to the sea.

After they completed their phony inspection, Lin and his associates called Dr. Hook and his team to a meeting in the main conference room. He had Dr. Hook and his team sit and then he addressed them, shouting and gesticulating in a frenzy. "This facility is a leaky bucket! You are all suspect of providing secrets to the enemies of the Dear Leader. Captain Lik, your security is far from perfect and we will outline this in our report. Rest assured, a full team from State Security will be here tomorrow morning to conduct a more detailed investigation based on our initial findings. You are all to stay here tonight. No one goes home. State Security will be here at 0700 sharp to interview you all again."

Lin then summoned a captain from the North Korean militia who was in charge of security details and instructed him to ensure that Dr. Hook's executive team did not leave or communicate with anyone outside the facility before State Security arrived in the morning.

Turning on his heel, he marched out of the room. His bootheels clicked like gunshots on the tiled floor. The noise was even more noticeable since there was not a sound out of the stunned and terrorized personnel in the conference room. They looked around at each other in wide-eyed silence, each contemplating if they had inadvertently caused a security leak. They were all resigned to a night of terror and stress such as they had never experienced before, and each feared imminent execution. The mere contemplation of a full-on investigation by State Security was enough to cause nervous breakdowns.

Little did they know that State Security would be swarming all over the facility in the morning, but for a very different reason. Some hours after the Israeli impersonators had departed, the devices they had placed activated and destroyed all the memory and files in the centre's mainframe. Dr. Hook and his technicians had no choice other than to report the disastrous effects to Pyongyang.

CHAPTER 53

Tehran, 0430 hrs

As Ari and Sarah were coordinating their exfil, the air above Tehran was shattered by Israeli fighter jets screaming over their targets. Colonel Lieberman in the lead F-16I swept in low over the Basij headquarters and fired two Hellfire missiles into the top floor. His wingman, Lieutenant Ben Weizmann, followed behind Lieberman and strafed the parking lot with the Gatling cannon where hundreds of militiamen were scrambling, panic-stricken, to mount their motorcycles and spread out through the city to control the ordinary citizens.

Two more F-16I jets piloted by Lieutenant Daran Majofski and Lieutenant Mendel (Mendy) Wolfing successfully destroyed over fifty trucks and APC vehicles at the IRGC headquarters, which was already on fire from the earlier attacks by Ari's teams. Other F-16I jets sought out targets of opportunity at all the IRGC defences.

Sarah and her group, having achieved mission success by capturing the leadership of the Basij, pulled back and took up defensive positions to prevent any of the Basij from leaving the compound. Sarah's commandos, code-named Sparrows, had stormed from the trucks after they crashed through the gates and raced fifty feet for the entrance of the building, just as they had practised at Rosh Pinah. During the drive from the warehouse, Sarah and her squad had been mostly silent, dealing with their individual thoughts of armed conflict in a foreign country. Sarah's mouth was dry, and every nerve was taut as a bow. She was keenly aware of the consequences once they exited the truck. Looking to her right, she tentatively smiled at Sergeant Alli Landa, her second in command and whispered, "Alli, we've got this."

"Piece of cake," grinned Alli. Their orders were to shoot any enemy who tried to stop them.

The whole squad tensed as they felt the truck shift down and sharply change direction to accelerate for the gates. All were locked and loaded, checking their weapons for the umpteenth time as the four GAZ-modified armoured trucks drew level with the main gates. The driver of the lead truck with Sarah riding in back made a sharp turn to the left and mashed the gas pedal. By the time the truck had covered the hundred yards to the gates, it was gaining speed and crashed through the wrought iron gates at over twenty-five miles per hour. The four gate guards were crushed under the wheels of the massive trucks. As they burst through and came to a halt, the commandos leaped out of the rear bed and raced for the building. The element of surprise was on Sarah's side and within fifteen seconds, the special forces were out of the trucks. Sarah was shouting, "Go, go, go!"

Sarah rushed up the steps, leading her team from the front with Sergeant Alli Landa covering her as they had practised so many times. Sarah was keyed for combat. As she reached the top of the steps to enter the building, she observed a Basij fighter pointing an AK-74 directly at her. She was zigzagging and his aim was poor. Then she heard the dreaded sound of bullets impacting flesh behind her and a muted scream; she knew right away that Alli Landa had been hit. Sarah eliminated the Basij fighter with a three-shot burst to his head. There was no time to check on Sergeant Landa, but she felt an awful foreboding. Pressing on with even more determination, she energized her command and her team swept into the building. As she advanced with her troops, she knew her biggest fear had been realized. She would lose one of her charges who was also a dear friend. Sick to her stomach, Sarah became a woman possessed. Any Basij that didn't surrender immediately, she shot without a shadow of remorse.

Once inside the auditorium-style main lobby, Sarah marshalled her squad leaders and directed them to the upper floors. "Bar-Nedar, take six troopers and clear the north stairwell. Be careful of booby traps. These bastards will try and string grenades on the turns or in doorways. Kill them on sight. Remember, we need the leadership alive, particularly Gholamhossein Gheybparvar." Each commando had cards with photos of the HVT's (high value targets).

The Basij fighter who had unleashed a burst of AK-74 fire directly at Sarah and Alli had hit Alli in both thighs and one had somehow eluded her Kevlar vest and entered her stomach. Her wounds were catastrophic. One of the medics attached to Sarah's squads, Nathan Gross, risked his own life to run and drag Alli to comparative safety behind the truck she and Sarah had jumped from. Desperately working to stanch the massive wound to her right thigh, Gross enlisted help from another medic. "Hold this battle compress on her thigh while I get a tourniquet on. Then we'll check this torso wound."

"Nathan, I can't stop the bleeding. Shit! The bullet has severed her femoral artery!"

"Keep the compress on! I need to get the tourniquet as tight as I can."

Gross then removed the sling from his weapon and, using it as a supplemental tourniquet, he pulled his combat knife from his thigh scabbard and used it as handle to tighten the sling around Alli's thigh. The bleeding slowed considerably.

Nathan then removed Alli's Kevlar vest and cut away her fatigues to examine the stomach wound.

"This is really bad. Pray for her! We have to get her to the aid station, now!"

Placing Alli gently on a litter, the two medics ran to the makeshift aid station set up in a commandeered Mercedes Sprinter van just outside the perimeter wall.

CHAPTER 54

Islamic Republican Guards Corps Headquarters

Ari Lazarus and Dov Horowitz had trained two Sayeret teams in Rosh Pina to attack and occupy the headquarters of the IRGC in Tehran. Their objectives were clear. They would take over the building and capture as many of the leadership as possible. Their two primary HVT individuals were the commanding general, Mohamed Ali Jafari, who was the overall commander of the entire IRGC, and General Ali Fadavi, Chief of the Joint Chiefs.

Corporal Yussi Nehrman, the driver of the modified Russian GAZ truck, made the turn across from the main gates of the HQ building and accelerated straight at them. The largely ceremonial guards realized too late that they were under attack and were crushed under the churning wheels of the giant vehicle. At the same moment, Col Lieberman's flight of F-16I fighter-bombers unleashed a flurry of missiles at the top floors. The commandos leaped from the vehicles and rushed for the entrance. Another two GAZ trucks forced their way into the rear area of the parade ground of the complex and those commandos were leapfrogging each other as they broke into the rear entrances of the building. The attack happened so fast with the coordinated air assault, the IRGC troops inside were completely disoriented; their initial resistance was slight.

Ari's first stop was the basement, where all the sophisticated communication equipment was housed. He led a troop of ten down two flights of stairs and was met by some token resistance from a half dozen security guards. They were quickly eliminated.

The communication centre was behind sealed doors, which took three minutes to blow open. Two troopers placed high-explosive Semtex around the locks and the hinges and retreated back down the corridor. Ari directed two troopers to keep a sharp lookout for any guards who might attempt to surprise the team by rushing down the stairs. They positioned themselves just at the turn between the first and second levels. While the Israelis were waiting for the doors to blow open, the guards threw two grenades down the stairs from the main floor. Each of the troopers immediately picked up one and threw it back up the stairs. As they were in the air at the entrance to the basement, they both exploded, causing some casualties among the guards. The lead sergeant, Evram Nussbinder, triggered the electronic fuse and the Semtex exploded, destroying the doors and their surrounding infrastructure. Several security guards immediately behind the doors were killed.

Once inside the communication centre, the Sayeret, under Col. Lazarus's direction, destroyed all the equipment, thus inhibiting the IRGC's ability to communicate with their satellite hubs and with General Soleimani in Lebanon.

With the damage done to the upper floors, any surviving IRGC commanders were prevented from escaping. Those not injured or killed were rounded up and placed in restraints, then led out of the building to the waiting transport. Among them were Mohamed Ali Jafari and Ali Fadari, the two most senior IRGC generals stationed in Iran. Both HVTs would be taken back to Israel and tried alongside the government leadership captured by Col. Dov Horowitz in Qom.

General Jafari was in a complete state of shock. He was easily subjugated and offering no resistance as his hands were placed in restraints. What was going through his mind was the fact that he and Fadari commanded a force of over 150,000 supposedly elite troops, and yet it appeared that less than one hundred Israelis had overwhelmed his headquarters.

As Ari and his men began to exfiltrate, the guards started to recover. Returning to the main lobby of the building, Ari and his men were met by a hail of automatic fire coming from outside the entrance to the building. A platoon of Guards, ably assembled and directed by a seasoned officer, Captain Mahmed Ahlavi, were attempting to trap and detain the Israelis inside the building until reinforcements arrived.

Ari communicated to the AWAC that they needed air support in a hurry. Colonel Lieberman came on his comms immediately, "Khihl to Macha1…"

"Go, Khihl."

"Heads down. I'm coming in from the east and will lay down a strafing run."

In less than two minutes, Ari and his men heard the roar of a low-flying supersonic fighter approaching. Then the air was shattered by the sound of the F-16I Gatling guns firing on the Iranians. Within seconds, the threat was removed and the fighter flew away to aid Sarah Holzman's forces.

"Macha 1 to Khihl; Todah rabah (thank you)."

Now that their way out was secured, the Sayeret teams began their exfiltration from the destroyed IRGC headquarters. They had the two HVT Iranian generals in restraints, as well as four other senior officers.

As they made their way to the vehicles that had been commandeered to take them to the airport, Ari was getting updates on how the operation on the Basij headquarters was unfolding. The teams led by Sarah Holzman had been successful in capturing two HVT individuals, and although they had sustained some casualties, one serious, they were now exfiltrating and loading into their trucks, ready to travel to the airport.

CHAPTER 55

Alli Landa was bright and vivacious and had grown up a tomboy in a family of four brothers where she was the youngest sibling. Her grandparents, Chaim and Zivia Bergman, had somehow survived the horrors of the Theresienstadt extermination camp because they had both been accomplished musicians. Their SS captors kept the talented musicians alive so that when the camp was inspected by the Red Cross, they could claim it was a work camp with many cultural events and activities for the inmates. It was a charade. Chaim had been a lead violinist in the Prague Philharmonic Orchestra while Zivia had played harp with the symphony orchestra before they were rounded up and sent to the camp.

They had arrived in Israel broken in body and spirit from the DP camps and slowly rebuilt their lives. After settling in Tel Aviv, they involved themselves in the thriving cultural life of the growing metropolis. Chaim had a position at a private school teaching music and Zivia worked for a medical office as a receptionist. To their great joy, Zivia gave birth to a healthy boy. They named him Moshe and watched with supreme pride as he grew into a strong and handsome young man.

Moshe served in the IDF as a tank commander. He met and eventually married a beautiful third-generation Israeli girl, Shoshanna Barents. They settled near Moshe's parents in Tel Aviv and Moshe started a small company that became very successful guiding tourists from the Diaspora around Israel. Moshe and Shoshanna—or Shoshie, as she was fondly called—had five children—four strapping sons and a daughter, Alli. Alli was quick-witted and an excellent student. As her brothers all rotated through their military service with outstanding records, she was in no way going to be left out. When her turn came to serve, after completing one year in the regular army, she applied to and was accepted into the Sayeret commandos.

As her three years of service was coming to an end, Alli was offered a permanent position as a ranking sergeant in the special force for women. By that time, she had met her future husband, Pesach Landa, and they were married soon after. Pesach was a talented engineer; he worked in a research lab associated with the Technion in Haifa. Alli and Pesach led a unique life. He was the homemaker as well as the breadwinner, while she was always on standby for a special mission. They were deeply in love and their relationship worked, especially after Alli gave birth to their two children, Micha and Avielle. Pesach and Alli knew that her commitment to the safety and protection of the State of Israel carried a risk of danger and perhaps fatality.

The two medics desperately kept trying to control the hemorrhaging from Alli's grievous injuries. Sarah continued to lead her team up to the top floors while others waited in concealed positions. The elite female commandos flushed any remaining Basij out of the offices and dormitories and down the stairs. Sarah was careful to seek out the leadership. When possible, she captured them, concentrating primarily on locating the Basij commander, Gholamhossein Gheybparvar. She and two of her commandos finally located him cowering in a stall in a women's bathroom on the second floor. Attempting to conceal his identity, he had stripped off his uniform, but Sarah easily recognized him from his photo card. He was in total denial. He could not believe his office building was being overrun by Israeli women!

As Sarah's troopers struggled to get him out of the washroom, he became violent, struggling and lashing out at his captors. Sergeant Leila Adon, using a Krav Maga technique, placed him a painful hold that ensured his complete compliance.

"Ok you bastard, now you'll cooperate. If you don't, I'll break your shoulder!"

He ceased struggling and collapsed, screaming in agony on the stairs leading down to the main entrance. Three troopers carried him out and down the stairs. By the time they forced him down to the lobby, he had pissed in his pants and was on the verge of passing out.

Any Basij that showed the slightest resistance were immediately cut down. There was no time to waste fighting them. Gheybparvar was really brave when he could order beatings of civilians, but as soon as he faced real opposition, he tried to flee.

Most of the building had been cleared and the Basij eliminated or rounded up, allowing Sarah to order a controlled withdrawal back to the street where their transport waited.

"Leader S to Sparrows! Pull back to exfil! Keep sharp. Leader S out."

The medics transported Alli back to their exfil vehicle—the Sprinter van that had been appropriated by some of Ari's men.

"Aid to Leader One! It is not looking good for Alli!" the medic said. "Can you break off now and withdraw with all of us to the exfil location?"

"Leader S to Macha One. We are taking some small arms fire. They are trying to set up a sniper on the third-floor northeast end window!"

"Gheybparvar, that fat piece of shit is trying to slow down our withdrawal. We are pinned down with him and don't want to expose ourselves crossing the forecourt. Can Khihl take out the snipers and get us clear passage to exfil? Besides the sniper there are probably one or two slime balls sitting back behind the third-floor windows with RPGs. I need the fly-boys to eliminate these pieces of crap ASAP."

Sarah and Ari could still hear the F-16Is circling overhead. They had broken off and ducked across to the Caspian Sea to refuel from an Israeli air tanker based out of the Azerbaijan airfield. When they returned, they were looking for targets of opportunity. Ari called Colonel Lieberman's call sign Khihl on the secure network. "Macha 1 to Khihl! The Sparrows need some more heavy strafing at the Basij target. Deploy your Gatling cannons on to the third-floor northeast windows. Leader S has identified at least one sniper and possibly two more. Khihl, we need this *now*!"

The conversation was being heard by all the leaders on the closed communication channel.

"Khihl to Leader Sparrow S. Stand by. Heads down we are coming in hot on the target in one minute."

Lieberman and his wingman flew in low at almost supersonic speed, just above the rooftops of nearby buildings. The sonic waves and sounds from their massive engines shattered windows and caused the ground to shake as they directed the fire of the Gatling cannons to the two top floors of the building. Within seconds, the two floors were reduced to rubble as the .50 mm Gatling shells destroyed everything in their path.

Both Ari and Sarah were awestruck at the devastation. Concrete was turned to powder by the high impact and any person caught in the line of fire was shredded into a dismembered pile of flesh, gore, and bones.

The vaunted IRGC and the Basij were reduced to a cowering, shell-shocked band. There was no leadership left and their will to fight back against the Israelis was gone.

CHAPTER 56

Once the threat from the Basij snipers was eliminated, Sarah and her team began to withdraw back down the street from where they had been driven in the GAZ trucks. They had not planned to use those trucks in case they were damaged or disabled during the firefight. The default was for some of Ari's team to commandeer trucks from the streets and take the teams to the airport.

They dragged Gheybparvar with them. At this point he was alternately screaming with rage and whimpering in fear. Once all teams were accounted for and ready, they set off for the Tehran airport, where two IAF C-130 aircraft were waiting to fly them back to Israel. They had clearance to fly over Saudi Arabia and on over the Red Sea to Rosh Pina. Ever since the 2015 Nuclear Treaty with Iran, the Sunni Saudi government had a secret pact with Israel that, in the event of hostilities between Israel and the Shi'ite Iran, they would permit the IAF over flight freedom in Saudi skies.

"We need to get her to the hospital and the surgeons on board the air transport now!" Gross urged Ari.

By now, Sarah had joined Ari in the aid van, and she was crouched down beside Alli's head as the medics worked to save her. Alli's eyes never left Sarah's.

"The docs have got you. Just hang in and we'll be sharing a Shabbat soon enough."

"Sar..." Alli wheezed through painkillers as she reached for Sarah's hand.

"Shh! Don't speak," Sarah whispered as she gently squeezed her hand. Alli drifted off into a semiconscious state and Sarah knew her friend's life was hanging in the balance.

CHAPTER 57

The trip to the airport played out exactly as planned. The hour was still early, and the heavy Tehran rush hour traffic had not yet materialized, so they made good time. Ari's eight drivers, who had acquired seven trucks, and the van drove directly out on to the airside hardstand where the C-130s were spooling over, watched by hundreds of civilian passengers through the terminal windows. Many believed these happenings were part of some military training exercise until they realized, some in shock, that the two C-130s proudly displayed the Israeli Magen David on their distinctive tails.

All incoming flights had been diverted to airports in neighbouring countries and all outgoing traffic had been grounded by the Israeli AWAC. Stranded passengers were nervously discussing among themselves that some serious event had occurred. They soon concluded that the smoke rising from the city centre and some of the suburbs were IRGC bases that had been attacked by an Israeli air raid. Many were beginning to show fear and concern as to what might happen at the terminal. They worried that the IRGC would mount an attack on the Israeli planes and they could be caught in the crossfire.

Many older travellers began to compare this raid to the Entebbe rescue many years ago. Even though modern civilians were concerned for their safety, it was clear that the Israeli soldiers were not paying any heed to them. Their only concern was the security perimeter around their two C-130 aircraft. Incredibly, other than a small contingent of regular Iranian military and a detachment of border police, there were no visible signs of Iranian forces who could threaten the Israelis.

As they prepared to unload the vehicles and board the planes, word was received from one of the F-16I pilots that there appeared to be a column of Iranian armoured cars and tanks racing down the highway toward the airport. The pilot was immediately patched through to the circling Spooky and alerted its crew to the potential threat. It was clear that the Islamic Revolutionary Guards had managed to organize the armoured column and were attempting to head off the Israelis at the airport. Within minutes, "Mr. Spooky" was over the column, hosing the tanks with the Gatling guns and Bofors cannons. It was all over in less than two minutes. Fifteen 70s-era Russian-supplied tanks were smoking heaps of scrap metal. The twelve armoured troop carriers were skeletal hulks of scorched steel. There were no survivors.

From the lack of presence of the local forces at the airport, it didn't appear that there would be any more interference. The local regular Iranian forces, observing the extent of the smoke from the attacks in the city and news filtering back about the swiftness and strength of the Israeli attacks, decided they were not about to make any overt moves against the Israelis, especially after the news of the destruction of the armoured column spread very quickly among them. Even though radio and cell phone communications were down, the Iranian forces were still able to communicate among themselves via walkie-talkies.

Most onlookers were curious about the handcuffed prisoners with black bags over their heads—particularly the one, Gheybparvar, who was being supported by two of the other prisoners. Many were guessing—and some even hoping—that it was one of the senior mullahs, or even General Soleimani.

The prisoners were escorted off the bus and hustled on to one of the waiting aircraft. The prisoners were in fact Gholamhossein Gheybparvar, the Basij commander; Generals Ali Jafari and Ali Fadari, the two most senior commanders of the IGRC; and some senior officers, including Ali Nazir Ruahi, who was probably one of the most feared men in Iran. Ruahi had taken great pleasure in administering life-threatening beatings for perceived dress code infractions on the streets of Tehran, but now he was a scrawny man fearing for his life as he was roughly pushed onto the ramp and into the transport.

Sarah and Ari's teams basically emasculated the IRGC and Basij leadership; as forces, they were no longer a factor.

It wasn't lost on the surviving Basij and IRGC that their headquarters had been destroyed and their leaders taken down by the hated Israelis.

Once the eight vehicles were abandoned on the tarmac, Ari and Sarah directed their teams to load onto the waiting aircraft. Each plane could accommodate more than eighty soldiers. In one designated as a medical evacuation craft, medics and a flight surgeon anxiously continued to work on Alli Landa. But she died shortly after lift-off, her hand in Sarah's.

Sarah sat by the side of the gurney as still as a stone. The medic, Nathan Gross, his uniform covered in Alli's blood, folded over with rasping sobs. "Her wounds were too devastating. I'm so sorry. I tried. I'm so sorry…"

Sarah brushed aside his arm and said, "Alli knew the risks. We all did. When we land, the teams and Colonel Lazarus need to see you as a strong, proud leader. Now get that piece of blubber squared away." Sarah knew she had to be strong and show the leadership she was recognized for in the Sayeret. She then helped Nathan Gross to his feet and walked toward the cockpit. Before returning to his duties to aid the injured, he reverently covered Sgt. Alli Landa's body.

CHAPTER 58

Suburb of Beirut, Lebanon, 0400 hrs

As news of the attacks broke throughout the Middle East and Europe as the world woke up, the Sayeret team in Lebanon had stealthily surrounded the house of Leila Adnan, the TV anchor. They waited until 0400hrs, and when the general's security team was at its most vulnerable, they stormed the house where General Soleimani was being energetically serviced by his mistress. Leila was sitting astride his chest with her lustrous black hair flowing over his crotch as her head bobbed up and down. Just as he began to climax for the second time that night, one of his aides urgently rushed into the room to deliver the news about the attacks on Qom and Tehran.

General Soleimani tried to ignore the compromising position he had been found in. He pushed Leila off him and started bellowing orders. As he did so, the Israelis charged into the bedroom, knocking the aide aside, and dragged Soleimani naked from the bed. Leila began screaming in abject terror. The TV anchor recovered enough to cloak herself in some sheets while Soleimani was unceremoniously hustled down the stairs. There, the commandos helped him put on underpants and a shirt, and then they paraded him in handcuffs and chains through the lobby and across the courtyard in front of the shocked and stunned household staff.

Leila Adnan continued to shriek from the upstairs bedroom as Soleimani was roughly dragged off toward his own special automobile newly manned by Sayeret. The three IRGC men who formed Soleimani's protective detail were dead.

Soleimani, manacled in his briefs with dishevelled hair and bare feet, looked nothing like a general in command of the Iranian forces in Lebanon and Syria.

The Iranian general, who was known for a haughty air of supreme arrogance and unprecedented brutality, recovered enough to begin making demands of his captors. He questioned who they were and where they had come from.

"Do you know who I am? I am the revered General Hussein Soleimani, Commander of the Quds Force. My men will hunt you down all over the world for your cowardly Zionist attack on the armies of God and the great Iranian Revolution!!"

One of the Sayeret commandos, Staff Sergeant Emmanuel "Manny" Ungerman, who was over 6 feet 4 inches tall and weighed 275 pounds of solid muscle, grabbed the general by his crotch and neck and threw him unceremoniously into the back of his Mercedes GL 550 SUV. Soleimani was shaken to the core over how easily he had been captured and deposited in his own vehicle.

Ungerman climbed in the rear door and seated himself next to Soleimani, then leaned in until he was face-to-face with him. He said to him in perfect Farsi, "Listen, you piece of shit, I am Staff Sergeant Emmanuel Ungerman of the Israeli Sayeret. You're going to Israel. Aren't you lucky? You get a free ride courtesy of the IDF."

Soleimani was apoplectic. He began snarling and then he lunged at Ungerman. The Israeli giant held him back with one hand and continued in Farsi. "You don't command anything anymore. You are now a captured war criminal. Any hanging or executions you attend will be your own, you slimy bastard. Your own people will celebrate."

The Sayeret had landed on the Lebanese coast and rendezvoused with an advance team, which had commandeered a series of vehicles for Major Avigold's team. The team, code-named "Hijack," had delivered several vehicles without injuring their hapless occupants, who then were restrained in plastic cuffs, gagged, and held in a storage warehouse where they were guarded by Hijack until the mission was over.

Once General Soleimani was secured, he was driven to the Israeli border through Hezbollah-controlled villages in his own Mercedes G550 SUV.

The Hezbollah troops believed he was on one of his snap inspections and stood in awe as the great man raced by. The Hezbollah commanders were fearful of providing any cause for the general to unleash his notorious temper on them. They were totally unaware of what was transpiring.

Major Benyamin Avigold led the kidnap raid and was seated next to General Soleimani with Sergeant Ungerman on the other side in the armoured Mercedes. Avigold helped Ungerman check the chains and manacles. The massive sergeant made sure that he yanked the chains as hard as he could.

"Major, he's not much of a general now, is he?" Ungerman addressed Major Avigold in Farsi.

Soleimani had difficulty comprehending the recent chain of events. As much as anything, he was struggling to reconcile what had happened to him with where he had just been. He was stunned and disoriented after his rough treatment at the hands of Ungerman. The Iranian general could not process what had occurred. Then the enormity of it all began to sink in. Here he was, captured by the hated Zionists, riding in his own special vehicle next to one of the most intimidating men he had ever seen, a giant of a Zionist who spoke fluent Farsi. Soleimani's wrists felt like they would separate from his arms. Then, to add insult to injury, here he was being driven away by Israeli commandos in his own special and distinctive automobile.

What distressed him the most was the complete lack of protection from his personal bodyguards and protective detail. Other than the three security men who had been minding his Mercedes, there had been no resistance.

CHAPTER 59

Musudan-ri Missile Facility, North Korea

Six kilometres outside the Musudan-ri missile testing site, a team of four Mossad agents led by another Israeli Vietnamese, Nuc Phonh Ven, and eight South Korean Seals worked their way down a steep embankment to the tracks of a dedicated rail line running directly into the site. Nuc Phonh with his team—Jona Bilt, Sasha Berkman, and Nahum Davitz, each of whom had taken on Israeli names—had identified the railroad as being the one that carried all supplies and personnel into Musudan-ri.

The South Korean Seals had extensive knowledge of the tracks and train operations. While at Rosh Pinah during their training and again in South Korea before departing to North Korea, they had studied real-time satellite imagery to acquire detailed intelligence. The live footage showed trains slowing down for the steep hill and curve at the foot of the embankment they had just descended.

The train was carrying bomb components and the missile's second- and third-stage assemblies and a senior delegation of Iranian and North Korean engineers and scientists. The North Korean operation was under the direct command of General Ri-Yong-Gil, the top military commander in the North Korean armed forces. Kim had specifically charged Gil with ensuring the success of the operation; as a result, he was travelling with his aides and the scientists. The train was heavily guarded by special forces and also was being provided air cover by helicopters carrying more special forces in case of any attack.

The South Korean Seals, with Nuc Phonh and his team, had hidden at the foot of the embankment for twelve hours. Their plan was to climb under the carriage trucks of the train as it moved slowly round the curve and place explosives under each compartment. Their primary targets were the car carrying the general and his staff, the one carrying the Iranians, and the special transporter with the missile and bomb components. This was fraught with risk, since discovery would mean instant death at the hands of the North Koreans.

Before the train approached and slowed to less than ten kilometres an hour, Phonh and his men moved down to the side of the tracks and hid under Ghillie suits (seasonal camouflage) to await the train. They had trained for this in Israel and Greece and were confident that they would be practically invisible in the darkness.

As the train lumbered by, each operator ran and climbed under the carriages. They had packs of Semtex and pencil fuses, which they proceeded to attach to the underside of the cars. The DM62 locomotive was required to be destroyed and this presented a challenge, since there was no way for the operators to gain access to the engineers' cabin. During training, one of the commandos in Israel remembered the details of sabotage operations carried out in France by the Resistance against the Nazis during the Second World War. At that time, Resistance fighters had managed to attach explosive charges on the tracks that would be set off as the locomotive crossed over them, derailing the train and destroying it.

The destruction of the locomotive was crucial for the Mossad, since it was feared that the North Koreans would simply deploy it again for replacement components and missiles. Without the DM62 heavy-duty locomotive—one of only three North Korea had obtained from Russia—their ability to deploy another train quickly would be difficult. Phonh and his crew had practised the operation so many times that they had their actions timed down to the last second.

Before they set up by the tracks to wait for the train, two operators placed the special explosive charges down the track exactly where the locomotive would be as the rest of the charges went off. Once the charges on the undercarriages were attached, the Mossad and Korean

Seal teams dropped down to the tracks and timed their escape as they rolled away from the under carriages. As soon as the train was past, they evacuated the area and waited for the huge engine to be derailed. Within two minutes of the team's retreating from the area, so far unseen, the huge Russian-supplied locomotive triggered a massive explosion on the tracks and immediately derailed and rolled over onto its side, dragging two other cars with it. Within seconds, all the other cars erupted in explosions that destroyed the missiles and their equipment. All but one of the Iranians were killed in the explosions, as were most of the North Koreans on the train. General Ri-Yon-Gil was severely wounded and would ultimately succumb to his wounds.

As the ambush on the train was taking place, a second team, led by Hoc Un Pho, hijacked three trucks, eliminating the guards assigned to protect them. Later they determined that several of the special forces guarding the trucks were members of the Quds Force. This of course was even more confirmation of the close strategic alliance between North Korea and Iran. The transport trucks were carrying critical casings and castings from the Yeongjeo-ri facility. The Israelis then drove the trucks into the missile firing site and abandoned them.

The operators had been forced to improvise once they gained access to the site. While the three trucks were being parked and abandoned as close to critical infrastructure as possible, three of the Israelis had managed to set explosive charges on two of the missile transporters. They continued to be undetected during the ensuing chaos, when the military commander of the facility was informed of the train derailment and explosions. Once inside the missile centre, the Mossad team deployed high-explosive satchel charges on centrifuge banks and key buildings around the site. They achieved this by racing around, adding to the chaos as the North Korean major in charge of the military garrison tried to marshal enough forces to go to the site of the train derailment and explosions.

Once the North Koreans organized and raced off to the train, Hoc and his team liberated one of the trucks and began the drive back to their exit point twenty-five miles down the coast. Explosive charges set in the two remaining trucks and the key placements around the facility were timed to detonate twenty minutes after the Israelis departed. Once they cleared the facility, the Mossad team set off south and east from Musudan-ri. As they were driving away to their exfil point, they heard the massive explosions in the distance caused by the two trucks detonating followed by a continuous string of even larger explosions as the charges they had set detonated and destroyed the critical infrastructure at the testing site.

The damage was immense. Storage tanks containing volatile liquid propellants for rockets were destroyed, which alone caused devastating explosions and damage.

In the immediate chaos after the train derailment, two South Korean Seals and one of Phonh's commandos managed to gain entrance to the missile bunkers that had been bored into one side of the mountain facility. They were able to attach satchel charges and some Semtex charges to the missiles being stored out of sight of passing American satellites.

Satellite images would later show that, besides the ICBM destroyed on the train, there were seven other missiles of various sizes already deployed on mobile transporters. Analysts back in Israel and at Langley observed that the whole side of the mountain had collapsed under tons of rock as a result of the massive explosions inside the bunkers. Coupled with the initial explosions, volatile rocket fuel being loaded on to the missiles blew up, and because of the confined spaces, massive fireballs of intensely heated fuel barreled through the chambers, destroying everything and everybody in their paths.

At the time of the explosions, seismologists in Japan and Guam registered a 5.2 earthquake in the North Korean region of Musudan-ri.

CHAPTER 60

After arriving at a deserted beach area, the Musudan-ri team, as planned, lay hidden among the shoreline rocks and scrub for one full day. Intelligence coordinated from the South Koreans had correctly led them to understand that as soon as any breach occurred at Musudan-ri, the North Koreans would deploy aircraft, ground vehicles, and dozens of heavily armed foot patrols.

The South Koreans had agreed to operate decoy activities further north, close to the Chinese and Russian borders, which would pull northern forces away from the area and allow the Israelis to extract at night. It would also confuse the North Koreans, who were always suspicious of their neighbours. They never knew if, how, or when China would move to eliminate the North Korean nuclear threat.

The South Korean Special Forces, who had accompanied the Mossad teams as far as the train derailment, had positioned three large Zodiacs at the extraction beach, each equipped with three 250-horsepower outboard engines capable of fifty-plus knots. Once the northern boats and aircraft cleared the area, the group boarded the Zodiacs and raced out to sea. After an uncomfortable ninety minutes, the three Zodiac craft completed a prearranged rendezvous with a Panamanian coal carrier destined to unload its cargo in Vietnam. Once aboard the freighter, the ship's course was altered, and it headed for Japan. After the freighter docked in Kyoto, the commando teams were quietly ferried to a waiting chartered plane that transported them back to Rosh Pinah. The South Korean Seals would accompany them to guard and escort the captured Kim Jong-un leadership when they arrived from Australia.

CHAPTER 61

Israel/Lebanon Metula border crossing

Soleimani's dark, hate-filled eyes drilled into Major Avigold's. Finally, still living in delusion, Soleimani hissed, "Who do you think you are, you Zionist pig? Stop this car immediately! That is an order!"

Staff Sergeant Ungermann jabbed the general in the ribs so hard with his right elbow that Soleimani doubled over in pain, attempting to catch his breath. Ungermann growled in Farsi, "Listen you piece of garbage, we do the commanding from now on."

The look of incredulity on Soleimani's face said it all. He was so used to being in charge and ordering all around him to do his bidding that his current circumstances simply did not register. At the same time, Major Avigold rapped on the divider window in the car and spoke in Hebrew to the driver and commando in the front seats. "Our client is a general and I am a major. He has ordered us to stop the car."

Soleimani, who spoke and understood some Hebrew, was surprised and it showed on his arrogant face. "I am glad you understand the chain of command, Major," he spat out.

Macha had the border crossing between Lebanon and Israel at Metula alerted and the Mercedes was now at the border. As they crossed into Israel, Major Avigold, the commander of the kidnap operation, notified Hijack that they could release their civilian captives and reunite them with their "borrowed" vehicles.

The Lebanese guards at the Metula crossing were regular Lebanese soldiers, not Hezbollah or Islamic militia. When they understood what was unfolding, they had no problem cooperating with the Israelis. They hated and despised the IRGC and Hezbollah and had a great loathing for General Soleimani. Some of them actually cheered when they saw he had been captured. This only added to Soleimani's boiling fury.

At Major Avigold's command, the car stopped, and the general was allowed to alight. Major Avigold saluted him and said, "General, it has been a pleasure escorting you. Soon you will join your masters, after a short helicopter ride courtesy of the IDF."

The hard mask of anger and disgust on Soleimani's face said it all. As Avigold's driver and Sergeant Ungermann hauled him, still struggling against the shackles, to the waiting helicopter, they noticed that Soleimani had soiled himself. The great general was a very different person than the one who had been bedding his mistress three hours ago.

For the Israelis, this was vindication. Soleimani had been in their sights for a long time. For twelve years, he had been a dictator ruling Lebanon with an iron hand, and for the past seven years, he had been the guiding force behind the Assad forces in Syria, who were just puppets on the Islamic Revolutionary Guards' string.

Israel had had Soleimani scheduled for assassination by the Mossad in 2011. Somehow, the information leaked to the Americans, and the US president and his secretary of state were furious. They knew it would jeopardize the secret nuclear deal they were negotiating with Iran. The United States had passed the information through the secretary of state to the Iranians. Iran made it clear that they would immediately break off the secret talks if anything happened to Soleimani as a result of Israeli actions. The US president was emphatic in a direct discussion with the prime minister—all hands off Soleimani. This single action cost the American president all his political capital with Israel.

CHAPTER 62

Tehran and Bandar Bushehr, two hours later

Word filtered back to the remainder of the Iranian military leadership that there had been massive explosions and destruction at all seven nuclear facilities. The only exception was Bandar Bushehr, where the Sayeret team were compromised by a patrol and had to fight their way out to the extraction point. Otherwise all teams had been successful.

The Bandar Bushehr team, led by Lt. Aaron Lazar, had set up their overwatch sniper, Trooper Jona Grosner, and were working their way down a hill to the main gate of the facility when an Iranian patrol spotted them. Trooper Grosner was able to keep the Iranians at bay and disabled their vehicle, but the alarm was called in and Lt. Lazar determined that they would not have time to enter the main electrical controls area to place their explosives. They quickly set explosives with a detonator for fifteen minutes in a main air duct over the counters of the control room, then scurried away toward their extraction point.

Surprisingly, security at the plant was relatively light and at first hesitant to react to the warning from the jeep patrol. This allowed Lt. Lazar and his men to get in and out without any serious opposition.

Since Bandar Bushehr was on the western side of Iran, their extraction plan had been to be picked up by Israeli navy commandos from the coast and transported to one of the Israeli submarines lurking in the Persian Gulf.

Unfortunately, their hastily deployed explosives had not been properly located in the key target areas, so the resulting explosion was only a third as great as it should have been. Even so, it caused tremendous damage, and when the other six sites exploded more or less at the same time, the Iranian regime realized that their long-term nuclear strategy was in tatters and no longer viable.

After eluding Iranian military patrols, the team lay low for one full day and night in an abandoned industrial building near the Bandar Bushehr harbour. At one point around 1800hrs, a small Quds Force patrol of four men entered the building searching for the team. Sergeant Lazar and three of his commandos moved quietly behind the Iranians and silently dispatched them with their combat knives. Trooper Nahum Weiss quickly slipped outside the building and checked for any reinforcements that may have been on their way. After staying concealed behind some discarded oil drums, he came back inside and reported to Lazar that all was clear. The Israelis then collected the bodies of the Quds soldiers and hid them under corrugated metal sheets that were lying around the floor of the building. Until they ripened and the flies gave away their location, they would remain hidden for forty-eight hours, giving the Israeli team time to extract.

Later in the night, once they had established communication with the submarine via the AWACS, they quickly made their way to the beach and were picked up by two Zodiacs, which carried them out to the submarine *Rahav.*

Iran was now in turmoil. The leadership had been kidnapped and was being held in the Little Satan's hands. Their nuclear plants, on which they had squandered billions of dollars in treasure and political capital, were totally destroyed. Their vaunted Republican Guards and the Basij had been decapitated; all of their leaders and commanders had either been killed or captured. Their one source of cash revenue— oil—was immobilized, since the Kharg terminal was destroyed and the oil storage facility at Bandas Abbas was a smoking ruin. Adding to the IRGC misery was the knowledge filtering in that similar destruction had happened in North Korea, thus cutting off any rescue of their nuclear plans and programs or an ability to threaten Israel and any other countries opposed to their terror regimes.

There was no guiding authority, and the various factions within the country would soon begin to squabble among themselves. They each vied for power as the Opposition Party coordinated its efforts to wrest control from the remaining clerics and mullahs.

CHAPTER 63

North Korea

Mossad operators of Vietnamese Chinese descent were finalizing their mission to decapitate the leadership of the Kim regime. For this operation, they had another team of agents hidden in plain sight in Pyongyang, where their objective was to destroy the seat of Kim Jong-un's government.

They recognized that getting up close to Kim and his cronies was not feasible. Eli Naftalin had acquired intelligence that indicated Kim and his leadership group would be celebrating the intended missile and hydrogen bomb test at the National Assembly parade. In Kim's usual bombastic fashion, he had ordered a series of parades to celebrate the planned nuclear missile launch and detonation.

Meanwhile, Naftalin had devised a plan in which his Vietnamese operators would infiltrate the depot where the parade was assembling, again posing as Chinese dignitaries. They had arrived with some pomp and circumstance, completely deceiving the North Koreans in charge. Once inside their trucks and SUVs, they had managed to gain access and then take control of two of the missile carriers and their missiles.

The Israelis had originally intended to fill the fuel containers of the missiles with thousands of ball bearings and metal shards as well as several kilograms of enhanced Semtex. The plan was that when the transporters passed beneath the reviewing stand where Kim would be celebrating, the explosives would detonate, sending ball bearings into the stands in a hail of death and destruction. After very careful due diligence, the plan was abandoned on two counts—first, the terrible toll in civilian and collateral lives, and second, the Israelis were not convinced the plan would sufficiently neuter the Kim regime.

After much review and often heated debate, another plan was conceived. The operators would release a noxious but nonlethal gas by way of several drones that would fly by the reviewing stand. The gas would incapacitate all the people and security forces on or around the stand, but only temporarily. Anyone inhaling the gas would involuntarily vomit and lose control of their bladder and bowels. Such physical acts, it was hoped, would psychologically affect the actions of the North Koreans. Analysts back in Israel had determined that when people, particularly men, uncontrollably urinated or defecated there was a feeling of shame which clouded their thinking; it made them less aggressive and more compliant.

The Mossad teams, in conjunction with the South Korean Special Forces, had set all the explosives on the Musudan-ri missile and nuclear site to explode after the initial parade in Pyongyang commenced. The Israelis, who were impersonating Chinese observers, had cleverly positioned themselves so as to release the drones carrying the gases as the missile transporters passed under the reviewing stands.

Pho Hoc Luong was keenly observing the stand where Kim and his generals were gathered and noticed a disturbance among the leadership. They had just been informed about the Iranian operation and, while digesting that news, word suddenly came in that the Musudan-ri missile facility had also just been attacked. For about thirty seconds, there was pandemonium on the stand where Kim was seen gesticulating wildly and yelling at one of his generals. The gas-bearing drones flew rapidly along the line of the reviewing stand. The drones had been engineered to fly at a high rate of speed. Because of their speed and size, they were almost invisible to the naked eye until it was too late to take any evasive action. Within seconds, the one hundred-plus people on the stands, including Kim, collapsed. The North Korean soldiers surrounding the stands were also incapacitated.

The initial shock and surprise allowed the Mossad and South Korean Seal teams to quickly insert themselves and collect the unconscious bodies of Kim and his key aides and military leaders. The sense of panic only increased as the North Korean soldiers were aghast at what they were witnessing and receiving no direction or orders.

The Israelis and South Koreans took advantage of the momentary breakdown and carried the inert North Korean leadership into their two trucks that were part of the parade, then immediately drove out of the capital for the coast. Most North Koreans who observed this at first believed that the evacuation of the leadership was for their safety. It was only after an hour or so, when some semblance of order was restored, that the remaining people in authority recognized what had actually happened.

The operators left the city unimpeded and continued west down the Youth Hero Highway that linked Pyongyang to the port of Namp'o. As their captives began to recover from the effects of the disabling gas, they struggled against their bonds and tried to understand what was happening to them. Kim and two of his aides were whispering, "Mok un Ling, where are we?"

"Dear Leader, we appear to be in an army truck travelling at high speed. I don't know where we are or where we're going."

All three men were sitting, bound, in their own filth on the floor of the truck.

"You are an imbecile!!" Kim shouted. "You are supposed to know where I am at all times!"

At this point, one of the South Korean Seals, Lieutenant Hoo Soo Luk, cuffed the aide around the side of the head, glared into the enraged eyes of the Dear Leader, and shouted at him in Korean, "Shut the fuck up, you piece of blubbery trash! Your time has come, Dear Fucking Leader. Where you are is on your way to the International Court in The Hague, to be held to account for the thousands of crimes you have committed against humanity."

Then, with a vicious kick to Kim's side, he exclaimed again, "Now, *shut the fuck up!*"

Kim and his aides were so shocked by this attack on his Dear Leadership that they recoiled against the sides of the truck and remained silent for the balance of the road trip. The more time spent on the road, the greater the stench from urine, vomit, and feces in the prisoner transport.

Kim the Dear Leader was so traumatized that he had become virtually incoherent. His shouting and attempted intimidation were not getting any results. The realization was sinking in that he was completely stripped of any power. Combined with the total humiliation of sitting in his own excrement in a vomit stained uniform, the cold truth hit hard — he was no longer the Dear Leader.

CHAPTER 64

Port of Namp'o, North Korea

When they arrived dockside in Namp'o, the trucks drove directly alongside the Monrovian flagged freighter, *Jubilant*. The *Jubilant* had unloaded grain from Argentina and was waiting at the docks. In reality, the freighter and its crew were a deep cover Mossad asset regularly deployed to track illegal arms shipments from North Korea to Sudan and destined for Gaza and Hamas. Once the teams and their human cargo arrived at the dockside where the freighter was berthed, they quickly embarked.

Surprisingly, the raids in the capital and destruction at the Musudan-ri missile facility had completely disoriented the military infrastructure of North Korea. During the drive from Pyongyang, there had been a total absence of military roadblocks and checkpoints. As they drove through, the Mossad operators observed they all appeared abandoned and deserted.

Back in Pyongyang, the remnants of North Korean leadership were in such shock that their mounting fear caused them to delay issuing orders and implementing actions to stabilize the situation. So great was their fear of the Kim family and their ferocious outbursts that they were petrified of issuing any actionable order lest they be criticized or worse, countermanded by Kim or one of his family. The generals and military experts were still unaware of Kim's capture and abduction and lived in fear of Kim and his sister.

Once on board the freighter, Pho Huc Luong gave orders to the captain to release the mooring hawsers and begin setting a course for

Darwin, Australia. The freighter was riding high without any cargo and could easily travel at 25 knots. Pho Luc wanted to get out of the harbour into international waters as quickly as possible, in the unlikely event that the North Koreans would connect the dots and try to restrain the vessel from leaving. Once in international waters, the freighter would be shadowed by South Korean naval assets and protected until she was well on her way into the South Pacific. The anticipated voyage would be six days.

During this time, Kim and his entourage were kept in solitary confinement, in small, specially constructed holding cells. They would be watched and guarded 24 hours a day by members of the South Korean Special Forces. The cells were only eight feet square, each equipped with a straw mattress, a galvanized steel bucket for use as a toilet, and another chipped and rusty bowl filled with water of dubious cleanliness. There were no toiletries such as soap or toothbrushes and toothpaste. Toilet paper consisted of a few sheets of Chinese newsprint, which was rough and mostly ineffective. To round out the prisoners' misery, their captors had also introduced a number of rats into the cells.

The prisoners were fed a meal of tainted fish and maggot-infested rice once a day, accompanied by a small plastic bottle of stagnant water. Each prisoner competed with the rats for their meagre rations. A single caged low wattage light bulb burned 24 hours a day. The idea was to totally demoralize Kim and his group by exposing them to the similar treatment his own imprisoned citizens had experienced.

By the third day, Kim and his top generals were feeling the pain of solitary and abusive confinement coupled with seasickness as the ship plowed through the rough Southern Seas. Each morning, they were awakened at 0500hrs and ordered out of their cells for interrogation. They were paraded individually to a small cabin where they sat in front of three military officers who proceeded to shout and scream at them. They were ordered to answer questions about the cruel and wicked behaviour of the regime. After each interrogation, they were taken back to their cells and, as they entered, they would be beaten with bamboo clubs. On occasion, the South Korean Seals would throw the prisoners to the hard steel floor and beat the soles of their feet just as the North Korean guards did in their prison camps.

On the fourth day, Kim was totally demoralized and disoriented when he was abruptly dragged off his toilet bucket and paraded to the interrogation room. He had lost any semblance of bombast or dignity. As the guards dragged him to the interrogation room, he began to whimper and moan. The interrogating officers again unleashed furious shouting and screaming at him until he fell off the chair he had been placed on and curled into a fetal ball on the harsh steel deck, moaning and crying like a child. This was the Great Dear Leader. Now the South Koreans observed him as the Big Sack of Shit.

By the time the ship docked in Darwin, Kim and his fellow prisoners were but shadows of their former selves. Completely broken in spirit and physically humiliated, they limped off the freighter in chains and onto a prison bus that drove them to the Darwin International Airport. The Israelis had arranged with the Australian government for an Israeli government plane to land at Darwin International. The prisoners were then shown to a secluded area within the airport, where they were allowed to shower and don clean blue prison garb, all the time under heavy guard of the South Koreans, who continually threatened and intimidated the prisoners.

The South Korean Special Forces would accompany the Mossad operatives on the flight back to Rosh Pina as guards and escorts for their very important prisoners.

During the voyage from Namp'o to Darwin, Kim had gone through many stages of disbelief, raging anger, and abject depression, exactly what Eli Naftalin had planned for him at Rosh Pinah all those months ago.

At least now as he recognized and understood who his captors were, a great fear seized Kim Jong-un. All the sabotage and attacks on his nuclear operations have been carried out by only one nation, Israel. His understanding was that the ayatollahs in Iran would be wiping Israel off the map. That plan obviously had not materialized.

Finally, comprehending that he was a captive of the Israelis and knowing his whole nuclear enterprise was in ruins, Kim Jong-un became deathly afraid. After his six days of solitary confinement and harsh interrogation, he began to understand that beyond his own self-aggrandizement he was an unimportant and sorry excuse for a human being, let alone a world leader. This hated tiny country of apes and dogs had destroyed him. His opportunity for world dominance in conjunction with the ayatollahs was now a distant dream.

As he was being led up the embarkation stairs to the aircraft, the dire situation he was in finally registered. By the time he was roughly bundled and shackled into his seat, essentially a metal chair bolted to the floor of the aircraft, he was shaking and trembling alternately from fear and suppressed anger.

Many hours later, when the plane landed at Rosh Pinah airport after a refuelling stop in Mumbai, the prisoners were disembarked from the plane and transported in a heavily guarded prison bus to the military prison on the base where the 9 and Mossad leaders were waiting for them.

CHAPTER 65

Rosh Pinah, Israel

Most of the North Korean Politburo and leadership had by now all been killed or arrested and the senior survivors including Kim, the Dear Leader, had been flown to Israel and then they would eventually be transferred to the ICC at The Hague, where they would be tried for human rights violations and murder.

With the arrival of the North Koreans, most of the leaders of world terrorism were gathered in one place. The Israelis had prepared a compound specifically to house all of these men while they made arrangements for the trials. The Iranians would first be tried in Israel and then later also sent to The Hague.

The day after Kim's arrival, all were lined up in humiliating prison garb and photographed for the world to see that the heads of these state terror organizations were not supermen, but just a plain ordinary group of cowards. Front and centre in the group photo were the Ayatollah Khamenei, President Rouhani, Foreign Minister Javad Zarif, General Soleimani, and Kim Jong-un.

On October 29, Israel announced to the world that it indeed had captured the Iranian and North Korean leadership and destroyed the nuclear facilities of both nations. The Iranian and North Korean leadership were being held at an undisclosed location awaiting trial on charges of terrorism, murder, and corruption. The news was electrifying and reactions from world capitals were, to say the least, interesting.

The Leftist anti-Israel countries in Europe, along with the EU in Brussels were apoplectic. They had been completely blindsided and their elitist anti-Israel plans destroyed. The covert cooperation between certain European countries and Iran was over for the time being.

In North America there were some half-hearted efforts by the Radical Progressive Left, the BDS movement, and Students for Justice in Palestine to organize nationwide protests against Israel on campuses and in the streets. They failed miserably.

Many Jewish students and non-Jewish sympathizers, realizing that these organizations were so corrupt, resorted to the tactics of their grandfathers during the 1930s, when they had to deal with Nazi sympathizers. The clinics and hospitals around many university campuses received a number of sorely hurt leaders after these protests. No one, not the press nor the politically correct watchdogs, batted an eyelid. They all finally realized that these movements were finished. No one wanted to be associated with them, much less be their champion as they had been in the past.

The presidents of the United States, China, and Russia were completely astounded by the daring speed and success of the Israeli attacks on Iran and North Korea. There were no major civilian casualties or serious damage to civilian infrastructure. The Israelis had learned very hard lessons in their various wars and operations in Gaza, where the Hamas terrorists had hidden behind civilians and even produced photographs and videos of civilians being shot or killed, which were later identified as news clips from the civil war in Syria. This careful attention to potential harm to civilians neutered any of the usual media attacks on Israel for disproportionate military force.

All three presidents, in a hastily convened joint conference in Moscow, Russia, agreed that the political dynamics of the Middle East and Southeast Asia had changed forever, and although the Americans were not particularly happy that they'd had no prior knowledge of the Israeli operations, they recognized that this result was better for overall peace in the world.

CHAPTER 66

Iran and North Korea, months later

Under China's direction, the country of North Korea became a Chinese protectorate and China was reassured that there would be no attempts at reunification on the Korean peninsula. The hope was that the Republic of South Korea would aid in developing a vibrant economic North Korean Protectorate of China. The Chinese Politburo had strongly reiterated to Japan, South Korea, and the United States that they would under no circumstances tolerate any military forces from these nations on their borders.

Out of respect to the Chinese, the United States and ASEA nations agreed to these conditions. They collectively believed that going along to get along was far better than confrontation. The mitigating factor was that the Chinese recognized that entering into a military standoff with the United States and NATO was a lose-lose situation. They deemed it much more profitable to remain wary friends with the United States and NATO countries than to enter into a round of military and political conflict. They also agreed with the United States that a mutually protective, newly proposed SINO–US Trade Pact was a much greater benefit to the world economy. The Chinese leaders understood all too well that a well-oiled economic relationship was far superior to military confrontation. Trading and people exchange from all the world's nations would be accepted and actually welcome in developing the new North Korean economy, much along the same lines as China's had developed.

Now, in adhering to the Begin doctrine, Israel also issued a stern and nonnegotiable ultimatum to the remnants of the Iranian government and people. They had forty-eight hours to begin shipping all of their uranium and plutonium to the United States and Canada. At the same time, all of their nuclear facilities, as well as those damaged by the Israeli raids, were to be completely destroyed. This would be overseen by demolition experts from the United States, Germany, India, and Australia. There would be no remnants of these facilities left. The centrifuges and isotopes would be destroyed and melted down. All control and computer centres would be irreparably destroyed.

Besides eliminating these dangerous facilities, the world powers wanted to reinforce a strong message to any rogue nation that regardless of how much national treasure was spent, ultimately the free world would defeat them. The cost would be total bankruptcy and being loathed by their citizenry for arrogant and reckless leadership.

The efforts of the Nazis and the Imperial Japanese for world domination before and during World War II had ended in the total destruction of their countries and elimination of their ruthless leaders. The West had bankrupted the Soviet Union and brought down the diabolical Soviet Communist regime. Besides these countries, there were other examples: Khaddaffi in Libya, Pol Pot in Cambodia, Assad in Syria, and Saddam Hussein in Iraq. Many were still attempting to recover from the heinous abuses of these despicable dictators.

The Iranians would be coerced into once again entering the community of nations as a secular democracy. Iran was no longer a looming nuclear-equipped hegemon threatening all of the Middle East. The terror organizations of Hezbollah and Hamas no longer had a patron to fund and direct them. In Lebanon, the might of the Israeli armed forces targeted and destroyed all Hezbollah infrastructure with little or no resistance, since without the support and guidance from the IRGC and Iran, they were rudderless. Each of the other Iranian terror proxy organizations was delivered a discreet message endorsed by the

Russian and US presidents that they had to destroy all of their missiles and heavy weapons or face overwhelming US and Allied forces. The Chinese entered North Korea with massive amounts of humanitarian aid and began to offer the ordinary citizens hope as they rebuilt the country into a vibrant and enlightened Chinese Communist-style country. The examples being China itself and Vietnam. China sought expertise from Israel and Canada on installing sophisticated agricultural programs to lift the country into the twenty-first century; the assistance was readily and eagerly supplied.

Even more humiliating for Khamenei and Kim Jong-un were the thousands of their citizens dancing in the streets of their respective countries, celebrating the collapse of the two regimes. More devastating for Khamenei was the news that in what was once Iran's colony of Lebanon, ordinary citizens were chasing the Hezbollah and Iranian guards out of the country—in some cases, even capturing them and administering swift street justice by hanging them from cranes and lampposts, Iranian-style. The pent-up loathing of the people who had been under Soleimani's yoke in Lebanon and the IRGC in Iran was akin to a tsunami that began to cleanse both countries of corruption and subjugation enforced with terror.

CHAPTER 67

South America

Recognizing an opportunity to cripple the drug cartels in Central and South America, the United States gained access to the Hezbollah leadership, which they were well aware had been the conduit for the cocaine trade with the cartels. What had also been suspected for years was that Hezbollah was the leading world trader in cocaine and other drugs, which they marketed through their tentacles in the United States and Western Europe.

The head of Hezbollah, Hassan Nasrallah, was personally estimated to be a billionaire as a result of the percentage he was keeping from all Hezbollah transactions. The Hezbollah organization was finally outed as being not only a self-funded terror network, but the world's largest drug and arms dealer.

With the treasure trove of information acquired by the DEA, FBI, and CIA from the Hezbollah's own files and electronic data, a fast and coordinated series of raids began rolling up the distribution channels of drugs coming into North America. What was unbelievable was the depth of Hezbollah's reach. They had influenced and corrupted many politicians in Mexico, Peru, Bolivia, Venezuela, Colombia, and the United States. The tragedy of all this was that during the six years that the US administration had been secretly negotiating the Iranian Nuclear Deal with Iran, extreme pressure had been placed on the United States by the Iranians to back off and desist from investigating and ultimately attempting to apprehend and disrupt the Hezbollah drug channels.

CHAPTER 68

One of the strangest happenings in both Iran and North Korea was the initially tentative efforts to remove all vestiges of the dictators and their enterprises. Their citizens were at first skeptical that all the sudden changes had occurred with little or no upheaval. As they began to understand what had occurred, both countries moved quickly to adapt to the changes. In Iran, the civil government, now removed from under the yoke of the clerics and their draconian rule, began to establish a new, republican-style government based on a similar model to that of the United States—a republic of states, each with local government overseen by a democratically elected central government. The government would be secular and have clear lines of separation between religion and state.

The ayatollahs and mullahs, along with senior IRGC officers, especially General Soleimani, would be tried in Israel for war crimes and acts of terror. It was unbelievable news to the ordinary citizens of Iran that they no longer had to fear the long reach of Soleimani and the Quds Force. If found guilty, they would be sent to The Hague to face further charges and sentencing, which could include the death penalty. Many in Iran, Lebanon, and Syria fervently hoped this would come to pass.

The ramifications of these surprise actions caused the UN and the rest of the world to sit up and take notice. Many UN bureaucrats who had previously been paid hundreds of millions of dollars to censure Israel now not only feared for their employment but also their lives. Mossad and 9 had them clearly identified and had a host of "thank-you receipts" to hand out. These were not handshakes or acknowledgements for good behaviour. Once the really bad actors were outed, they either had to resign from their positions at the UN, or in some cases flee back to their countries, where unbeknownst to them they were still on a 9 watch list.

The EU and UN at first attempted to interject themselves into the discussions but were harshly rebuffed by the Arabs. Within the Arab society that had been established in Judea and Samaria and Gaza was a cadre of citizens who had recognized for years that the Iranian hold on Hamas and Hezbollah—aided by the UN and EU—had chilled any attempts to negotiate a peaceful solution to the Israeli–Palestinian crisis.

These reasonable and wise leaders, who had been waiting quietly in the background, had long ago understood the reality on the ground. There would never be a "right of return" for five million "refugees," as constantly promoted by the Palestinian Authority and UNRWA. The eight tribal leaders, who ever since 1967 had exceedingly close—albeit clandestine—ties with the Israeli authorities and government, believed in the emergence of Israel as a Middle East powerhouse, both militarily and economically. There was no doubt that they wanted to participate.

In the disputed territory known as the West Bank, the civilian governance was placed in the hands of these eight Arab tribes that had lived there for centuries. The whole West Bank, Judea and Samaria, was now fully recognized as belonging to Israel, as was the original intent of the Balfour Declaration until the Jordanians overran and occupied the territory in 1948. It only became disputed after the Israeli victory in 1967. All of the approximately one million West Bank Arab citizens were offered Israeli citizenship and those who did not wish to be Israeli-Arabs were given the opportunity to close up their homes and businesses and leave the country with fair market value compensation paid by the Israeli government. This stands in marked contrast to what the Arab nations had done to the Jews in 1948, when they threw them out with just the clothes on their back. It was interesting that for seventy years, there was no UNRWA collecting hundreds of millions of dollars and promoting a right of return every year for Jewish refugees.

In many ways, the Israeli operations in Iran and North Korea had finally ended the diabolical and corrupt narrative encouraged by the liberal Western media. Organizations and agencies within the UN had fostered lies about Israeli occupation and apartheid to the media and even at the UN itself caused incitement by terrorists against Israel. To the Israelis, this had been terror in another guise.

In Gaza, the citizens, with Israeli assistance, turned on the Hamas gangsters and either executed them or deported them to Israel or Egypt for trial. Egypt and Israel had agreed to jointly provide governance and security to Gaza until free elections could be held in both Gaza and Lebanon without intimidation and threats. In the case of the Gazans, they would be given three ballot options.

First: Would you wish Gaza to be part of the State of Israel?

Second: Would you wish Gaza to be part of the State of Egypt?

Third: Would you wish Gaza to be an international territory governed by Egypt and Israel?

One of the most difficult and critical issues the UN and Israel had to overcome was the fifty years of PLO propaganda disseminated in the general Arab population. The message was that Israel was never a home for the Jewish people. For all these years they had played the world with statements of wishing for a two-state solution and a willingness to live alongside Israel in peace. Nothing was further from the truth. They were educating their people that Israel was one big settlement which had to be cleansed of Jews. They used the power of the radical Islamic clerics in the Muslim Brotherhood and other terror organizations around the world to deliver a ridiculous interpretation of the Quran, which declared that any Muslim-occupied land could not be surrendered or even negotiated away from Muslim ownership. Their strict interpretation was such that even Spain and Portugal, which had both been occupied by Muslims in the twelfth century, were eventually to be reconquered, since the Kuffirs had no rights there anymore as it was once Muslim territory.

Modern-day Israel was occupied as recently as the end of World War I by the Turkish Ottoman Empire, which was Muslim; and more recently, the disputed West Bank had been occupied by the Arab

League Jordanians, also Muslim. The propaganda of the radical clerics brainwashed Palestinian Arabs into believing that the Jews should and would be driven out of the Land of Israel. For fourteen hundred years, the practitioners of Islam, Shi'ite and Sunni, had hung onto their beliefs that this dogma was sacrosanct. Unless the Jihad to reconquer the lands was carried out, there could be no settlement with Allah.

Furthermore, the two sects each had a hard core of radical clerics who preached daily that the followers of Allah and Muhammad had a religious duty to kill the infidels and kill the Jews. Sadly, the Saudi Wahhabis and the Muslim Brotherhood in Egypt preached this radical form of Islam daily. In the contentious West Bank and Gaza, as well as Lebanon, Jordan, and Syria, this was taught in all the schools. Then, in a most surprising move, a group of progressive, modern-thinking Islamic clerics from Egypt and Saudi Arabia formed a committee to begin the daunting task of eliminating hate curricula in Arab schools. They did this at great personal risk, but they had the total support of the Saudi and Egyptian governments, who jointly had defanged the radical Wahabis and Muslim Brotherhood, both of whom were responsible for preaching hateful radical Islamic dogma.

The greatest task of the UN was to clean out all the corruption and dishonesty within its ranks. The United States, Canada, Australia, China, and Russia let it be known that the Muslim Bloc and their supporters, countries like Venezuela, Cuba, Bolivia, Paraguay, Norway and The Republic of Ireland, would no longer be recognized when they attempted to block or vote against resolutions in support of Israel. The United States, Canada, Australia, China, and Russia also engaged Egypt, Indonesia, and Saudi Arabia to begin a reeducation of their populaces; it was imperative to communicate that Middle Age thinking and philosophy did not reconcile with modern beliefs.

CHAPTER 69

Israeli leaders made it clear to the UN and the world that they would no longer sit by and have the radical clerics urge incitement against Jews, which called for their murder and destruction. Israel would ignore the UN calls for calm and the accusations of disproportionate responses. Any radical Islamic individual or group calling for the destruction of Israel and the Jews would be targeted for elimination by Israel regardless of where in the world they were. At first, there was abject horror and outrage from the Liberal Left, especially in the EU, Canada, the UK, and the United States. Israel ignored them, and when a well-known radical cleric engaged in incitement to murder Jews and Israelis from a pulpit in Paris, he was summarily assassinated in broad daylight by a 9 team. Another in Malaysia who committed incitement on television to murder Jews and Israelis was terminated in his bathtub by a female team from 9. This added insult to injury as the Israelis loudly publicized how he died.

Even in Washington DC, the Israelis, under the auspices of 9, led by Ari and Noah, carried out their retribution agenda on a well-known Muslim cleric, Ali Muhammad ibn Saya, who would espouse calls every week from his pulpit for the indiscriminate slaughter of Jews wherever they lived.

Ari and Noah flew into Baltimore International from Montreal on a Delta flight. They were met by a nondescript limo driver holding a sign with the name *Mr. Landau* written on it. With the support of the resident Mossad team attached to the Israeli Embassy, they had accommodation arranged in an Airbnb just outside Georgetown. In fact, the limo driver was a Mossad operative on the ground in DC. If the FBI and CIA had watchers on him, they would soon realize he was just an errand boy for the embassy supplementing his meagre income by moonlighting as a limo driver.

The Mr. Landau the driver was meeting would have easily been picked out on security cameras at BIA, which continuously ran facial recognition software comparisons. The software would have identified Ari as Mordechai Landau, a software engineer from Montreal and Frankfurt. If they had more than a passing interest, the FBI would have identified him as a senior development engineer working for a large multinational software company. In the interests of financial prudence, he had Netta Levi, posing as his assistant, rent an apartment on a long-term contract. This made sense, since extended stays at any of the more comfortable hotels in DC were upwards of $600 per night.

Two days after Ari and Noah arrived, two more engineers, Eli Gershon and Adam Mervish, arrived at Dulles International Airport from Milan. The Vienna team was on the ground and ready to pay some Israeli antiterror retribution on one Ali Muhammad ibn Saya.

After all the agents were settled, Ari and Noah went for a walk around Georgetown. Once they ascertained they were not under any kind of surveillance, they walked into an Avis car rental office and rented a small transit van and a Dodge Caravan minivan. Noah drove the Caravan back to the home while Ari drove across the Potomac into DC, then past the mosque several times over a one-hour period.

Returning to the house in Georgetown, the four 9 operators prepared their plans. Over the next five days, they determined that the best way to eliminate Ali Muhammad ibn Saya was to assassinate him in broad daylight, inside or outside the mosque, whichever scenario presented the best opportunity. They wanted to send a clear message. Ari advised the team that he would make one more trip into DC to check the entrances of the mosque yet again and locate the security cameras. When he returned, he called the group together.

"The mosque has a perimeter covered by at least a dozen cameras. Eli, we are going to need you to hack into those and make them inoperable for twelve hours. I don't want the people and security in the mosque to be suspicious, so you need to disable them without it appearing to be a malfunction. Can you do that?"

"Not a problem, boss. The mosque is easy. Their system isn't much better than a residential system from Best Buy. What are we doing about the DC cameras at the immediate intersections and subway entrances?"

"Good point. We will have to hack those as well. Are you able to handle them?"

"No, boss. I will have the IT boys at the embassy take care of those."

Ari continued fine tuning the plan. "OK. We know ibn Saya, that bastard, will be arriving at the mosque at 1000hrs as per his regular schedule. Unless he changes his security routine, he will have an SUV in front of his armoured Jaguar and another SUV behind. Typically, there have been four security people in each of the SUVs, including the drivers. So, we will be up against at least six armed security guards and possibly two more from his Jaguar.

"We will be dressed as worshippers in keffiyehs and thobes. Each of us will carry the suppressed HK machine pistols with thirty round magazines under the thobes."

"What if we're stopped at the doors?" Noah questioned Ari.

"I've selected the side entrance, where he always has his vehicle stop, so we will not be entering the building. We will carry out the attack outside on the street, just as he alights from the car and prepares to walk into the building." The other operators nodded in agreement.

"We know that ibn Saya will be travelling as usual in his armoured Jaguar. His security guys are reasonably professional, but they will be slow. They are very protective of him and the only real opportunity will be when he gets out of the car to enter the mosque. He always uses the side entrance, so that's where we will set up. His driver will stay in the Jag. The bodyguard will jump out and open the rear right door for him. The muscle in the two SUVs will alight also, but our customer is very impatient. It will be that impatience that gets him killed."

As he walks between the car and the side door, we will hose them from just outside the door. Eli, you will have the transit ready. Adam, Noah, and I will direct our first shots in controlled and deadly fire on ibn Saya. Then we'll each take a target vehicle and spray full auto fire at the security detail. When they duck for cover, we will run for our vehicle."

They knew that Ali Muhammad ibn Saya had a community meeting at the mosque that morning. As the convoy pulled up to the side entrance, three men, apparently humble worshippers dressed in long, flowing white thobes and keffiyehs stepped out from the entryway and devastated the imam and his guards before they had time to react. Ali ibn Saya collapsed on the spot, instantly dead from three bullets to the head.

Each of the 9 operators unloaded the remainder of their thirty-shot magazines at the three vehicles. The bodyguard from the sedan died as he was closing the door, instructing the driver to wait. The driver, who was the only survivor, was too traumatized to be of any assistance. All eight of the security detail were either dead or severely wounded.

The entire action was over within ten seconds. By the time any bystanders, of which there were few, could react, the three men took off walking fast down the side streets that surrounded the mosque. As soon as they were out of sight, they discarded their robes and headgear and quietly evacuated the area in the transit van driven by Eli.

Once again, Ari and his 9 team had eliminated a terrorist who otherwise would have continued to incite terrorist attacks against Jews. One less enemy of Israel and peace. This assassination caused tension between the United States and Israel; the Americans were convinced it was the Israelis who had engineered the hit on US soil. The US president called Prime Minister Mendelsohn to express his outrage and displeasure. But there was no proof.

After the call terminated, the US president was furious as he recounted the details of his conversation to his aides and national security advisers. "The son of a bitch knows exactly who is responsible! I want a full press on this to catch the people involved."

Nathan Levi, the national security adviser, gently began to calm his president down, saying, "Mr. President, that imam has been inciting his flock to murder Jews for years. Our administration, like previous administrations, have turned a blind eye to his incitement. Frankly, the genuflecting that we in particular and the West in general have addressed to the destabilizing forces of terrorism is over, thanks to the Israeli actions in Iran and North Korea. My advice to you, sir, is go with the flow. If the Israelis are indeed responsible for the killing of the imam, so be it. Perhaps you should express your displeasure with the random shootings that take lives on the streets of Washington, DC. There were thirteen shootings with nine fatalities, besides the imam and his people, in DC in the last 24 hours. Four of those killed were under the age of fifteen."

The president and secretary of state were not enamoured by Levi's statement. Levi calmly continued, even though he recognized that he had earned the ire of the president. "The DC police chief informed me that besides the imam and his personal bodyguard, three of his security detail died and five others are all in serious condition. The only witness was the imam's driver, and he described the killers as 'Bedouin-like assassins.' He was convinced they were Arabs from a rival sect."

The president glared at Levi, but his sense of political survival prevailed. He knew that Levi was ultimately correct. Another, albeit famous, radical imam and four of his security detail killed on the streets of Washington, DC was not going to cause a war in the Middle East, Eastern Europe, or even the South China Seas.

CHAPTER 70

Bolivia, South America, and Jerusalem, Israel, two months later

In Bolivia, there was a radical Hezbollah branch fomenting hatred against not only Israel and the Jews, but all infidels, especially North Americans. The Hezbollah cell was now led by Hashim Safi Al Din, a cousin of Nasrallah, the former leader of Hezbollah in Lebanon. Nasrallah was on the run, believed to be hiding somewhere in Syria or Iraq. A combined Israeli and US special forces detachment was actively hunting for him to bring him to justice.

The South American Hezbollah cell had been embedded in Bolivia for over twenty-five years, slowly spreading tentacles throughout Venezuela, Peru, and Guatemala. The cell also had strong ties to the Colombian and Mexican drug cartels. The terror group, with limitless access to Iranian cash and drug cartel distribution proceeds, was feared all over South America because of their indiscriminate brutality—including against law enforcement and government members who opposed them. Safi Al Din reported directly to General Hussein Soleimani, the mastermind behind the whole Hezbollah drug operation.

Macha and his 9 teams deemed this group the most dangerous terror cadre in the world now that the threats from Iran and North Korea had been eliminated. Over the past number of years, Israeli Mossad had been observing the group and their offshoots all over South America.

Macha requested a secure meeting with Prime Minister Mendelsohn and Defense Minister Melnik. The following day, his request was granted and at 0900hrs he was ushered into the PM's private office in Jerusalem.

"So, Macha, to what do we owe the pleasure of your company? I suspect, knowing your proclivity for trouble, that you don't have much for us to be happy about."

Macha smiled and responded, "Happy, no, but excited, yes, because between Naftalin's Mossad and my sources we have definitively identified the heart and head of Hezbollah outside of Lebanon. Nasrallah's cousin, Safi Al Din, is their top man running all Hezbollah operations worldwide since we chased Nasrallah out of Beirut and sent him into hiding. Ali Din reported directly to that bastard Soleimani. Frankly, Gershon, we consider this extension arm of Hezbollah more dangerous and more of a threat to peace than the Lebanese group was. Ari, Dov, and Eli have prepared an intriguing operation plan that we believe will take these bastards out once and for all. Unlike Lebanon, South America is a huge geographical area and these *momserim* are all over. We do not have the resources to cover all the bases, so our plan calls for a singular large-scale attack on their Bolivian headquarters, with further actions against their satellite operations in Chile, Peru, Venezuela, Mexico, and Colombia. We have all the locations detailed and our satellite imagery, which we have been sharing with the Americans, confirms that they are gearing up for a major operation."

Prime Minister Mendelsohn looked at Macha momentarily, and then growled, "And what is it you are proposing?"

"Gershon, we need you to sell the Americans on conducting a wide-ranging attack on these guys. Optimally, we believe if you can convince the Americans, Canadians, and Mexicans to develop a large special forces operation utilizing our intelligence to neutralize these bad guys, we will not be seen in the Arab world as the aggressors."

PM Gershon Mendelsohn scrunched his eyebrows. "That's it?! You want me to call up that skinny prick of a US president and basically ask him if we can borrow his Delta and Seal teams, so we appear clean as we orchestrate the takedown of Hezbollah? My dear Benyamin, just wait one moment while I pick up the phone and call him right now!"

Macha realized that he had pushed some wrong buttons but observing the hint of a smile on Melnik's face, he rebutted. "Prime Minister, we have the advantage after Iran and North Korea. Once we present the operational intelligence on this Bolivian Hezbollah organization to the US and Mexican presidents as well as the Canadian PM, they will come on board."

After Macha finished detailing some of the logistical support he required to get the operation in gear, he left the PM's office and returned to his headquarters.

Meanwhile, both Mendelsohn and Melnik began working the phones. Eli Naftalin, head of Mossad, and General Mordechai Nudelman, the Chief of the IDF, flew to Washington, where they were joined by their Canadian and American counterparts. They had all agreed to leave the Mexicans out of the operation since the drug cartels and Hezbollah had infiltrated all levels of government in Mexico. After they made their presentation to the Joint Chiefs and the heads of the CIA and DEA, to their utmost surprise, the United States and Canadian special forces commanders formally requested that Israeli operatives and Sayeret commandos be attached to their forces.

Two months after the capture of the Iranian clerics, the Americans led a raid with assistance from Israeli Sayeret and Canadian JTF2 special forces on the Bolivian Hezbollah headquarters. They also hit two mosques that were nothing more than armed camps. The combined special forces secretly entered Bolivia at Villazón, across from Argentina. The mosques and Hezbollah infrastructure were sited some 10 miles from the centre of Villazón. After assembling around the sites, especially at the larger of the two mosques, the United States, Israeli, and Canadian special forces first deployed drones to unleash missiles into the buildings. The terrorists came rushing out into the square in front of the building, as expected. The specialists fired controlled bursts of automatic weapons fire on the radicals and in short order there were none left standing.

A joint Israeli and Canadian JTF2 team commanded by Captain Michel (Wolfman) Leroux entered the remains of the damaged mosque to search for any terrorists who may have been hiding.

Wolfman was a ferocious warrior. He had deployed to Afghanistan soon after 9/11 as a trooper in JTF2. He was highly motivated, since his elder brother, Jean-George, had died in the 9/11 attacks on the World Trade Center. JG, as the elder Leroux was called, had been a successful financial trader at an international brokerage house on the 76th floor of the South Tower when it was struck by United Airlines Flight 175. The Boeing 767 slammed into the 60th floor below JG's offices and he perished along with so many others who could not evacuate the upper floors. "Wolfman" Leroux had idolized his brother, and once he knew of JG's fate, he vowed revenge. He had already been serving in the Canadian Armed Forces and immediately volunteered for the JTF2 detachment. He was accepted and deployed soon after to Afghanistan. There he garnered a reputation as a fierce and uncompromising soldier. He was equally at home killing Taliban and Al Qaeda terrorists with his McMillan TAC-50 sniper rifle, his sidearm, or even his bare hands. "Wolfman" Leroux now commanded one of the most elite units ever assembled and his team made quick work of the Hezbollah terrorists.

Over at the office and school buildings, US Navy Seal Teams used devastating fire from two drones to smash their way into the halls and rooms that were not destroyed. Seal Team leader Lt. John Daker and his number two, Petty Officer Norman Haspell, with Israeli Sayeret commando, Senior Sergeant Alon Lasky, resolved not to let any terrorists survive.

Daker deployed his teams on the perimeter of the buildings to prevent any terrorists from escaping. He ordered Haspell and Lasky to clean out the buildings. Taking six men with them, four Seals and two Sayeret, they conducted a room-to-room search. A good amount of the infrastructure was fairly damaged from the drone strikes, but the central core and offices leading from it were still standing. Sergeant Lasky began to climb the stairs to flush out any terrorists still hiding when he heard suspicious sounds. Mindful of not being ambushed, the team held still while Lasky and Haspell counselled. Suspecting that some terrorists would be hiding, they withdrew down the stairs and ordered up a pinpoint strike on the top floor. After the drone unleashed its intensely accurate missiles, the teams entered the building once more and climbed to the third floor to search for any terrorist survivors. There were none. As they descended to the second floor, they soon located Safi Al Din hiding in a cleaning supply locker. He was cowering behind some cartons of paper supplies and since he had no civilians to hide behind, he was terrified.

When he lived in Lebanon and Gaza, Ali Din had been identified by Israeli intelligence services as responsible for planning and participating in several brutal murders of innocent civilians within Israel and in France. Defense Minister Melnik, who had assisted in planning the assault, had made it clear to the Sayeret that no prisoners were to be taken. The US and Canadian forces simply removed themselves from direct involvement as the Sayeret eliminated the radical terrorists. As Sergeant Alon Lasky explained to his Canadian and US counterparts after he shot Ali Din in the head, "We used to capture these bastards and put them in jail. Then, one day we were held ransom by their groups to release hundreds of the bastards for Gilad Shalit. We know that this garbage was directly responsible by his own hand for the killing of at least eight Israeli women and young children."

No mercy or quarter was shown, and all of the radicals were killed. At the same moment, other teams hit the satellite operations all over Central and South America.

By the time all of the operations were completed, the Canadian and US government agencies responsible for drug interdiction were completely awed by the amounts of cash and drugs either seized or destroyed. The DEA confiscated $24 billion USD and another €12 billion. Over fifteen thousand tons of cocaine and five thousand tons of oxycontin and methamphetamine were also seized.

Notwithstanding the blistering editorials in *The New York Times* and the *Guardian* and the talking heads on CNN and MSNBC decrying the use of "disproportionate responses" and the "slaughter of unarmed combatants," the majority of ordinary citizens in North America and Western Europe wholeheartedly endorsed the operations.

CHAPTER 71

Within many countries—France, Belgium, Germany, Sweden, Denmark, and the Netherlands—the native citizens demanded that their governments take similar action on the radicals in their midst. In some countries, especially Sweden, some of the most violent radical quarters in cities such as Malmö were paid a visit by strange-speaking hard men from 9. After these visits, those inciting the murder of civilians were assassinated with no questions asked.

It did not take long for the world to appreciate the serious effort to end terror. The Left howled, calling for emergency debates and enquiries to any organization that would listen to them. Their narrative had been eliminated. No one was going to pay attention to their demands for political correctness and spurious rights. The only rights being addressed were those that allowed every country and its citizens to live free of terror.

In Lebanon, Hezbollah was totally defanged and removed from their control of the Lebanese government. Israel made peace overtures to the Lebanese and offered a formal peace treaty and cessation of the state of war that had existed since 1980. This was joyously accepted by the Lebanese people. The Hezbollah cadres and terrorists were all rounded up and placed in detention camps until they could be interviewed by the UN under Israeli supervision. The majority were found guilty of war crimes and exploitation of government resources. As much as there was a loud exclamation from the liberal Western media and countries like France and Sweden, many were sentenced to death.

The United States was ecstatic by the sudden success of this daring plan that 9, led by Macha, Eli, Ari, and Dov had created. For too long, political posturing and self-aggrandizement in Washington had held back the power of US agencies such as the DEA and CIA, enlisting the overwhelming power of the military to eliminate drug and terror organizations. The US State Department, historically anti-Israel, had no avenue to call for their usual punishment for disobeying Uncle Sam. Egypt and Saudi Arabia, the two leading Sunni Arab Muslim nations in the Middle East, celebrated the success of the Israeli mission. Not wanting to be left on the sidelines after Israel had seized the initiative, Russia and the United States together carpet-bombed the remnants of ISIS in Iraq and Syria. The United States and NATO, with overwhelming support from the UN, went after the various strongholds of Al Qaeda in Yemen and Al Shabbab in Somalia, destroying their infrastructure and camps. It became very clear that without the backing and support of Iran, these entities were rendered ineffective.

One major revelation of Iran's vicious involvement in the world was the Iranian Hezbollah roots and involvement in Venezuela, where a diabolical regime had taken over the country. The long-term objective there was to unleash Hezbollah and Iran-financed terrorists on the United States and Canada.

The Turkish strongman, Erdoğan, suddenly realized the fact that he wasn't important anymore. After a brief period of bluster and empty threats about liberating Jerusalem from the Jews, he was surprised and chastened when an elite Israeli Special Forces team entered Turkey and rounded up some key members of his party, took them back to Israel, and gave them a tour of the "occupied cities" of Jerusalem, Tel Aviv, and Haifa. This was of course broadly televised so that the Turkish people could see for themselves. It especially hurt that Israeli forces had easily entered Turkey and captured key leaders, and Erdoğan's vaunted security forces had no clue until they learned of it at the same time as the rest of the world.

Erdoğan, understanding that he was now an emperor with no clothes, began to negotiate properly with the Kurds and Israel. A gentle but not so subtle message from the UN and the United States had him release all of the political prisoners he had rounded up several years ago. He was also forced into holding tamper-free elections, which was something not seen in Turkey since his rise to power. All of his grandiose plans for a new Turkish Empire with him as the new Sultan were dashed. Very quietly, the Israelis and Saudis delivered a message to him that any attempts to reestablish a Turkish Caliphate would be met with swift retribution.

Erdoğan also failed to take into account that the British had long memories and even more than a hundred years later still harboured bad feelings toward Turkey on several accounts; their defeat at Gallipoli still stung and the sacrifices made there and in Palestine during the First World War to bring down and defeat the Ottoman Empire were well remembered; the Armenian Genocide carried out by the Turks in the early years after WWI, which Erdoğan categorically denied, was a real source of outrage for the British, since it happened under their watch in Turkey. Further, the belligerence shown toward the British by Turkey in general was not appreciated. Unfortunately for Recep Tayyip Erdoğan, the British were only too happy to engage with the Israelis and Saudis in reinforcing the message.

The EU led by the French also attempted to salvage some pride out of the sudden change in dynamics and concluded that the best thing they could do was to close down all their NGOs in Israel, the West Bank, and Gaza. At last, the descendants of Monsieur Picot would disengage from the region.

One of the most inspiring results of the change in dynamics in the Middle East was the relationship between Egypt and Israel. For years there had been a cold peace between the two neighbours. Egypt's economy was weak and without aid from abroad the country could not sustain itself. Common Egyptians had long been led to believe that their problems were because the Jews controlled Palestine and the Al-Aqsa mosque in Jerusalem. The leadership of Israel and Egypt determined to break that destabilizing myth once and for all. The Egyptian government had finally eliminated the strength of the Muslim Brotherhood, who had for almost a century promulgated this myth. They had many times issued draconian orders to police and internal security forces that imams or sheikhs preaching vitriolic lies and sermons would be arrested, tried, and if found guilty, executed and their mosques destroyed.

Ever since Egypt and Israel joined forces to thwart Iranian expansion in Gaza and Sinai, which was using Hamas and Islamic Jihad as pseudonyms for the Muslim Brotherhood, both countries had implemented coordinated attacks on these terrorist organizations. Egypt's secret services, Mossad, and 9 identified the terrorists and simply assassinated them.

The two governments also encouraged Egyptian and Israeli businesses to joint venture in establishing the types of high-tech agribusinesses that were so successful in Israel. This initiative would help thousands of small farmers develop and sell their crops into world markets, instead of living at a subsistence level for lack of investment. The intent was to show the ordinary Egyptian that Jews were their friends and allies, not a mortal enemy. The Egyptian military had already experienced this since the two countries allied to fight against Hamas and ISIS in the Sinai. With Israel's assistance, Egypt had been able to finally destroy the two terrorist entities, but not without terrible losses to their armed forces. The returning soldiers spoke highly of the cooperation and resolved to help their Jewish neighbour.

Since the downfall of the Kim regime, China had been imposing a rule of law on North Korea. Recognizing that the eyes of the world were watching, the Chinese government cleverly enlisted aid from Australia, Canada, and Israel to develop the country's agriculture. At the same time, they recognized that the North Korean population had been programmed to believe Americans were the worst people on earth, so they requested the United States to keep a very low profile in the initial rebuilding of the country.

The Koreans were equally wary of the Chinese. Beijing recalled the aftermath of the Hiroshima atomic bombing at the end of World War II. The first Allied troops into Hiroshima were the Australians, who had brought immediate aid and succour to the civilian population. They were regarded as being neutral and less feared than the Americans. The Chinese also enlisted help from the Australians in establishing health clinics and transportation infrastructure in the early days of the transition.

CHAPTER 72

9 Headquarters, Tel Aviv, March the following year

Macha sat in his office and reflected on the events of the past few months. He was waiting for Ari and Dov to meet with him, to sign off on their successful mission. As with all 9 operations, there would be no singular recognition outside 9 for their success. As far as Israelis and the world knew, Israel had launched preemptive strikes on Iranian and North Korean facilities to end the nuclear threat as they had done against Iraq and Syria in years past. The fact that their tiny country had eliminated one of the greatest threats to world peace with a series of daring and stunning raids was beside the point. The usual cast of spin-masters on the BBC, CNN, FOX, and MSNBC all jockeyed for interviews with Israeli ministers and military spokespeople. All to no avail. 9 operations did not exist. A blanket of silence settled over the nation beyond a general celebration that the Iranian and North Korean nuclear threats were over.

CNN in particular spent days trying to ferret out information. Their news anchors tried valiantly to put a US flavour on the story because their friends in the White House looked so inadequate when the news first broke. They were unsuccessful.

Dov and Ari arrived separately and were welcomed into Macha's office. Eli Naftalin joined them shortly after. They shared coffee, brioche, and an assortment of fruit as they discussed and reviewed the mission. Soon they were joined by Sarah, Colonel Lieberman, Captain Einhorn, and Major Avigold.

They were elated by their success, but also terribly saddened by the loss of Alli Landa. They had all attended the military funeral accorded to her and shared the sorrow of loss equally with her family. Alli's husband, parents, grandparents, and two small children had all been at the graveside. The grief etched in their faces was something Ari and Sarah would never forget.

Alli's bravery under fire was exemplary, but all the words and eulogies would not replace a lost mother, wife, daughter, and granddaughter. As if to add to Ari's despondency, it turned out that Alli's grandparents had arrived in Israel after the Shoah in the same group as his. Nothing would ever erase the memories of the grief at Alli's funeral. It confirmed in his mind that as long as terror was on the march, wherever in the world, he would continue in the services of 9, prepared to carry out orders as designated by Macha.

After the news of the operation's success had become public knowledge, Prime Minister Gershon Mendelsohn visited the offices of 9 to congratulate Macha and his team. At first, Macha was apprehensive about the visit because of his concern that the media would accidently be able to question where the PM was going and what he was doing. Understanding this, the prime minister was driven from his office to the offices of Defense Minister Melnik, ostensibly for lunch. After briefly meeting with Melnik, he joined a group of lower-level assistants leaving the offices and took a taxi driven by a 9 operator to the 9 building, completely unobserved. There, seated in the simple conference room, Macha introduced all of his team that the PM had not previously met. Looking out from his hooded eyes, the PM addressed Dov Horowitz, Eli Naftalin, and Ari Lazarus. "You must realize that in my wildest dreams I never expected you to succeed so brilliantly. A century from now, military colleges will study your operations and refer to them as the benchmark for boldness, decisiveness, and courage."

CHAPTER 73

Washington DC, later that year

Prime Minister Mendelsohn was just reelected in a landslide victory. He was making an obligatory trip to the United States, to repair his testy relationship with the US president. The president was nearing the end of his second term and another US election was soon to be held. Gershon Mendelsohn wanted to set the record straight with the president face-to-face. His closest advisers had begged him not to, as one phrased it, poke the bear.

Not one to back down from a confrontation, especially when he knew in his heart of hearts that he had right on his side, Prime Minister Mendelsohn met with the US president one on one in the Oval Office.

The PM quickly set aside pleasantries and faced the president directly. "Mr. President, why did you ever believe we would allow those bastards in Iran to even get close to eliminating us from the face of the earth? You sold us down the river at the UN and the EU; you concluded that ridiculous treaty with them; you gave them billions in gold and cash, which they used to fund Hezbollah and Hamas to attack us. You allowed those Iranian thugs to take over Syria and threaten our very existence. I am here today to ask for… no, to demand an answer."

The president was rocked back in his chair opposite PM Mendelsohn. No one had ever sat in his office and been so abrasive.

Barely containing his anger, he replied, "My dear Gershon, you wouldn't understand…"

"Don't you dare dear Gershon me! You have had an obvious anti-Israel perspective ever since you took office. You and that pissant of a secretary of state backstabbed us at every opportunity…"

"I am the President of the United States…!"

"You know I couldn't give a shit about who you are! To me you are a double-dealing anti-Semite and thank God you will be out of office soon enough! I needed to tell you this to your face and to let you know that anyone who incites the murder of Jews or engages in terrorism will get the same ticket to the seventy-two virgins that Ali Muhammad ibn Saya received last month."

On that note, PM Mendelsohn stood and bid the president a good morning, then let himself out of the Oval Office.

EPILOGUE

Paris, one year later

Ari, Leah, and Esther strolled through the Tuileries gardens admiring the magnificent architecture of the Louvre and the Quai d'Orsay. Leah was happy to have her husband back, unencumbered by the security concerns of their beloved Israel, at least for the moment.

Arm in arm with Ari, she asked him, "Isn't Paris the most beautiful city you have ever been in?"

"Leah, my love, yes Paris is beautiful, but it will never be as beautiful for me as Jerusalem. Paris has magnificent galleries and palaces and wide boulevards, and of course the fine French cuisine, but there are too many terrible ghosts surrounding Paris, particularly for the Jewish people."

Esther chimed in and asked Ari for an explanation. "What do you mean by ghosts, Abba?"

"Dear daughter, have you heard of the Dreyfus affair? It started in 1894 and it would go on until 1906. The French government and military tried a Jewish artillery officer, Captain Alfred Dreyfus, for treason, and he was imprisoned for life. The charges were bogus and eventually he was exonerated, but the blatant anti-Semitism always below the surface in France was there for the world to see. Sweetheart, the French have never been our friends politically, although I have some very fine French business associates. As a matter of fact, some of them are meeting us for lunch tomorrow. My associate, Laurent Tremblay, is as fine a man as any and we had many good times at McGill when we studied there. Over the years since then, he and I have concluded some very, very successful deals."

Ari continued, "Perhaps one of the greatest tragedies of the Second World War was when the Parisian Gendarmes rounded up 13,000 Jews living in Paris in July 1942 and held them in horrendous conditions for several days in the Vel' D'Hiv cycling stadium. They were held under a blazing hot sun in confined spaces with little or no food and water, with no toilet or bathing facilities, before being driven off to the concentration camps of Drancy, and then they were turned over to the Gestapo and SS for transport to Auschwitz."

"It was only in 1996 that President Jacques Chirac of France fully apologized to the Jewish communities of France for the French government's involvement in the deaths of over 76,000 French and foreign Jews sent to the death camps. Even during our little countries' wars, we could never trust the French. They were with us at Suez in 1956 because it suited their need for oil. Later, to curry favour with the Arabs, they denied us planes and armaments we had already contracted and paid for.

"In the Yom Kippur War in 1973, in which your Zaide Eli fought so bravely on the Golan, they would not let the US Air Force fly over French territory to resupply us. In one high-powered diplomatic conference discussing Israel and the Palestinian Intifadas, a senior French diplomat said, 'All the current troubles in the world are because of that shitty little country Israel.' Yes! my dear daughter and wife, Paris is a city of beauty, but there is too much unpleasant history for me here, both modern and ancient."

The three Israeli tourists strolled on in contemplative silence for several minutes. Finally, Esther broke the silence. "Abba, why have people all over the world, for centuries hated us? Why do they want to destroy us?" She was visibly distraught, with tears welling up in her eyes.

"Listen, my darling, there has been a worldwide hatred of Jews for over two thousand years," Leah explained.

"But why? What did we do?"

Ari interceded, "Esther dear, because for all those centuries we had no country. We were driven out of our ancestral home by the Romans. We were scattered all over the world. Europe, Spain, South America, Russia. Wherever our ancestors found a safe haven for a few years or a few centuries, we were eventually persecuted because, with our Talmudic education and penchant for study and learning, people feared us. Without a country to call our own, we were always going to be under attack. You are only slightly aware of what happened to your great-grandparents a little over eighty years ago."

"Why, Abba? What happened to them? Zaide always steered me away from asking too many questions, but I wonder. Why?"

"Ephraim and Miriam Lazarus, your great-grandparents, were originally from one of greatest cultural centres of Europe, Vienna. They were both brilliant doctors and leaders in their field. They were well established in the upper echelons of Viennese society. That all changed when Hitler and the Nazis took over. Almost overnight, your great-grandparents were beaten, all their possessions stolen or confiscated, and they were sent in filthy stinking cattle cars to the death camps."

"Oh, Abba, I had no idea. How awful! Why didn't you or Zaide ever tell me this?"

By now Esther was visibly upset. Leah, meanwhile, was concerned that their Paris visit would become a total disaster.

"Esther, so much has been written and said about the Shoah that I know you are aware of what happened. Ephraim and Miriam never wanted to discuss their very personal experiences. They felt that there was nothing more to be gained. In fact, your Zaide Eli told me a long time ago that when his parents finally reached Haifa, immediately after Israel became a state in 1948, they refused to talk about it because they couldn't bear it. They made a commitment to leave the horrors of the Shoah behind them even though they would never forget them. Your great-grandmother Miriam told Zaide Eli that she made an affirmation of life to only go forward as they stepped off the ship that brought them to Israel."

Ari then took his tearful daughter in his arms and hugged her tightly. He stroked the tears from her cheeks and kissed the top of her head, then proclaimed to both Leah and Esther that in previous centuries and decades, Jews all over the world would recite the prayer, "Next year in Jerusalem," but now because of the daring Israeli men and women under arms, Jews could say and pray emphatically without fear of terror: "Always in Jerusalem."

ACKNOWLEDGEMENTS

I want to thank all the wonderful people who have helped me through the trials and tribulations of writing and publishing a first book.

A big shout out to Beth Kalman Werner of Author Connections, who held my hand through the entire process. Without her encouragement and constructive criticism this novel would never have been published.

A very special thank you to Karin Cather, whose brilliant suggestions with regard to Israeli culture and Jewish tradition enhanced the integrity of my narrative.

Many thanks to Meghan Behse and all the folks at Iguana Books, who have taken me from manuscript to final publication.

Without the creative skill of Ruth Dwight from Design Playground the cover would not have happened.

Finally, a huge thank you to my wife, Joan, who stood by me and encouraged me to carry on when I was suffering that awful "writers block." Her critiques and suggestions of the early manuscript are baked into *The End of Terror*.

www.ingramcontent.com/pod-product-compliance
Lightning Source LLC
Chambersburg PA
CBHW020557030726
47497CB00007B/1975